FOXY-T

TONY WHITE

Foxy-T

faber and faber

First published in 2003
by Faber and Faber Limited
3 Queen Square London WC1N 3AU

Typeset by Faber and Faber Limited
Printed in England by Mackays of Chatham plc,
Chatham, Kent

All rights reserved
© Tony White, 2003

The right of Tony White to be identified as author
of this work has been asserted in accordance with Section 77
of the Copyright, Designs and Patents Act 1988

*This book is sold subject to the condition that it shall not,
by way of trade or otherwise, be lent, resold, hired out or
otherwise circulated without the publisher's prior consent
in any form of binding or cover other than that in which it
is published and without a similar condition including this
condition being imposed on the subsequent purchaser*

A CIP record for this book
is available from the British Library

All characters in this novel are fictional and any resemblance
to actual persons or events is entirely coincidental

ISBN 0-571-21684-6

2 4 6 8 10 9 7 5 3 1

FOXY-T

They got proper names them two init but everyone still call them by there tags what are everywhere on all them like stairwell and flats and playground round here – least where they aint been wash off yet or paint over. And they are Ruji-Babes and Foxy-T.

Both of them girl work up the E-Z Call phone shop and internet up Cannon Street Road. That is they switch on all the computer them and log on or whatever then switch on the network and get them phone meter running so like at whatever time you can see who is in like booth number two calling Russia or back home wherever and how much it cost. And they make sure theres all the main phone cards in stock init and then order new ones in when there running out or whatever. And like switch on the photocopier since man can get them copy there and all. And make sure its got all paper in it and that. And they probaly thought since the E-Z Call is owned by Ruji-Babes uncle whose been out in Bangladesh or wherever for some little while that theyd be sorted there for as long as they want init. Because people have always got to get on the internet for there emails and do photocopying or buy phone cards or phone there families to make sure that the money they sent over got there OK and shit like that. Well all of thats true init thats what people have fe do every day specially round here. But if Ruji-Babes and Foxy-T thought that mean they was sorted they was wrong. Because that aint the way it work out seen.

Ruji-Babes is real skinny and small and she look much younger than she is. That girl use to wear glasses I think when she was at school. Man can tell because her eyes always look a bit too small and a bit watery and a bit dark and dry around her eyelid them like if you got flu. Only now she have like contacts what she always lose or stick on the end of her finger and wave around when she talking and thats probaly because she think it look cool to do that like on Friends or whatever. And because the E-Z Call is own by her uncle she is like the manager really until he come back at some point. Which mean that she probaly does all the stuff like pay bills and that. And thats just as well because Foxy-T some time act a bit scatty and a bit of a feather brain what is just useless at that kind of business side of thing. And Ruji-Babes uncle is like a business man init deal with property all over and like import export and him let her take over the shop while him away because him look out for him own family but also because him a bit worry about her long term prospect or whatever because she always been a bit sickly. And even when she got contact lenses she still look like a little girl with no tits. She really flat chested that Ruji-Babes init but Foxy-T is not she got massive tits man. And Ruji-Babes uncle probaly think that no gangster gonna want to marry him little neice let alone a good business man what can look after her while him away so he better open up the E-Z Call so she got some kind a security and a place to live yeah up in the flat. And him probaly figure that since Ruji-Babes and Foxy-T is like good mates or whatever and they both smart girl they would make like a good team init. And that way Ruji-Babes uncle no have fe worry about him neice when him go away is it.

What is now known as E-Z Call use to be the Cannon Street Cars for a few year init but him never make a load a money out a that cab company so him like put up the rent fe get them out then when him decide fe invest in like the E-Z Call him rip out all them fitting and dump that old drink machine and stuff and probaly sold the radio and whatever or maybe they took it with them yeah. And then him got someone in fe put up all booths and run all the wires in and shit and redecorate.

Ruji-Babes already done Business Study at school init so she went up the Tower Hamlets Community College for some like NVQ in accountancy because him say she better do that before he gonna let her run the place for him and not because him no have no confidence in her fe do them type a thing already but more so him knowed that Ruji-Babes was gonna take thing serious init. So all while that work was being done in the shop yeah she done her course and then them two move in and they open up the shop and that. That flat upstairs need a bit of work and all init but he give them money fe redecorate and get all furniture and that what they went up Ikea for in Ruji-Babes cousin van. Then her uncle send some like plumber and that round fe fix up the kitchen and that so them two can enjoy thereselves and he can protect him investment cause the place look well nice if him ever want fe sell up. Once all these thing sorted and him see that thing was looking well safe and Ruji-Babes running things the way him want him went off Bangla or whatever well I know it was.

First of all when them girl took it over and once Ruji-Babes uncle gone back or whatever I think her grandad would come in and just sit in that big chair they got in there next to the desk or whatever and he probaly come in like most day. Ruji-Babes grandad was like part of the furniture himself init. He never live there cause him have a old people flat down Miles Court there. Man would see him a walk slow up Cannon Street Road with him stick in the mornings when you was going to school or whatever and fe true him keep a eye on thing init but that man no understand what type a thing them a deal with in that shop so he aint gonna do nothing is it except just be sitting there and listen to the radio. Not because him stupid or whatever just cause him old and live him life by them old way. And also him never in a very good way is it. I mean him ill seen. So even though him dress up that he want him dad fe keep a eye on them two girl Ruji-Babes uncle a probaly thinking the other way around init. And probaly he plan that this way the old man have something fe keep him occupy and also him figure that them two girl is gonna keep a eye on Ruji-Babes grandad and look after him a bit which is what they done like fetch him tea and him lunch and that. But like I say him ill init and man could hear him cough and that and he always be spitting on the pavement outside and him die after about a year. So he didnt come in and sit there and sing under him breath like he use to no more. And this meant they could put on decent music init instead of that other like traditional music and cricket what him would a listen to all day.

 Not that they wasnt upset or nothing. Because believe me Ruji-Babes well upset and even Foxy-T was upset and they both miss him init only they was also a bit relieve seen since now they could talk about all kind of thing they couldnt of talk about before and also listen to them own kind a music like I say what is probaly better for like business and all and through

Ruji-Babes knowed business she would a think about them thing. Aint that them two dont like them old type a music sometime but not all day is it. So after that it was just Ruji-Babes and Foxy-T in the shop except every now and then one of her cousin or whatever would drive up in him big beemer. Trust me everyone knowed Ruji-Babes cousin init through him use fe drive her uncle around on him business call only now her uncle gone back home then is him son what take over them type of runnings and man seen him around the area doing them thing like collect rent and tax off all them shop. When him come over E-Z Call one a them like him mate or whatever what was usually drive would stay outside in the car or whatever and the other one would go in and look through the books for like an hour and then stand up and shake his head an go, 'Well Rooj I dont know how you done it man but this place certainly doing good business seen,' and him count out some of the money out the safe yeah and go up the bank or whatever. Except normally that was Foxy-T job fe cash up and go up the HSBC on Commercial Road but only that bank now close down init and when this cousin or whatever would come around then it was his job. But if at least you can say well that way there was still some one keep a eye on things even when her grandad didnt do that no more.

They wasnt young them two is it. They must of been like twenty something because Ruji-Babes was in year nine up Mulberry even when my cousin Naz first went there and Naz marry now and got a kid an shit and she live out Lakeside in Thurrock. But they wasnt too old neither. And them both well into it and figure this business suit them and they settle right into it believe me.

I dont know where Ruji-Babes uncle got all them computers from but they had quite good computer init what must have cost him. But him a business man init so him probaly know you have fe pay top dollar for quality PC with all windows 98 and shit. But also because him a business man him probaly also know what him want fe pay and how man can make money out a pay what them can rather than what them should. But even if him get them cheap or whatever they was alright them PC. There was also like a Canon copier init and Fax Service and all the top up cards. Like Vodafone and T-Mobile and BT Cellnet and Orange you name it man. Them have this colour copier and all when them first start up but it was shit man. Them copy always come out looking wrong and all the colour them was faded. So them make a call and aks someone fe come and take it away fe get repair or whatever and that was when Ruji-Babes grandad died I think around about that time and the colour copier never come back neither. So that mean them just have black and white copy and the internet and the phones and its OK yeah cause if anyone want colour copies like mainly restaurants or whatever fe put them menu in the window they go down Ekota Stationer because they got colour copying in there and a laminating machine and different colour paper and them do colour copy up to A3 and even if you want it bigger like A1 or whatever Ekota can do that in a week.

 I dont think Ruji-Babes and Foxy-T even mind not having colour copies no more. Them not in competition with Ekota Stationer is it. Not many people ever come in and use even the black and white one is it. Most people just want fe use like the internet or the phones or by there top ups. Or sometimes man just come in an look at Foxy-T tits an try fe chat her up or aks her out even though we all think them two is gay. And I think they was probaly happy just having the internet and phones init because they wasnt out fe start a chain like them Snack Palace or whatever they was happy just having there E-Z Call and knowing that however many people would need to come in for there top ups and send there emails and that was probaly enough work just doing that. And that make it sound like Foxy-T was thick or something because I just said she got big tits and act like a feather brain but she wasnt thick at all man is it. And its Foxy-T what knowed about computers and that through she done computer study at the Keen Student Centre up Vallance Road cause even though Ruji-Babes good with them business side of thing she never knowed the first thing about computer and it was all like some big mystery to her init and the way them PC just break down and crash all the time make Ruji-Babes nervous like she afraid of them. But thats what this Foxy-T good at seen. Foxy-T can do all that stuff believe me and she know about all them thing more than most boys do probaly because she never play games or nothing like what all boys want to do mostly just play games init but she wasnt even into them games like you or me would be or like man would think most computer people would be always playing games or whatever. Cause Foxy-T she just like doing all the programming and figure out how it all work and make it even work better. And thats how they done everything what you need to do if your running a phone shop through share out the job them according to what them two is good at. And even though they look different and them two different kind of girl but they fit well with each other in that place believe me. And probaly none of us really knowed if they was gay or not is it but we just say that because Foxy-T woudnt ever go out with no one and we never seen her with like a boyfriend which is surprising yeah since she so fit though it aint so surprise with Ruji-Babes since she aint all that even though there someone for everyone init. And also we say they is gay because them live in the same flat and they wasnt married as well as they didnt have boyfriends or nothing like I say so thinking about it they probaly was gay init. Though fe true most a them people down this way never think about them type a thing. Least them never talk about them type a thing in the open. Cause most a them like shop keeper and whatever is rent there shop from Ruji-Babes uncle and borrow money off him for one thing. So they aint gonna aks too many question about him family is it. And also is enough for some a them type a man fe take that them two girl in business let alone think about whether them gay or not. But I reckon they is gay. But mainly like I say them girl just be left alone fe do them own thing seen. Also dress wise that Foxy-T always wear boy type clothes init like some trackie bottom and just a fleece or whatever like a polo shirt type of thing so if you wasnt really looking at her or whatever like out the corner a your eye she just look like some boy with her hair tie back or whatever. Least till she like turn round or whatever and then you see her big tits even with that fleece on. An if you seen her face youd know she werent just a boy is it. Because she got them big eyes with like long eye lash and a girlish way of looking at you like she was a bit shy or whatever. But also like she was laugh at you inside a bit and it make you feel like a fool or whatever sometime when she look at you like that like she know what your thinking. And if she concentrate like on them computer or something she have a way fe do this init where she untie her pony tail and shake out her hair and be like standing there on one foot with her hand clasp upon her head and just look at the computers and thinking and then sit back down and do whatever she figure out she have fe do. Trust me when she done that it make her tits look even bigger init. An she have that same kind of look on her face if she was looking at them PC like when she looking at you init like she smiling in secret even though she would probaly never like smile at you or laugh at you there was some way that you thought she might do that and if she did say something that would show she knowed what you was thinking just like she knowed what that computer might be doing and why its going wrong or whatever.

And they was always going wrong them PC believe me. But she must generally have thing under control because I never seen any of them computer missing like they been sent off fe repair. So like I say Foxy-T good with computer and keep it all running on that side of thing. But she have her funny ways init. Like stand on one foot with her hand clasp upon her head when she try fe figure something technical. And like she might have a particular way of switching them on in a certain order or whatever starting with the ones nearest the door or starting with the ones farthest away from the door or whatever. Or turning on the lights in them phone booth first and then like switch on that server or whatever and getting the network up and running before she done the photocopier and then like do the individual PC. I dont know which way she done it cause that type a thing is all before the E-Z Call open up in the morning init. But you know that probaly that girl have some kind a nack fe do them thing. But in spite of she had some kind of nack or whatever them PC was always going wrong and this aint cause Foxy-T was shit at computer just because thats what computers is like init. And if one of them went wrong then all them others would probaly crash init. There screens would freeze or whatever. Well when I say always I mean probaly once a day or something. And even if you wasnt using them PC at the time like if you just got there or whatever man could always tell when they was start fe go wrong like that cause she just be standing there in the middle a the E-Z Call on one leg or whatever with her hand clasp upon her head and staring into space like she a look at them call charge and tariff what they got stuck up on the wall in them shops. And man would just be turn round where them sit and look at her tits and keep them finger cross that she a go fix it but believe me them no mind wait five minutes is it. And at time like that you never want fe disturb Foxy-T is it. And even if Ruji-Babes would say something like, 'T what you think we should do about this, girl?' or aks her if she want a coffee or whatever then Foxy-T just wave her hand as if to say like, 'Dont talk to me now man I'm thinking init.' Then after a while she would probaly try whatever it was she been a think about and it would generally get everything back up again and hopefully no one what was working on the computer would lose there like work what they been sitting there for the past couple of hour and doing for like £3 or whatever. But then the next day something else would go wrong init. And thats just the way it go with computers seen. Man can sort them out for a bit but there like anything you have fe always be look after them type a thing like animal or whatever. Them thing dont just run on there own is it. You have fe look after them all the time init. You got to reboot them or start them up again with there software CD and check the cables aint come loose or nothing like general wear and tear. And you have fe dust them and all init because if you got the door open like in the summer then all that black dust come in the shop and its like attract to them through magnetic or whatever and them PC get right filthy init and that black dust all get suck up inside there workings. And none of that stuff last for ever is it. You have fe replace this bit and that bit when them wear out or like some customer spill him drink on the keyboard. Then you have fe get a upgrade or whatever when some new version of Windows come out and read them manuals and shit and remember whats so different about this new software and whats the same as on the old software. Trust me is a lot of work doing all that seen. It aint just switch them PC on in the morning and remembering fe switch them off at night. Though obviously you must have fe do that and also make sure them phone meter get save on the back up init so you aint lose all them figures about who a call where and when them do it so that Ruji-Babes can do the books and work out what it all cost and how much them owe like the phone company and how much them get fe keep. Listen man is just like selling anything init. Them proabaly get them phone call cheap and like sell them a bit more expensive than that but still make it sound cheap compare with all them other call shop. And because Ruji-Babes good at business side of thing and Foxy-T good at deal with them computer and that this is how them make there living seen.

Only you aint go make a million running a call shop and internet is it. Unless you got a chain a them place. And them two didnt want a chain a E-Z Call. Them no build no empire is it. Them two just want there E-Z Call and each other init probaly. Cause otherwise if they had like another one up Stepney Green or wherever they need to get like other people work for them and all and thats not the way them girl like it which is with just the two a them at home and in there shop because otherwise like basically Ruji-Babes would have fe go up there other shop all the time and like do them books and pay them bills and all and Foxy-T would have fe look after all them other computer them. And even if you get other staff fe do some a them thing you know that none of them new staff is gonna be so into it as you are is it. And one a them might even be rip you off or whatever and them two Ruji-Babes and Foxy-T no want them kind of scene and not even know if them can trust there staff or whatever. Its nuff stress that type of thing believe me.

And you know maybe Ruji-Babes cousin might come in one day when him pass cause he have some new idea fe make them more dollar cause fe true him learn nuff thing off him dad init and understand them bigger type a picture of how money work and the way it move around and what it make people do and what type a thing you have fe do when you got it. So him say, 'Eh Rooj me think you should start fe do them Money Gram init what you say man? Me a talk with them man up Tele-International on Mile End and them make nuff money out a that. Man say just have them sign up outside good for business init and them all part a the deal there.' And Ruji-Babes well cautious about them business and how much them can invest in them new idea so she go like, 'Let me look at them detail man I aint go make up me mind just like that is it. Them type a franchise a big commitment man.' And fe true is cause she careful they is make money in the first place init and her cousin knowed this and respect her way but still when she act like that him look over where Foxy-T and roll him eye so Ruji-Babes no see him do it while she fuss over something and him go, 'What you think about them Money Gram T?' But Foxy-T aint stupid is it and go, 'Listen man is Rooj you a fe deal with on them type a thing. I dont know is it.' Then she go back to what she was do before. Other time him driver park up outside and Ruji-Babes cousin a come in and go, 'Look Rooj, I got this little property up Vallance Road you know the Sari Centre opposite the Snack Palace and I know fe true we a go make more dollar if it was a E-Z Call init what you say man?'

And Ruji B would like look around and it would be all them customer chatting away and looking up there emails on the internet and stuff and she probaly go, 'Look man we got enough to do here already init. Plus is all them man down there go up Whitechapel for them thing already.' Then she maybe check him new clothes and go, 'Anyway nice suit man.'

And Ruji-Babes no joke when she say them have nuff fe do already init cause specially in like the summer time they might be work there till like nine at night. And even then right they wouldnt get no time for there selves till they shut up shop and gone upstairs which might be like ten ten thirty. And it wasnt like they didnt have nothing else to do is it because they both of them know it aint just work make life worth living seen. Both a them girl know its all them other thing like maybe sit and chat or eat some nice take out in front of the telly is what life all about and thats why them two enjoy work init as well as because them like there jobs or whatever its also because of the time when you aint working but yet you know you is got food in the fridge and a nice place and you aint vex and all stress about them basics so you can relax and know you in control a things.

Or like maybe Foxy-T would enjoy just be sit there upstairs in the evening and fiddle around with some other kind of computer stuff what she got a idea about like how it might work or how she can make it work better and them kind a time she just be fiddling around with like her laptop or whatever and sing under her breath to herself for like hours init and Ruji-Babes might bring her a cup of tea or whatever because she know that when Foxy-T got some kind a idea from nowhere she aint gonna get no decent conversation out of her till she done it or at least had a go and most a the time she was trying to get all them stupid PC downstairs working init so it aint like she got a load of time to just get on with her own stuff she used to call it. And if they had like a chain a E-Z Call then this kind a time just fe spend on there own thing would just be take up with running all them other place init and them two rather have the time than all that extra stress.

One big problem though round here for Ruji-Babes and Foxy-T was that they didn't have that good security and it can be well quiet round them streets at night. None of them sweet centre and fry chicken shop was open all night so after about like eleven or something its like a ghost town down Cannon Street Road and even down Commercial Road what is like one of them big main road into London. Aint like west London where every main road just pure shop and bar and restaurant seen. Even now they open that drive in MacDonald on Commercial Road in the old Jet garage opposite Watney Market there aint nothing else just a load a fashion business what is busy in the day but close up about five. So its well dark and quiet like I say and as you might expect theres nuff robberies and shit.

And now there plenty a them yellow sign appear init all chain up to the lamp post them what say 'Police Notice: thief operate in this area. Please lock your car and keep your valuables and your mobile out of sight' what no one take no notice of let alone them thief. Couple a notice aint put them off is it. And also in like the last couple of year them robbers get well cheeky init. And this aint just at night neither. Them two could be both sitting there in the E-Z Call and someone would go, 'Right look this phone aint working man' or something or go, 'Can you help me with this computer I think it just crash init,' and whichever one a them is working might turn around for a second and someone else will just come in and nick a handful of one particular phone card or something. Like they'll take all the Speak and Save £10 cards one day. Or try and get some Vodafone top ups or whatever right from under there noses. And by the time they got back to the front or whatever them thief will be gone and just some empty display box them on the floor and no one in sight or just some car already turning round the corner into Commercial Road and like well out of it.

They got well vex them two and try all kind a stuff fe stop them robbers. First of all Ruji-Babes was like looking through the books and working out what money was over that month after they paid all them rates and rent and bills or whatever and things was look OK money wise so she maybe say, 'Listen T, we need one a them lock-up cabinet init. Them glass ones so all them phone card can be put away till we need them.' And buying this counter mean that Ruji-Babes aint got the money fe get like a drink machine like what she had plan fe do but she probaly figure no point have a drink machine if you stock is always get nick is it. And they went up the shop fitters init on the corner of New Road fe check them different type a counter they got up there and they got this like secondhand one what them shop fitter just take out a some place they was doing a refit or whatever. So cause it like second hand maybe them knock a bit off the price init so you see that Ruji-Babes aint stupid when it come to business. And once that was deliver and put up there in the E-Z Call by the window they put all them phone card and them top ups in there. But it aint that simple is it because you aint gonna keep that thing lock up all day is you man. If someone a come in and say, 'Give me one a them ten pound Talk is Cheap', or like aks for maybe a twenty pound Call Me or a five pound Talking Drums or whatever and you get that out and then straight away there be some other customer going like, 'Do you do them Why You Never Phone? I'd like a twenty pound one please.' What you a go do then man? You aint gonna lock up that cabinet and then open it again in between each one of them customer is you because if you do that them customers are gonna just walk down the road and get there cards or there top ups or whatever down at the One Stop in it. Least they would probaly get there top ups down the One Stop because them do Vodafone and T-Mobile down there. And you no want them customer what come to you fe buy them phone card to change them habit is it. So most of the time them still have fe keep that cabinet unlock and that mean they was still getting rob init. And what if someone come in like some schoolboy gangster what has got a knife or whatever and a bit of a attitude and he still gonna get them cards off you whether you keep that cabinet lock or not. And thats just in the day init when there plenty people about and everything. Cause theres nuff passer by on Cannon Street Road in the day time init. But at night is worse cause even though them got like one a them roller shutter on the front or whatever its just some mash up old shutter whats been there for years since before it was even the Cannon Street Car and Ruji-Babes uncle never got it fix when he buy the place in the first place and he never got it fix when he decide fe open up the E-Z Call. So that shutter would roll down but man could see it never shut properly. Them hole on the bottom for the padlock them they wasnt line up or nothing so it never lock properly and is all plant and leaf is grow in the bottom of them runner. That shutter just there for appearances init but you aint go look too close. Like they try fe make it look like they got a proper shutter and them things cost man believe me. Like five thousand dollar plus for just some steel shutter on your front window. And that aint even the best ones thats just the basic ones. And whatever happen Ruji-Babes know they aint making enough dollar for one a them new shutter is it. So it seem like them robber just another fact of life. Even though there was like a baseball bat down behind the counter there and some big machete behind the upstairs door what they got off the butchers opposite. Neither of them was right up for using none of them weapon. Though sometime Foxy-T would be a stand behind the upstairs door with that machete heavy in her hand and listen to them robbers whisper while them nicking whatever and just hoping them thief no wreck her system or nick that server and pull no plug out the wall or whatever and she just be hope that them thief aint gonna try fe come upstairs and see if theres anything worth jacking from there. But usually they never did them thief. Cause mainly them thief was like after stuff from the E-Z Call what is small and easy fe sell and what they come in and scope some other time like when they come in fe buy some kind of little five pound Vodafone top up or fe aks Ruji-Babes if they done stamps or whatever and she go, 'No but they do them book of six stamp down Ekota Stationer there though init,' or whatever and them customer go, 'Right. Oh seen, cheers man,' or whatever but them thief aint really after buy stamps or shit they was just lookin at the PC them or the stock in that lock up cabinet. So eventually them two start fe put them card and top up and that in the safe at nights but you aint gonna put computers or whatever in the safe is it. And also they was always careful not to put all them card in the safe cause if they done that then some robber or whatever is gonna do more damage init if him have fe broke up the cabinet fe even get one little box a top ups. So them always start fe leave some out. Like they'll leave out all the Speak and Save ones some night or them Dirty Talks and one of them boxes has got to have like a couple hundred dollar worth a cards init so man can understand why them rude boy want fe nick them init.

So like I say Foxy-T and Ruji-Babes is the best of friend since school. And them two is always use fe run together in them day not with no other posse or gang or whatever just the two a them. And even though Ruji-Babes was always a little weakling Foxy-T was well tough even though she had like big tits or whatever. She big for her age seen and plenty boy know she could have them easy if she want so most a them just know fe leave them two alone. And when they wasnt working or whatever or if they was bunking off a class them two would go and sit on the steps of one of the flats and smoke and chat and write there names. Or they probaly go and sit on the climbing frame over Bigland. And you could probaly hear them a climb up that like squeaky bridge on that climbing frame at lunch times or before school init and like laughing and talking from in the flats if you had like your window open or you was out on the balcony. Or man would like find some cigarette end in your stair well in the morning where they was hang out before school and find they done there tags on the wall there by your rubbish chute. None of them girl done like big dub plate and that is it just one a them would probaly of nick some blue marker at school or whatever so there be just maybe a empty B&H packet and just 'Foxy-T' and 'Ruji-Babes' writ up there in blue pen and all neat type a girl writing.

And like I say they was best of friends and looking back we is all think they was gay since time init though maybe them no realise and we didnt really know are selves even though they probaly wasnt really gay not like that they just didnt have boy friend and that though there plenty man who want to see Foxy-T tits or give her them cock fe suck or whatever believe me. Nuff man dream about that init. Cause like the name say she well foxy man. So they wasnt really gay most probaly just kind of a bit gay but man never see them two a kiss or whatever. And Ruji-Babes was a bit of a weakling like I say but she would always give Foxy-T the time of day and even though Foxy-T was a bit of a day dreamer she always have a minute for that Ruji-Babes mainly even if she never had no time fe none a them other girl in them two class.

But even though they been best friend from time sometimes on them long nights when there just the two of them in the E-Z Call on there own or whatever and it seem like no customer a go come in and it aint even like six o clock yet or whatever and things was a bit tight money wise then they might argue init or get a bit feisty with one another. And this wasnt help by the fact that sometime Foxy-T would feel like she was the one what done all the work just fe keep them computer and phone run smooth and all Ruji-Babes done was sit at the front and be chatting with them regular customer or whatever and not really be doing nothing or thats what it seem like to Foxy-T on them kind of long winter nights when everything seem to be breaking down all the time. And Foxy-T like all that kind of work really but it seem like it would never stop sometimes and she maybe get a bit angry at nothing man or have some type of expression on her face as if to say like, 'Ruji-Babes you better not aks me no damn fool question right now.' And Ruji-Babes would want fe chat with Foxy-T and aks her if she alright or whatever and she be feel really tired and them dark rings round her eyes would make her look right worry and vex and she wouldnt be able to stop herself from aksing Foxy-T if there was anything the matter and when she done that you know that Foxy-T would just shout at her or whatever init.

And on them kind of nights they felt like they was fight some kind a losing battle and it was just tax them man. And it felt like they was the only ones was try fe make some kind a honest living cause nothing else would be open except right up Whitechapel and there probaly wasnt even enough money fe one a them a go up Tayyabs and pick up some like kebab and naan and some dal or whatever which was there favourite meal from up there. It seemed like they was the only things they had only each other in the whole world. And sometimes they might think that was a good thing like at least they got each other but on them dark nights it might seem like well whats the point and why is we bother.

And even if them kind a time when it all seem like a waste a energy no come too often them robbers was enough fe drive them up the wall believe me. There was some times when they didnt really have any reason fe think it but just it feel like something gonna happen. And them feel it in the air. And on them days it be hot yeah and the mood would be well tense out in the street and there be lot of bad tempered people like shouting or whatever and bad traffic all back up down Cannon Street Road like if there some road work them go on up Vallance Road or like some van a try fe park outside the butcher them like the traffic be back up all the way down to Cable Street init and all them driver like honk there horn and get well stress. And them big plastic meat bins of all like bones and skin or whatever would be on the pavement outside the butchers there and them blue bins is well rank believe me. And there be some a them junky out the hostel on the pavement and standing around the old payphone up the road and on them days Ruji-Babes would be sit at the front with one hand on that baseball bat all day and even Foxy-T might have that machete tuck away inside a Metro next to whatever computer she happen to be a fix that day. And they was just like that all day cause on them kind of long day you never know when some rude boy is gonna come fe rob you. And believe me them robber can be quick init and just blend in with the background like they is any other person going about there business and going down the shop or something fe get there fags. And on days like them Ruji-Babes might be just shake with the nerves of it all and Foxy-T would be about ready fe cut someone up just fe look in the window funny when they walk past. And usually on them kind of day nothing would happen at all even though them two could feel that some one was definitely out fe try and rob them. Just for some reason they never. Like them rude boy change there mind or whatever at the last minute yeah. But believe me them no let up is it. Man cant relax when them run a shop cause you never know when them thief a go come seen.

One a them type a afternoon was when Ruji-Babes had gone up the bank with her cousin fe do some business cause him a drive pass after collect him tax off them other business there and then they was plan fe go up the cash and carry and buy them few box a top ups or whatever and it was just Foxy-T in the E-Z Call by herself. And she sitting at the front of the shop with that machete hid under some paper or whatever and the sunlight was come in low over the roof of the Nagina Sweet Centre init and it be that type of thick gold light what just seem to hang in the air like man can reach out and touch init and she was just sort a day dream and not even really keep much of a eye on thing because perhaps she be like think about some problem with them computer or whatever. And Foxy-T always a bit like that init not really pay too much attention to anything. Like she was a million miles away and I dont know what she was think about but she was probaly listen a bit of chatter outside in the street or whatever. And there be music a come out the door a the Cannon Video like normal and them play some film music init and she be think about that film cause she knowed it and knowed them scene what go with that music where some man and woman them play hide and seek around some garden and maybe she also be like half listening to someone talking in one a them booth in the shop but not even able fe really hear what them a say just there tone a voice or whatever. And perhaps Foxy-T also just be listen to the sound a that guy in the empty factory opposite a play basketball like he done most afternoon and just listen to the sound a that ball bouncing on the concrete floor there. And the air be thick with all them sound and that type a gold light what catch all the dust in the air and she was look at them long shadow cast on the woodchip paper by that low golden sun or the shadows of them phone card poster in the window as they fell on the top of that lockup cabinet where she was a sit only just think about them man and woman in that film init.

I dont know maybe she look up for like a second or something anyway and there was a thief just stand right in front of her. She didnt even know how long him been standing there he might a been there for like five minutes or something. And she never seen this rude boy before but him stand there and look at Foxy-T like him try fe read her face init and for some reason that girl think him look nervous way him do that. And him just stand there looking at her right in her eyes man. And it was like this rude boy see right inside her in the way like she could see right inside them computer them or whatever and know whats going on in there well thats the way this thief was look at her init and it was like him maybe forgot what him plan fe rob or whatever cause them both just froze and looking into each other eyes for what seem like hours but was probaly only like a minute. And Foxy-T aint notice that music no more is it she just be look at him and notice that this thief wearing nice jeans and a Giorgio top and over that a short black leather jacket but good quality. And she even had one hand on that machete under the Metro what a fold up there on the top of the lockup cabinet but Foxy-T couldnt move or nothing and she felt like she being strip open and expose by this young thief and like she fill up with him eyes and like she cant breathe init. And this thief still just stand there and aint afraid of her at all believe me. And through all a this Foxy-T aint quite all there is it. It was still feel like she was day dream and she was probaly try fe make herself pick up that machete and tell him to like fuck off out of it but before she could even move or think straight or whatever him just turn and slowly walk out of the shop there. And him walk out real slow through that thick gold air init as if him have all the time in the world and nothing she could do was ever go make him do nothing him no want. And what shake up Foxy-T so bad was that she knowed this was what him a thinking and she knowed that he was right. She couldnt a done nothing even if she wanted to and the worse part of all this was that she knowed she never want fe do nothing anyway. Believe me there was no fight left in that girl or nothing. And by the time she like pull her self together and get out the door him half way down to the One Stop and she just watch him look back at her then get in him Golf or whatever and slowly drive away. And then him gone and Foxy-T is left just stand there and stare down Cannon Street Road at him indicator light flash as him turn left into Bigland Street and never even think fe check him registration or nothing. She want fe run after him init but she know that she couldnt even have caught him now because him long gone and she couldnt leave the shop without no one at the front or some other robber might come in and try fe nick whatever. So she just stand there and think about what she would maybe do if she found him or if she had of chase after him. But she knowed that if he come back again when she was in the shop on her own she wouldnt be able to do nothing then neither. Cause this thief a seen right inside her init and him knowed just like she knowed that she couldnt do nothing about him. And if you saw her then you probaly only think she look a bit more dreamy than usual and a bit blotchy on her neck and a bit wild eyed like only now him gone was she getting afraid of what might of happen or what she wanted to happen. What she knowed she wanted.

She was so out of it just standing there in the doorway like that that she probaly didnt even notice that Ruji-Babes and them was back and them two is get out of him car. And Ruji-Babes cousin say 'Yes T' nuff time init before that girl wake up and check them two is reach. But she still distract init and dont say nothing only smile and step back in the E-Z Call. And he look at Ruji-Babes and raise him eyebrow in Foxy-T direction but then him mobile ring and him say, 'Listen Rooj something come up man. Later yeah,' and then him get back in the car and them gone.

Ruji-Babes follow Foxy-T back in when him gone and say, 'You alright T? What's going on man?'

And thats when Foxy-T wake up init and probaly look around and see all them computer screen working normally and a couple a people checking fe them email or whatever and that old Somali guy what live in them old people flat down Miles Court where Ruji-Babes grandad live before him die is still talk in the booth and the gold light still coming in low through the window and she just go, 'Yeah Rooj safe man,' and didnt say nothing about that thief at all is it.

And Ruji-Babes is got some take out on her way back from the bank init. Only normally them two would try and eat after work cause them no like eat together in the shop. This is partly because them two like there privacy or whatever and partly because it felt a bit rude fe sit there and eat in front of your customer and have fe wipe your hand before you serve them and not wanting to eat and deal with other people money and then go back to eating when you dont know where there money been or if them guys wash there hands. But right now them no care about them thing cause them miss lunch init so is like a early tea and once she put them new box a top ups in the cabinet there Ruji-Babes just clear some space on the top a that lock up cabinet and spread out the Metro on the top and tear open that bag and lay out them naan breads and some little bag of salad or whatever like chop up lettuce and tomato and carrot and cucumber. And she also got some kebab and a tin-foil container with some tarka dal in it and them two just sat there in what left a that golden sun init and broke off bits a there naan and be dipping them in that dal and eating bits of salad with there fingers or whatever and while they was eating Ruji-Babes was chat away about something or other what the bank had said and this and that like something what happen or what they seen from the car up Romford Road and Foxy-T was just eat like automatic init and she be listening and day dreaming in that boyish way that she had of not really listening and not really saying much except to say yeah or seen or whatever. And thats what she was sometimes like anyway so Ruji-Babes didnt think anything different than usual but believe me Foxy-T was well distract and shook up inside and trembling with the memory of that thief and still feel that way him a look right inside her. And when they finish eating and all them food containers was chuck in the bin outside and Ruji-Babes a screw up that newspaper and then wipe down the top a the counter or whatever Foxy-T just went and stand in the doorway looking back down the street the way that thief had driven off in him Golf. That little robber what had look right inside her and understood what she was all about or so it seem to her when she was standing there. And she reckonise that way he had of look at her because that was the way she had of look at thing sometimes when she knowed everything about it and understood it and felt like it was a part of her or something she had control over like them computer what she knowed everything about and can see what they is doing and what they is try fe do and what they is gonna do in spite a that. She could remember him eyes and the way him look at her and the way she felt that she was part of him. And the way him look over him shoulder at her from down the street before he got in him Golf as if he was invite her fe follow him. Like him invite her fe come join him but also like him a laugh at her inside the same way that she would sometimes have that secret smile on her face and all when she looked at them computer or at some stupid boy what is try fe chat her up. So she was shake up cause she recognise him manner in herself init.

And the sun going down by this time and that golden light disappeared init. And it getting cold and start fe get dark and from inside the shop Ruji-Babes is call her name and going, 'T! I think this phone is busted because that call what that old guy was making didn't come up on the screen is it. Was it working when you log him in?'

And that Foxy-T probaly couldnt even remember if she even logged that man in fe start with though she must of init because otherwise him wouldnt of been able to make him call or nothing but fe true she couldnt remember nothing else about it and she knowed that she didnt keep a check on the screen or whatever when him talking or even probaly look fe check the time him hung up and finish or whatever. So she couldnt say nothing really to Ruji-Babes except like shrug her shoulder and go, 'Yeah.'

But she come back in the shop and step over anyway fe take a look at the phone then she come over fe check it up on the screen and then she found it and say to Ruji-Babes, 'Oh yeah look man I just save it to the wrong account init.' Then she just drag it over the right account and everything sorted. Only it wasnt sort is it since her mind still out there in the evening streets where them buses was going past with there lights on and people all coming home from work and shutting up them shop and a wait fe them chicken and chip or whatever and she just thinking about that cheeky little thief and she want fe grab that machete and slash that vinyl on the roof of him Golf or smash him tinted window them with the baseball bat.

She didnt say nothing to Ruji-Babes about it that night when they was upstairs after they done all the locking up and shutting up shop and pulling down the shutter. She didnt say nothing at all not till like on Sunday when they was watching Antique Roadshow and she just went, 'Yeah Rooj, this thief come in the other day but he didnt nick nothing.'

And Ruji-Babes was like surprise and goes, 'When was this? Why didnt you say nothing T?'

And Foxy-T was like, 'Well him no try fe nick anything but I know say him a robber init but I was like too surprise to do nothing. I dont know man.'

Ruji-Babes couldnt believe her ears probaly and she went like, 'What you didnt do nothing at all? Not even phone the police them?'

'No,' says Foxy-T. 'Him just a stand there lookin at me like him daring me fe pick up that machete init only him knowed I wouldnt do nothing.'

Ruji-Babes was getting right jumpy and going, 'Them little bastard thief aint afraid of nothin T! What we gonna do when they aint even afraid of us is it. What use are them baseball bat and machete when they aint even afraid a them thing. I wish youd a took that knife like in Crocodile Dundee init and scared the shit out of him. That fuckin little thief I tell you!'

'No I know man,' says Foxy-T. 'But I been keeping my eye out for if I see him again so I can make a note of him registration or whatever but I aint seen him at all is it. I dont think that thief from round here cause I aint seen him before. Maybe he come from up Whitechapel or something.'

'Well I dont think he be coming back now is it,' says Ruji-Babes. 'Cause him know we know what him a look like. The cheeky little bastard! Fucking hell man I tell you if I see him I'm gonna cuff him one with my baseball bat init. That would get him well scare init.'

But after that Ruji-Babes probaly forgot about him really. Just got angry when she think about thief in general not nothing special about this one robber what Foxy-T was talking about.

And Foxy-T probaly didnt even think about him much neither not on purpose anyway. Just when she was shake out her pony tail and stand there on one leg with her hands clasp upon her head and try fe like figure out what was wrong with one a them computer she would be day dreaming in another part of her head because thats the way she used to think by half thinking about something and then half not thinking about it. And whenever she was do this she wouldnt be able to help it but that little thief looking over him shoulder at her like he was invite her to get in his car was what pop into her head. That and the way him just stand there and stare straight in her eyes across the lock up cabinet as if to say him knowed everything about her. And this went on for ages man. Like if she was changing the tariffs on the database for all them different phone cards when the rates went up or whatever she probaly find herself thinking about that thief. Or if she standing on the counter and stickin up them new A4 sheets on the window what advertise them different rates then she maybe find herself thinking about that thief. And even just when she wasnt doing nothing but like check her hair in the mirror in there downstairs toilet out the back of the shop it would sometimes be just like it was that litle thief what was look back out the mirror at her. And them kind of time she could smell him hair gel and him leather jacket and everything. And remember thing she hadnt even notice at the time like him gold earring them and the sleepy dust in the corner of him eye. Like if she was make some coffee upstairs to bring one down to Ruji-Babes at the front when it was a bit quiet and there was nothing on the radio then it would probaly be that fucking thief she was think about. It was doing her head in man believe me.

She soon start and find some reason fe go down Bigland way what she never done since she left school. If she was going up town or whatever instead of going up Whitechapel and catch the 25 she change her habit and start fe go down Shadwell and get the DLR just cause thats the way that him drive away init. She would tell Ruji-Babes that it was quicker and that fe go this way but really it was because she a look for that thief even though she never knowed what she gonna do if she seen him.

And after a while just going down that way by Watney Market was enough fe make Foxy-T feel that same way as when him looking at her up the E-Z Call. She just feel all strip open and expose init. Like he could see everything she a think even though him not there. It was like over them few weeks that way of feeling become a part of her personality and it was addictive man. She kind of half like feeling that way and all init though she probaly didnt admit it to no one. Not to herself and certainly not Ruji-Babes. But she found all kind a reason fe go down Shadwell. Believe me whether she knowed it or not she was hook man. Like crack only she didnt know it seen.

And Foxy-T was also start fe look at like other man she seen around the place whether customer or whatever just fe check them and see if she feel that same type of feeling what that thief make her feel. She never say nothing to Ruji-Babes about it and probaly didnt even think about it herself is it just she was doing this automatic and probaly never knowed she was doing it. And if Ruji-Babes a notice the way Foxy-T behave she didnt say nothing even if she was feel a bit panic or whatever cause man know that Ruji-Babes pay nuff attention to Foxy-T she have fe notice init but this would happen whether they was in the Quality Food Store or up the cash and carry or whatever. But also even though Foxy-T a tell Ruji-Babes about that thief she never tell her how him make her feel is it. So this was a big part of Foxy-T what she was hide from Ruji-Babes all through the rest of that summer whether she mean to keep thing from Ruji-Babes or not. And sometime like if they was on one of there walks what they might take on a Sunday and go down by the river it be like Foxy-T head was spinning around cause she just have fe check each and every one a them man she see. And also since Foxy-T well fit nuff man was always look at her and all init and she not afraid to catch there eye that Foxy-T only what she was a look for in them eyes she never find so them bloke would be cant believe there luck init to get some fit girl eye them up they think and them man try fe smile at her or whatever only by the time they done that she already knowed that they aint that type of man what make her feel like that thief done and she aint even look at them no more. And man know that Ruji-Babes must a notice this init only she never say nothing. And all the rest of that summer Foxy-T was act like this and just like look at nuff man init where ever they was and each time she was like hope and expect them fe have that same type of effect on her what that thief done only they never is it.

And them week go pass and soon it be like autumn again and the two a them hate that time of year man because you always have fe keep that door shut and it was a drafty cold place E-Z Call was. They had a couple of them Calor gas heaters what they could wheel around and heat the place up and that but if you got the door shut them things are rank and make your eyes sting and your throat all dry init. And them fume make Ruji-Babes contacts hurt and all and she just be sit there and her eyes is all red and stinging man and she just feel like cry with frustration sometimes. And them two a hate that time of year cause it mean winter on the way and thats even worse cause it felt like they was living in the dark init. Cause by the time it got light in the morning they be open up the shop and then it soon be dark again and they never got out in the light during the day so by the time they shut up shop and that it was like another day gone by and they never seen the sun. They was both the kind of people what at least like to get out for some kind of walk in the day whether its just down the Quality Food Store fe get some biscuits or whatever or one a them longer walks what they would take in the summer on like a Sunday when they shut up shop for the day and walk down Tower Bridge and just stand on them jetty out over the river down by the OXO and just look at the water and have some kind of quiet chat between the two of them. Both a them love them kind of walks by the river and they was them special kind of time init but in the winter it seem like you never get a chance fe get out and when you did man you was freezing whatever way you wrap up. Aint worth a walk down the river in that kind of rain and wind is it. And the worse thing about them dark days and long nights was that Ruji-Babes got even more afraid of robbers and thief what might come in the shop after whatever them could carry away. Foxy-T wasnt so afraid of that as Ruji-Babes but she just felt slow and heavy in the winter and knowed that they probaly argue more than usual when they was all shut up inside like that with no easy way fe just chill.

Still they would enjoy some of them evenings when like they would shut up at maybe eight or something when it was obvious no one was gonna come and make no calls or whatever. On them rainy nights when you aint gonna go down the E-Z Call to get no photocopies or make no calls. Them kind of nights when everyone just want fe curl up warm at home and watch telly and turn up the heating on full. No one gonna go down the E-Z Call on a night like that unless its desperate or something is it. And them nights would get a bit heavy sometimes because Ruji-Babes would be all chit chat and bustling around. Like that one always have fe do something or be fussing over someone init and because it was just the two a them the person she usually be fuss over is Foxy-T. Whereas Foxy-T could just sit quiet in the warm and like read when them watch telly or something without feel no need for chat or fuss or nothing. But that telly would just make Ruji-Babes get even more fidgety. She was one of them kind of people what cant relax at all sometimes. And as them day pass and it get darker and darker it seem to them two that is more and more night like that and neither of them two is think anything a go change and them just in for pure hard winter seen.

But fe true man never know what come around the corner is it and them two no different. Them two never knowed that this one night a go be different cause it start off like all them other bad night seen. One a them rainy night in autumn when it just a piss down outside and no damn fool gonna go and check him email in that type a weather is it. And them two had eat something or whatever and Foxy-T was sit there with her feet up on the coffee table and read one of them big software manual and half the time just be staring at the telly but mainly not really looking at what was on just watching the pictures like they was far away and then every now and then she might look back down at this big book on her lap and turn over the page or look back at the end of the last page so she could try and find her place again. Only she wasnt really concentrate on either of them things. Ruji-Babes was sit there and wishing she could read something or whatever like a magazine or something but she took her contacts out because of the Calor gas fire make them feel dry and itchy so like I say it was impossible fe wear them things at time like this and there was no way she could read without them contacts and she didnt like wearing her old glasses cause for one thing they werent strong enough now is it. They was still the ones what she had at school and them glasses make her nose hurt and her head swim like she was back in double geography down Mulberry or something. And she never got a new pair or whatever because she decide long ago that she didnt want fe wear glasses ever again but then on nights like this when she couldnt wear contacts neither it was murder because she just want fe read and daydream like Foxy-T doing. Only cause she have fe wear them contacts all day down the E-Z Call now work a finish she aint go wear them is it. So she was watch the telly from as far away as she could without her eyes hurting even more and listening to the DLR going past in the distance and them kids down Bigland letting off fireworks what have been in the shop for like month already even though is only October and still like three week till bonfire night.

They wasnt expecting visitors that night or any other because they never got no one coming round in the evenings. Even Ruji-Babes cousin or whatever only come in the daytime init and always phone up first and never come round without arrange it first. So they was surprise to hear someone a knock on the security shutter down at the front of the shop.

Ruji-Babes look up and catch Foxy-T eye.

'Well I dont care who that is T,' she says, 'because I aint gonna open up shop this time of night for no one init.'

'Seen,' says Foxy-T. 'They can wait till morning or use the flipping pay phone.'

Then they both went back to what they was doing or not doing and think nothing more about it.

But just because they wasnt think about it doesnt mean it gone away does it. And sure enough like maybe twenty minutes later Foxy-T sat up and look over at Ruji-Babes. 'Did you hear that Rooj?' she aksed her. But there werent no answer cause Ruji-Babes was now sit up straight in her chair and all because she had hear it and all. And the thing what they both heard over the noise of the telly from up there in there sitting room above the shop was a footstep. And theres nothing strange about a footstep when its outside on the pavement or whatever or running down the street late at night cause thats the kind a thing you hear all the time around here believe me. Theres always someone running away from someone else round here. Some thief with a car radio or a video in a bin bag or whatever. Or just some rude boy a fool around with him mates and run fe catch up after stop and chat with one of him spar. But this footstep wasnt out the front of the shop in the street is it. This one was out the back and come in since the kitchen window a open fe get rid of them fume and the smell of cooking. It sound to the two a them like someone had gone round the back of the buildings and climb over that wall round there little back yard. Which would take some doing believe me because you have fe climb over a couple of other walls before you got there and nuff like barb wire and shit upon them wall out the back a the E-Z Call so it didnt sound like it was no accident that someone had jump over the wall into there little back yard. So they was well shock init. Trust me man would have fe make a big effort fe get into them yard.

Ruji-Babes made to get up but Foxy-T shush her down and like stared at her for a second like she heard something else and what she thought she heard was some footstep on them steps what went up to the back door what lead into that little hallway by there toilet downstairs. And next to the toilet door was that door they always call the upstairs door what leads from the shop to the flat or from the flat to the shop. And her and Ruji-Babes was just stare at each other right because they both heard that footstep on them steps what lead up to the back door. But it was what they heard next that got them shitting thereselves. Cause someone like maybe some thief or robber or whatever was putting a actual key in the lock and turning it real slow. And them both try and think is all next door init but you know the sound a your own lock init cause you hear them turn every day so aint no mistake is it both a them knowed is there back door what is be unlock. And they both heard that lock going and then they heard that familiar squeak what the back door makes when you open it and whatever oil or whatever Foxy-T might of put on them hinge is still gonna squeak and nothing you can do about it and thats what they heard next. They was really shitting it now for real and Ruji-Babes reach down beside her chair and pick up that baseball bat and same time as that Foxy-T was glancing over at the shelf where she put her machete when they come upstairs and she went and got that machete didnt she and they both just standing there in the middle a the room facing that door what they knowed was surely gonna open up any second. And this like there worse nightmare init some thief a come at night. But it seem like hours they was waiting there both a them shitting it and just looking at the door handle and waiting for it to turn.

And both a them knowed that some thief or other was coming up the stairs because they could hear that creaking as he come up. It was almost too much to bear believe me and Ruji-Babes being a bit of a weakling like I say was almost fainting with pure fear and half pissing herself probaly while she stood there waiting for that minute that they both knowed was gonna come when that thief open the door fe confront them in there own living room.

And they is both just stand there and looking at the door and they could feel the touch of someones hand on the door handle almost before they seen it move. It was like someone a touch them init and they both feel like them want fe just run away as far as they could from that room where they was standing. Both a them would a rather been anywhere else in the world at that moment but there was nowhere for them to go is it because the only door was the one that was just about to open. And thats what happen then. That door just start swing open real slow.

Ruji-Babes and Foxy-T was pale and shaking with terror by this time and it was Ruji-Babes was spoke first she say just, 'Who is it?'

She shout it out real fast and high pitch and the door stop opening for a second init but no thief come in yet.

And Ruji-Babes says, 'We is armed! What you want? Who are you?'

And this thief just say nothing and then the door open and he come in and he was some young man who was carrying one of them thin kind of carrier bags you get from the newsagent but they couldnt see what was in it and him have like a ruck sack on him back. He never have no weapon either is it. He look wet and cold and look first at Ruji-Babes with that baseball bat and then at Foxy-T with that machete what she was holding out towards him. And he could see she was shaking because that blade was shake and tremble even more than she but then him look again at Ruji-Babes and just walk them few step over to where she stand cause he seen the baseball bat init but him figure she aint never gonna use it so him just put him hand out and take hold of it so she knowed that if she try and move it him gonna catch it first. And this thief just stand there right in front of Ruji-Babes like this for a second and look at her like him try and figure something out init and the way them both hold that baseball bat it look a bit like them two is hold hands init and none of them move they all stand there like that for a few second until he say to them 'Who are you?'

And they both go, 'We live here!' and both a them speak at the same time. And when him hear this him look puzzled and look again at Foxy-T then back to Ruji-Babes and none of them is moved yet and none of them two is even try fe use them weapons is it.

'Who are you anyway?' Ruji-Babes aks him, 'and what do you want? You better tell us or we calling the police init. Why you want fe break in here eh?'

And he take a deep breath this young man standing there with that carrier bag in him hand and Foxy-T can see that him cold or whatever because hes only got on some t shirt and a little black jacket and his hands is all cold looking and all and cause Ruji-Babes so close to him she is like feel the cold night air come off him init. And he goes, 'What? Mr Iqbal no live here then?'

At the sound of him voice Ruji-Babes is just like step back and let go a the baseball bat and it drop on the floor by him feet cause he never expect her fe do that and him unprepare. But she aint make a move for that bat is it and him must figure that he have the upper hand there cause him no make a move neither. Both a them girl is pure puzzle init cause him no sound like a thief when him say that. And him no aks where them keep there money or whatever.

Then him think for a second and remember the key in him pocket and him fetch it out and like jangle it in front a Ruji-Babes and say, 'I never broke in man. I thought Mr Iqbal live here anyway. Who the fuck is you two?'

And Ruji-Babes says like, 'No, we live here init. Theres no Mr Iqbal here and it dont matter who we are.' She look quickly over at Foxy-T who also look like she about to faint only this aint going the way them two thought it was gonna go is it. You aint normally gonna chat with no robber so Ruji-Babes dont know what to say for a second. Then looking back at this youth she say again, 'Who are you? You better tell us man or we gonna call the police!'

And he goes, 'Well, Mr Iqbal lives here too. Wheres he gone man? He's my grandad and I use to live here too for a bit. Wheres he gone do you know?'

Then he drop him bag on the floor and Foxy-T felt completely lost because there she was all ready to defend them against some thief or robber and then there they are with some young man what is obviously lost init. And she was just a bit lost herself at the sound of him voice aksing for him grandad. So she just stood there but she didnt drop that machete she just stood there staring at this young man who was a bit younger than them two. Like maybe twenty or a bit younger. He wasnt nothing special is it just some young man you might pass in the street or down the shop without even look at him. But neither of them had seen some young man lost like this before. Young men was always the ones what was after something from you with there type of cockiness. But this boy what had lost him grandad was not doing none of that. He had a kind a sharp face with a longish black fringe just swept to one side a bit but not so slick and fashionable as them rude boy them round here what do burn ups along the walkways in the Bigland and practise there skids and play there music or whatever and act like dealers and players. And there was nothing particularly crisp about the way him dress is it. She look at him eyes which was bright and dark even by the light of that lamp they had by the telly. She could see them soft hairs on him cheek. He just stood there looking from Ruji-Babes to Foxy-T and back again. Ruji-Babes was wear just her normal kind of smart skirt and a blouse like a young woman might wear to work or whatever and Foxy-T was wear some Reebok Classics and a pair of trackie bottom and some big type of Adidas polo shirt. Boys clothes him think for a second. Then him look at that machete what she was still a hold in her hand. While he was look round at Foxy-T there was a noise as Ruji-Babes sit back down defeated. She was turn away and from the way her shoulder start fe shake it look like she might be crying. It was all too much for that Ruji-Babes.

'Is he dead do you think? My grandad?' the boy aksed after a bit.

'Well, we been here a couple of year now,' says Ruji-Babes who is not crying no more and pulling her self together and figure out this aint no thief just some lost boy or other.

'Yeah?' he says, 'Shit man I been away for about four year and he was here when I left. Shit man a couple of year? For real?'

'What use to be downstair in the shop in them day then?' aks Ruji-Babes. She start fe get her strength back init and decide fe test him a little.

'Was Cannon Street Car when I live here. My grandad use to rent this flat off them.'

Ruji-Babes almost sigh with relief init and say, 'Is it? No I think he die init that old man what live up here back then. Me uncle tell me them Cannon Street Car move out after that init.' Then she look at him and go, 'Sorry man I . . .'

'Shit man. Dead?' aks the young man again.

'Yeah. I think so,' says Ruji-Babes.

'Seen. Seen,' says the young man. He was still staring at them with this same kind of expression like half totally baffled and half like curious about them two and what have we got here then in him sharp young mind cause even though him a bit lost he was still a young man init and that side of him a start fe come out more and more with every second.

And Foxy-T was still just stand there with that machete in her hand and look at him that same way what she look at the thief a few month back on that summer evening. She saw him that same way no matter how hard she try fe think, 'Well its just some lost young man.' Seem like the air in the room go thick init like she cant breathe and nothing she can do about it.

Ruji-Babes was like, 'How comes you dont know if your own grandad dead or not then?' Because she was back to her normal fussing self and had start fe doubt this young man story by now. Everyone know it use to be Cannon Street Car downstairs. That aint prove nothing is it. Just mean that him could a pass this way before dont say that him must a fe live here or whatever. Any fool knowed this use to be Cannon Street Car init.

'I been up Feltham for about four years,' say the young man. Then him look a bit sheepish like him maybe regret a say that since going up Feltham aint something you is gonna admit to people what you dont know.

Both a them girls knowed what Feltham is and they stiffen a

bit cause perhaps him a thief after all and out fe rob them but he says like, 'I use fe nick cars and stuff when I was a kid but I aint gonna do that no more is it. I aint going up Feltham again. Its a nightmare up there for real especially fe them young Asian man with all them racist and shit. Man I aint going back there for real believe me.'

'Is it?' says Ruji-Babes taking charge again. 'So when you get out?'

'This afternoon man. Me just reach init.'

'Seen,' say Ruji-Babes. 'So what you get the train back? Feltham up pass Harrow way init.'

And hes like, 'Yeah them give you like a ticket home and tube fare and the stuff you come in with init then plus I got a giro fe cash tomorrow up Whitechapel post office. I just got the tube down from Kings Cross man.'

In fact him no take the tube him walk init fe save the fare since Kings Cross aint that far if you go up Pentonville and down City Road. And by save that tube fare him have enough money fe buy a pack a Lambert and Butler. Only he aint gonna admit that to them two girl is it.

No one said nothing now they just all stand there and stare at each other.

'You have somewhere fe stay then?' aksed Ruji-Babes.

'I don't know man maybe I can check me spar init and if not theres them empty flats down Shadwell,' he say. 'I figure me go and stay there then see if I can find my sisters place out Dagenham in the morning.'

'Is it?' aks Ruji-Babes.

This young man just don't say nothing but just look from one a them to the other and then back again and Ruji-Babes imagine how him feel just find out about him grandad like that. Then he break the silence and say, 'Well I don't know man. I just plan fe check me grandad init. I don't know. Me a go find somewhere.'

'Sit down for a bit man,' she say and point at the chair.

He pick up him carrier init then sit down and put it on the floor by him trainer. That baseball bat just left on the floor there.

'What them a call you?'

'Zafar.'

'Zafar! Shit we knowed a Zafar once init. Him a fool!'

'Well I aint no fool is it,' say the young man. 'That just me name seen. Zafar Iqbal. Same as me grandad init.'

Then him check both a them woman init and him aks them the same question.

'Man call me Ruji-Babes,' say Ruji-Babes. 'And this Foxy-T . . .'

And this Zafar laugh and say, 'Shit man them sound like tag init. So them you real name? Shit man.' And him a laugh again init.

Ruji-Babes look at Foxy-T and raise her eyebrow. 'When you ever meet someone with name like that eh?' Then she laugh and all. Is just Foxy-T no laugh.

'I'll make some coffee,' says Ruji-Babes then she look over where Foxy-T stand and say, 'I think you can put that down now T.'

And part of Foxy-T is think no way she can possibly put this machete down but she slowly reach and put it on the table next to the telly then she pick up that baseball bat and think for a second before she put it down on the table and all then sit down where Ruji-Babes was sit before and just sit there quiet for a second.

Neither of them two is say nothing now and Ruji-Babes is gone through the kitchen. And then Foxy-T thinks actually she cant bear fe sit in the same room as this thief cause thats how she thinks of him and now funny she cant remember what that thief look like before cause theres just this new young man who is filling up all them same bits of her like that other robber done before and like none a them other man done and she just feel like she have fe get out a that room before she bust init so she thinks maybe she'll make that coffee so she a stand up and say, 'I'll make that coffee,' then thinks for a second and say, 'You must be hungry init.'

And hes like, 'For real man! I'm starving!' And then he shake him head and start to laugh at what happen since him a bit freaked out as well init not just them two got a surprise tonight.

Then him say, 'Shit man! I wasnt expect this when I come out is it! I wasnt expecting this at all man.'

But he didnt seem sad about his grandad is it only kind a curious about the flat and about Ruji-Babes and Foxy-T.

Then him look around at there living room and goes, 'It looks a bit better in here and all init! My grandad never have much furniture and stuff is it. You know what old people are like from back home yeah. They happy with not much stuff init.' But them two girl have got there living room looking well nice init. Aint much furniture fe true but a couple a nice arm chair and a sofa and a telly then they got nuff big poster on the wall. When him check them film poster and that he say, 'This look much better now fe true. Where you get them poster man.'

'Cannon Video man. Next door neighbours init.'

Foxy-T was in the kitchen next door and sort out some food and coffee only there wasnt much in so she was just make beans on toast. But even in there she could still hear him voice in the other room. But it was more like when someone like some customer make a call downstairs and you can hear them voice but not really hear what them a say. And even though she was like open them beans and tipping them in the pan and putting some bread in the toaster and sorting out plates and cutlery and stuff and try fe concentrate on doing them things she felt that she was just as out of it as she was when that thief stood on the other side of the lock up cabinet downstairs and he seen what she was thinking inside. Stirring the beans and putting Flora on the toast this was all she was think about except that she felt slightly ashamed only fe give this young man something like beans on toast. 'He's probaly been eating beans on toast up Feltham for the past four years init,' she think to herself.

When the kettle boil she done there coffees and then she put him beans on toast and a coffee on to a tray. Her denim jacket was like drape over the back of the kitchen chair and she pick that up now and put it on init. Cause she felt a bit self conscious about this young man seeing her now for some reason. As she come back in the sitting room with him tray and that him sat up in the chair and look around fe watch her coming in. Believe me man she felt more faint now than she did when them think he was a robber or something.

That boy a watch her now as she bent down fe hand him the tray. She was just wearing her usual Fila trackie bottom and Reebok Classics and Adidas polo shirt but it felt to Foxy-T like she was wear some sexy gear or like she was pure undress the way him a look at her. Anyone would probaly say that him fancy her way him a look her up and down like that.

The room was a bit dingy init because there was just this lamp on next to the telly and him face was catch the light. It was almost like this Zafar was the only person in the room who was lit up. Ruji-Babes was sit on the sofa in the shadows and now she give him that tray Foxy-T went back out into the kitchen and get there beans on toast.

Ruji-Babes says, 'Hang on T. I think I'll have my tea on the table.' Then she stop for a second and look at that boy and say, 'You can come and sit at the table and all if you want.'

But that boy was already tucking into them beans on toast on him tray and he look up at where Ruji-Babes a sit in the shadows with him mouth full of beans on toast and says, 'Cool. No listen I'm fine here man.'

And Ruji-Babes says, 'Sorry is only beans on toast.' But she can see that him well enjoying it as much as if it been a big spread up Tayyabs and she knowed that even if him a sit down in front of a table that was groaning under the wait of loads of chicken tikka and lamb chop and seek kebab and dal and bhindi and a couple of naan and one of there big brass mug of mango lassi that he wouldnt enjoy that meal half so much as him enjoy just sit there and tucking in to them beans on toast in there sitting room. And Ruji-Babes felt like she was enjoying having someone round because they never did have anyone round for tea or nothing and fe true them two was hungry for company init. To Ruji-Babes having Zafar there feel easy init and like having her little brother round or something having this young man appear out a the blue and stopping for beans on toast. And even though she was as scared as she could of been when they heard him footsteps out the yard and they heard him put the key in the lock and when they heard him come up stairs and open the door – she was shitting herself then believe me but now she was just relax and enjoy having someone round for tea.

'What happen to that coffee, T?' she said.

And Foxy-T whose been sitting there quietly eating her beans on toast like a mouse say, 'There here init.'

When they all finish there beans on toast Foxy-T gather up them plate and put them in the sink. Then she go in the front room and she could see that the young bloke finished all him toast but still have some beans on his plate so she says, 'Would you like a slice of bread and butter fe mop up?'

And he says, 'Wicked man! Please!'

So she took another couple of slice of bread out the packet and got the Flora out of the fridge and make him a couple of slices bread and butter what she took in and give to him. He just start fe push loads of beans on to that bread and eat it like that with him fingers and just mop up all of the tomato sauce with them two slice of bread.

Foxy-T then fetch her coffee from the kitchen and went and sat down on the sofa again right over there in the shade. And she felt half dress even though she was wear her usual trackie bottoms and polo shirt and even though she got like her denim jacket on init. And she still felt half dress sitting there and so she sit back a bit and cross her legs but whatever she done that boy was just sit there wiping him plate with the last bit of bread and looking at her legs. And if the telly had been on she would have watched it and even though it was switch off she was sitting there looking at it but his reflection was all that she could see in that dark screen so that she didnt know where to look now. So she just sat there looking at the cup of coffee in her hand and drinking that.

The boy had finish up him tea now and him a sit there with that empty plate on him lap and that empty cup cause he drunk all his coffee now fe wash down the beans on toast and him just looking at her in the shadows on the other side of the room and it seem like he cant see her very clearly is it. So whatever chit chat Ruji-Babes was try fe make and whatever chat him give back him still mainly just try fe get a better look at that other one.

Still Ruji-Babes and all her fuss and question no give up. And soon that boy has tell them how him come from out Dagenham till he was like twelve or something and then him come and live with him grandad in this flat. Only he never really got on with him grandad because that man a bit strict and old fashioned in the way that lots of them old people are especially ones who spent most of there life back home. So he spent a lot a time running with some of them posse from down Shadwell and got into nicking and robbing cars and then doing burn ups down the walkways in the Bigland estate and doing skids and crashing them car in that playground down there or whatever. And whenever one of them car got wreck all the local kids would like get down off the climbing frame or whatever and rip off all the windscreen wiper and number plates. And this one little kid seen it was like him special job fe rip off the number plates them. And once he rip them off he go and put them down through the drain in Chapman Street then everyone smash them cars up man and someone might come down later on and torch it or whatever.

And Ruji-Babes was going, 'Yeah, yeah. Seen. I remember

that those was bad times round here man. And what so you get caught or something?'

And him say, 'Yeah. I was caught cause this one time some couple of Feds was walk through the estate and saw this going on and a couple of us got caught init.'

So this was when he went up Feltham Young Offenders. But he was out now and all that type of runnings was behind him fe true.

And Ruji-Babes is just like nod and go 'Seen' or whatever but she knowed man no get four year just through steal car is it. Only she no push it there just through be polite and through sympathy for him grandad dying.

Tell the truth though he was more interested in them girls than just talk about himself init. This Zafar was keen to know what they was doing here in him grandad flat and with there little business in E-Z Call. And they could tell he was a ghetto youth because of all him question them and the way he was slightly take the piss out of them but also keen fe check what kind of angle they was working. And when Ruji-Babes and Foxy-T start talking about them computer keep crash and that he was laughing and all because they was being quite funny about it all and slagging off Ruji-Babes uncle for buying shit PC to start with and telling all story about some of them customer and that and doing impression of some a them.

'Listen, though,' says Foxy-T. 'Cause we aint just interested in work all the time is it Rooj.'

'Is it?' aksed the youth laughing but still looking hard at Foxy-T over there in the shadows. 'But if them computer crash for good your fucked init. If you aint got a chain a these E-Z Call then you aint never gonna afford fe buy new machine is it? What you gonna do then?' he aksed.

'Dont know,' says Ruji-Babes. 'I think we gonna manage alright init.' But she got a bit of a funny look on her face when she say it like she might be worried that they wasnt gonna stay in business. At least thats what this boy think when him see her look like that only him dont know Ruji-Babes is it so him dont know what kind a business brain she got and how she probaly move there profit around and plan fe them type a thing.

'Listen man,' he says. 'You need a man around the place thats what you need.'

And when he say this Ruji-Babes bust out laughing dont she. And say, 'Listen. You little youth dont know what you a talk about is it. Fuck do you know? We is getting on just fine thank you. And what you know about business eh? Just got out a Feltham? Shit man. Init T?'

And Foxy-T look up pure startle like she never expect no one fe aks her nothing but go, 'Eh?'

And Ruji-Babes no pause for breath is it just go, 'Too right init and listen man you can have plenty people work here but still not run out a thing to do. But it just some little type a business seen. Like E-Z Call dont make enough money fe pay more than just us two is it. So we just happy to put in the hours and then take a little time off and enjoy ourselves sometime and all.'

'See thats what me say!' says the youth. 'You aint willing to put in the hours fe expand and make some more money out a this business is it.'

'You aint know shit man. We put in plenty hour and we dont need no lecture from some boy like you is it. But you got one thing right we aint into all that expanding talk,' says Ruji-Babes. 'We aint into all that shit fe true. But you aint know shit is it cause this a good business. Aks T man.'

But when him look at Foxy-T she no say nothing is it.

'All work and no play,' says Ruji-Babes, 'make jack a dull boy init.'

'Seen,' him say as him laugh at this. That youth was pissing himself now. The way them girl put him in his place have him crack up init. But then he stop laughing and goes, 'So why you start out in business then if you aint gonna make all them sacrifice and make a real go of it like. Tell me that!'

'Listen to this boy!' says Ruji-Babes. 'We make plenty sacrifice whatever that got to do with you man. And we making a go of it otherwise we wouldnt be here is it. But listen tell the truth we thought it might all be a bit easier than this. When we start out it seem like everyone making heap a money out a phone call and computers and we want some of that money for ourselves in it. But we know better now. Is only like your British Telecom and T-Mobiles is make any serious dollars out of phones. Dont talk to me about them global village and third generation mobile phones and shit.'

'Seem like you dont like that telephone industry there,' say the youth. 'You dont seem fe rate it.'

'Yeah we rate it alright,' say Ruji-Babes laughing. 'We just rate it low thats all.'

That youth laugh but Ruji-Babes carry on and no give him a chance fe talk now.

'Telephones, internet, top ups, phone cards,' says Ruji-Babes. 'Tell the truth I sometime think its all shit man. I tell you if there was money to be made in little shop like ours is bloody BT would be running them all init.'

'Seen,' says the youth. Then he start laugh again. And them girls start laughing too. Even Foxy-T was sit there and covering her mouth up with her hand like she no want that youth fe see her teeth.

'Still,' says Ruji-Babes. 'We dont fret. Do we T. We never vex. Easy come easy go, thats us.'

Sitting there in his chair this youth was well chuffed. That meal had sort him out. Ruji-Babes started aksing him a bit more about himself now and whenever she aksed him a question he was all polite and just answer quietly. He act like he didnt have nothing and no reason fe hide from them two it felt like. And him sitting in him grandad place after all init so in a way it was like them two girl was him guest and not the other way around.

Foxy-T aint say much is it. She no really a part a this conversation and she just sat and listen and maybe sip that coffee and look over at him occasionally from where she sat on the sofa there. And as he sat there chatting with Ruji-Babes by the light of that lamp by the telly she finally start fe chill init. And it was weird but she feel like that robber was round in there flat and like she didnt have fe go down Shadwell and look for him Golf no more. So she just sat there listening to him chatting away to Ruji-Babes only she didnt want to join in at all it was just like she want to sit there quietly in the corner and she can only do this when Zafar was a chat with Ruji-Babes and not glancing over at her where she sitting in the shade there on the sofa. There was something else and all which was that somehow this Zafar smelt a bit like that robber done. Perhaps it was him hair gel or something mixed up with how a young bloke what has had a long journey and walked a fair way in the fresh air might smell and it reminded her of that thief for some reason. This was a new kind of smell in this flat because them two

Ruji-Babes and Foxy-T just smelt of shampoo and conditioner and maybe a bit of perfume what Ruji-Babes sometimes wore since Foxy-T got her some for her birthday. But Foxy-T like them new smell and just sat there quietly.

The chat fizzled out after a while and that Zafar sat up a bit and looked over at Foxy-T all cosy on the sofa.

'I better go down Shadwell and check them place man. See if I can get in any of them empty flats down there for the night init.'

'You cant go down there,' says Ruji-Babes. 'Its just all junky and crackhead what doss in them flats. Most of them is brick up now any way.'

'Is it?' he aks.

And Ruji-Babes goes, 'Yeah.'

'Well me go sort something out,' says Zafar. 'Must be somewhere I can sleep for a bit.'

Ruji-Babes was thinking it aint a very good idea this Zafar going out and sleeping rough on him first night out of Feltham like this wasnt a very good start and he just probaly fall in with them crackhead and tramps wherever he went. Especially round here, she thought. Every little nook and cranny what could shelter some person from the rain and the cold night air would have been discover long ago init. You aint just gonna come out of Feltham and walk into some cushy little number what doesnt already have some mad rank old tramp or crackhead in it. The empty streets of the city at night is there neighbourhood them kind of people they know the runnings init and they gonna notice some new kid on the block just like we would in the day time if someone try fe move there family in the E-Z Call.

'You probaly better stay here for tonight,' she says. 'Till tomorrow init then you go over Dagenham and stop at your sisters or whatever. But tonight you can sleep on the sofa. But only tonight seen cause if my uncle found out he fucking do his nut init. And there a right bunch of nosy old women init them men what work in the sweet centre over the road and theyd soon notice and get on the phone to him believe me. Even if he is back home. Probaly use are own phone fe grass us up init.'

Then Ruji-Babes aksed Foxy-T what she think.

Foxy-T take a breath and look up a bit shock to hear her name init cause she just been sit there and listen to them but tell the truth she just been listen to the sound of them voice not what them a say since she lost in her thought. So Ruji-Babes go through it again and aks her what she think about them two may let Zafar stop on there sofa.

Foxy-T just want fe run init but she play it cool and say, 'Dont matter to me is it. I dont know man what business is it of your uncle if we put up a friend on the sofa for the night.'

'No thats right,' says Zafar. 'Its just for one night. Dont matter what he think about it. Whats he gonna do anyway. Is your flat aint it.'

'Well he could do a lot actually,' says Ruji-Babes. 'But what him dont know about wont hurt him is it. And like I say its just for tonight. I'll get the spare duvet out the cupboard man and then you can kip down on the sofa init.'

'You sure about this,' he says. 'You dont have fe put me up is it. I mean I dont want fe cause no trouble.'

And Ruji-B goes, 'No we sure man. You can stay here the night.' Foxy-T no say nothing is it and both him and Ruji-Babes take this to mean she agree.

He look at them both init and sigh like him grateful and him half laughing: 'Well thats a fucking relief then. Shit man me no look forward to kip down in some old doss hole down Shadwell or walk the streets all night and try fe stay out the way of the Feds is it.'

Foxy-T went up and got the spare duvet out the cupboard while Ruji-Babes fuss around and chatted. She make up a bed while them talk init and believe me that bed look well comfy to this Zafar. Nice clean sheet and pillow man and a clean duvet cover. Ruji-Babes was enjoy herself and all cause it feel just like having her little brother round for the night and all the attention what she might have want fe lavish on him somehow got lavish on this Zafar. He was grateful for this and it felt to him a bit like he had arrive at his sister place already only he knowed that when he did it wouldnt be half so comfy as this because him sister got a couple of kids and that now and it would be well noisy and crowded in her little flat out Dagenham.

Only that aint all him a think about. But the funny thing was that now she out the room when him try fe remember what Foxy-T look like he couldnt remember. That girl make some kind of a impression on him but him couldnt think what it was that she look like now that he didnt have her sitting in front of him. But even if she had of been there on the sofa still him might not have been able to get that good a look at her is it because it seem like she was kind of hide herself away from him in a funny sort of way what him couldnt figure out at all. Seem like even when she there in front of that Zafar and him just glance at her she get further away init and the more him try fe look at her was the more she hide herself away in them shadow.

When Ruji-Babes gone upstair Zafar get in bed and tuck

himself up init and aint long till him sleep. Believe me it was well comfy compare with them beds up Feltham. Him tired from him walk and the shock a getting out and him no believe him luck being in this flat and getting look after by them two girls. And he was just lay there for a bit and think about them two girl and wondering if they was gay and him just let him mind wander init and imagine what they might be doing up there in there bedroom. So he was just laying there on the sofa under that spare duvet and imagining them two going down on each other pussy or sucking on each other tits and it make him hard just lying there on the sofa. So he was laying there with his hand on him cock for a while and him just imagine that them two is lezzers and maybe one of them come down stairs and take him hand and lead him up them stairs so they could both play with him and let him fuck them both in all kind of way and he just drift off to sleep a happy man thinking about this probaly before he could even wank about it because him so tired and comfy after four years a them shit beds up Feltham.

But upstairs Foxy-T no sleep and when she did it was like she was just hear some man whistle in her dreams and she was walk all round Shadwell and in the Quality Food Store and up by Watney Market and by the rag and bone men and the Sari Centre and down the post office and the DLR station and yet where ever she go this whistling was always out of reach. Then she seen that robber again and him stand under a street lamp and just whistling and looking over at her in that slightly piss-taking way as if to say come and chat or whatever so she goes nearer but he aint really smiling and she see him picking him finger nail with like some little knife init so then she think better of it and turn fe walk away but him grab her wrist and wont let her go. And to Foxy-T in her dream it feel like him dig him nails into her wrist and she wake with a fright and just lay there in bed shaking.

In the morning Foxy-T is more or less forgot all about her bad dream though and she just get dress and make herself a coffee or whatever and then go down stairs to the E-Z Call without even look in fe see if that Zafar awake or not and she just switch on all the computer them and done her usual routine about switching on the server first or whatever then logging in and going in to the system fe check the phones all log in to the right networks and that all the phone cards and top ups is neatly stack inside that lock up counter and that they wasnt gonna run out of anything. Ruji-Babes go out early and all init because like a lot a woman Foxy-T and her no really eat big breakfast is it just have there coffees or whatever and like maybe one piece a toast but she figure that Zafar being a young man and just out a Feltham would probaly wake up starving and need a bit of breakfast inside him before he can go over him sister place up Dagenham. But is early init and none of them shop round here is open up before about ten o clock. Well the One Stop opens at eight o clock in term time fe sell sweets and fags to them school girls from up Mulberry with dinner money burning a hole in them pocket but they aint got much food in there is it so Ruji-Babes end up a walk all the way down the newsagents in Shadwell opposite the DLR there and fetch some cornflakes and a big carton of milk and another loaf since they use up most a that bread what they had last night. Normally her and Foxy-T would only get about a pint of milk because they only usually had it in there coffees or whatever but she figure she probaly better get a big two litre carton for

Zafar. When she reach back at the E-Z Call Foxy-T is already got the shutter up and is like fiddling around in the shop only the door still lock cause they aint open yet. Them two dont open E-Z Call up till about ten neither is it. But Ruji-Babes knock on the door and Foxy-T let her in and by the time she get upstairs and knock on the door what leads in to the sitting room and go, 'Eh Zafar you awake man?' that Zafar say, 'Come in man. Its OK I'm up now yeah.'

And he just sit there in a T-shirt with him like shorts on init and Ruji-Babes go, 'You sleep well?'

Zafar go up the bathroom fe get wash up and that while Ruji-Babes is put the kettle on fe make coffee and sort out a bowl for him cornflakes. Then she think for a second and like walk over by the kitchen door and say, 'Eh Zafar. You want a clean T-shirt man only you probaly about the same size as me init and I got a load. Shall I sort one out man?'

Zafar just go, 'Yeah nice.'

When him fresh Zafar put him clothes on and that T-shirt what Ruji-Babes lay out upon the sofa and then he go down stairs fe check the E-Z Call. He was look around at everything init and try fe remember where the old counter used to be when this still Cannon Street Cars and where that old drinks machine was and where the controller sat with him radio and Zafar remember all the calendar of like Mecca or whatever and map and shit on the walls. A lot had changed man you can depend on that. He was looking at all them computer which was all line up with there screen savers on and him look up when a bus went past. There never use to be a bus down here is it and he say to Foxy-T, 'Eh? What bus is that, man?'

And Foxy-T look up from where she sit and looking at a

screen on one a them PC and say, 'What? Oh is a D3 init.'

And that Zafar must have look a bit puzzle cause then she tell him it goes down Asda on the Isle of Dogs and up Bethnal Green the other way.

And he aksed her if it is a new bus and she says, 'Yeah couple of years man. But it aint very good is it. You can be standing out that bus stop for like an hour and its quicker fe walk sometimes and thats the truth because them roads aint wide enough for no bus especially when them lorries all park up on New Road. Takes ages man.'

And he look out at the bus stop over the road there and see some white bloke a stand there in him work clothes with a kid all dress up for school stand next to him. Then he look up at all them sign on the wall yeah. One a them say 'Strickly prohibited to access pornographic sites'. Another one say 'Polite notice. Please do not shut down the computer after you finished your job. Signed the Management'. Then he check all of them piece of A4 sellotape on the walls fe advertise all them different tariff what you pay fe call different countries. And it remind Zafar about the time when him use to look at all the map they use to have on the wall when it was still Cannon Street Cars init and how him would use to just look at all them different place on the map them or whatever and say them place names to himself and checking out how all cabs going to a particular distance would maybe like charge one uniform rate and then if you went over into the next area that was coloured in with a different colour marker pen the price went up. So still him couldnt think about some area in London like if one of him spar up Feltham say like him come from Edmonton without him automatically think of the price. The place and the price was all mix up in him head init. Only them price probaly well out a date now init. And is the same type a thing now init. Only when he look up at them telephone tariff and shit him couldnt understand what the reason is that mean a call to Lagos cost more than a call to the USA but him could see it did. But it aint like they is further away or whatever is it.

Zafar was look up at all of them tariff for ages and then out the corner of him eye he seen a D3 come the other way and stop at the bus stop there and that bloke and him kid getting on the bus and walking down the gangway to find thereselves a seat as the bus pull away up towards Whitechapel.

Then Ruji-Babes a shout down the stairs that coffee is ready and breakfast or whatever so him and Foxy-T stop what they was doing init and go upstairs.

'Its looking really different down there,' Zafar say when him reach the kitchen but he was thinking how it was kind of the same and still about travelling to them different place even if you was only talking to them different place and not actually driving to them place in the back of some old Cavalier with a air freshener in the shape of a no-smoking sign hanging off the mirror and some red-eye driver what you know has been kipping in him car because it still smell of sleep and sweat. It felt like him in the middle a some massive thing what is too big fe even grasp like a million time bigger than the Cannon Street Cars map of London and maybe more like a tube map or something init only bigger and with like Lagos and Karachi and New York instead of Tottenham Court Road or Finsbury Park and all them normal tube station. He was think about all them things while he munch him way through two bowl a cornflakes and heaping three sugars in him strong cup of Nescafe.

Foxy-T just sat quiet at the table and drank her coffee then had a bit of toast and Nutella when Ruji-Babes fix some. Foxy-T felt a bit like she did last night where she no want him fe look at her. But the smell of him hair gel never fail fe remind her of the thief again and it also remind her a bit of her dream. So that girl just sit there quiet and no say much is it. Ruji-Babes was the one fuss around and aks if anyone want more coffee and that.

It wasnt long til they have fe open up the E-Z Call is it. Ten o'clock soon come. Zafar done his bit to repay there kindness by sweeping up. Him also take a screwdriver and him scrape off some sticker what had make him laugh night before when he first come and knocking on the shutter before him come round the back way. That sticker had keep annoy Foxy-T and Ruji-Babes and all only them never get a chance fe scrape it off is it. That sticker right on the shutter there init and it say,

>'ABRAHAM IS NOT WAS A CHRISTIAN.
>MOSES IS NOT WAS A CHRISTIAN.
>JESUS IS NOT WAS A CHRISTIAN.
>I IS NOT A CHRISTIAN TOO. HA HA HA.'

When he done that Ruji-Babes aks him fe go over the £1 shop and fetch some heavy duty bin bag what he then fill up with all that rubbish what had been cluttering up that back yard for ages. Most of it was stuff from when Ruji-Babes uncle have the place refitted once he chuck the Cannon Street Cars out. There was a load of junk believe me. And Zafar found a bit of one a them old minicab office maps out there and before him broke it up fe stuff it in a rubbish bag he sat and look at it for a while and remembered him grandad. He check in that shed what use to be a air raid shelter cause him think maybe some stuff a go in there only it full a old sewing machine init. So he throw all them bin bag out the front next to the lamp post and when he finish sweep up him go back in and offer Ruji-Babes fe go up the shop for them and get some food in and them girls were going like, 'No, dont worry man. You is earned your keep already Zafar.'

But he was saying, 'No I might as well do something useful init.'

So they sent him down the Quality Food Store with a list of stuff what they need and Ruji-Babes count out some money carefully so there wouldnt be too much change and sent him away. He was back in about half an hour with some mango init and some frozen river fish from back home and some big flat breads and veg like tomato and cucumber. And then him pull out that couple a pounds in change from him pocket and tip it on the counter there where Ruji-Babes took it and put it back in her pocket. But he didnt say nothing about when he was gonna go up Dagenham to his sisters place is it.

In the afternoon he went out but Ruji-Babes and Foxy-T both notice that he didnt take him bag with him. He come back in the shop around five and look just as bright and cheery as he done the night before after him eaten that tea they give him. He take off him jacket and hang it on the back of a chair. They could see that him thinking about something or other.

'Did you call your sister?' aksed Ruji-Babes.

'No. I mean yes, I call but no answer this afternoon. So I call my cousin in Birmingham and he say yes Radya have split up with her husband and is staying up Birmingham with me auntie. But they both out when I phone init. My cousin say them gone fe see a solicitor or whatever. I dont know what I'm gonna do is it.'

'What do you mean do?' aksed Ruji-Babes.

'I mean where I man gonna stay,' says Zafar.

He didnt say nothing else is it. This was the boy in him they realise. And not only that but a boy who is been living somewhere he didnt need to think for himself. Where you knowed that you gonna get three square meal a day and a roof over your head whatever happen and without no need fe lift a finger. It was like that Zafar think that in making that call he had done him bit and now it was up to them what he done. And even though they wasnt even family and Zafar only meet them the evening before by pure accident init but somehow it seem like him think this was there problem and not his where he was gonna sleep that night. And both a them see this in him at that moment.

Foxy-T was sitting at the end of the counter and half listen to the radio and half listen to what Zafar been saying. Without really thinking about it she was looking at Zafar while him talking. He hadnt notice but look up and suddenly they was looking into each others eyes. Zafar and Foxy-T. They was both pretty surprise init and both felt like they jumped out there skins but truth be told they didnt move at all and Foxy-T felt that same look of slightly piss-takey whatever that she recognise in him the night before and what she recognise in the first place from that thief even if it was only her imagination which it might of been. And that look seem to burn right inside her and fill her up till she feel expose and strip open like she done with that thief init. And both a them was try fe turn away but neither of them can is it till Foxy-T made a funny expression like she was think about something else and look quickly out the window at the simple boy from the Nagina Sweet Centre over the road who was like stand there and shake some old box upside down over the gutter fe clean out all them scrap of food or whatever that was inside it. And she watch all them scrap fall down in the gutter then watch that simple kid go back in the sweet centre with him empty box and shut the door behind him.

Ruji-Babes was shake her head and look like she about to say something but she never. She certainly wasnt saying, 'Oh never mind Zafar. That dont matter is it. You can stay here another night.' She definitely wasnt saying that. She look over at Foxy-T but she didnt have her contacts in is it they was in there case on the counter there so she didnt see that Foxy-T look really out of it. That Foxy-T just look like normal to Ruji-Babes. Just like her normal dreamy self.

'What you think T?' she aksed.

But Foxy-T just say nothing and Zafar too just a sit there staring.

'You listening T?' aksed Ruji-Babes.

'Yeah?' says Foxy-T.

'Well what you think then?'

'What you want me fe say?' aksed Foxy-T without really thinking.

'What you think,' says Ruji-Babes.

'I dont know,' says Foxy-T. 'Whatever man.'

And then none of them says nothing for a bit init. And that Zafar just still sit there staring at Foxy-T like him eyes was the point of that knife what the thief might of had in Foxy-T dream last night.

'Yeah,' say Ruji-Babes eventually. 'Whatever init. I guess if you need to stop here another couple a night till your sister back then thats OK with me and all Zafar.'

Zafar didnt say nothing for a bit but just look out of the window or whatever then he just suddenly look up at Foxy-T and sort of half-smile at her again in that direct piss-takey way him have and she didnt know where fe look so she just look away. And Ruji-Babes dont know what to think. She just sat and watched the way that Zafar was look at Foxy-T but she couldnt really understand what that look mean because it wasnt like him a really smile just that this boy seem kind of intent on whatever it was. And him eyes was shine and all init.

Then he turn to Ruji-Babes and just goes, 'Listen I dont want to be no trouble to you two is it. Is nice you let me stop here last night man but I dont want to be no trouble.'

But Ruji-Babes goes, 'No its no trouble Zafar. Its like having my little brother to stay init that boy about the same age as you.'

'Well if you is both sure,' says Zafar. 'Only like I say I dont want to be no trouble believe me. But is nice of you to aks me and that would be brilliant man if your sure.'

'Course we do init. Make a change to have a bit of company dont it T.'

'Is that OK with you and all though?' he say turning to Foxy-T.

'Yeah whatever. I dont mind,' Foxy-T say in a half-hearted kind of way what Ruji-Babes never pick up on cause she aint got her contacts in yet like I say.

'Oh wicked man,' says Zafar.

Then him say, 'Listen man I was figure me go and check some of me spar this evening init. Is that OK. I mean I aint go be back late is it.'

'Seen,' say Ruji-Babes. 'Cause we don't got no spare key is it.'

And Zafar check him watch and say, 'Listen man they expecting me init. Later, yeah.' And saying that him stand up and pick up him jacket. 'Listen,' him say before him go. 'Thanks man.'

And all this happen right in the E-Z Call init where nuff man can hear them business. All the customer them is tap away an concentrate upon them email and shit like usual. But Foxy-T and Ruji-Babes is act like they aint there sometime. If them two want fe chat then they is chat init. And probaly is there life so them do what they want and like you aint go wait till like ten at night fe say something is it. You a just go say it when you think it seen. And them two is always like that believe me. Man can hear all type a thing them a talk about in the E-Z Call.

Cause tell the truth when Zafar a step out that afternoon and once him cash that giro up Whitechapel he probaly just been check around the place fe see him spar init. Listen man you been away four year that is what you a go do init. First thing man you go fe check you spar. Serious now. What else you a go do is it. And Zafar no different so probaly is man like Shabbaz and Ranky was who him a look for. Only maybe there aint no sign of either of them is it but still him just enjoy a walk around the Bigland and soak up the vibe. He just enjoy be back init. Just fe look down Cannon Street Road and see them DLR train cross the bridge. And walk where him want. Feel like home to Zafar seen. And trust me that Zafar is just pure enjoy the fact that he knowed he could walk as far as him please when him please init. And with that money in him pocket and all Zafar probaly feel like a king init. First thing him would a done is peel off some dollar fe buy a pack of Silk Cut, then him light up and step back down New Road. Fe true him never seen much a the area last night is it since it well late by the time him reach Cannon Street Road so now him just enjoy him freedom. Just fe hear man soundsystem when them drive pass feel good to Zafar now init. Aint too hard fe realise that he must a miss the area when him up Feltham is it. And him must bump into plenty people just walk around like that. But none a them is seen Shabbaz so Zafar figure him may check in the Golden Lion Social Club on the corner there. Place use to be ram init only now is quiet and just Jazeen there behind the bar like always. Even the pool table them is all stack up on there side. Jazeen just go, 'No man they is out of town init,' but Zafar aint stupid is it. He would a knowed that Jazeen knowed the runnings init and keep him eye open so Zafar probaly a go aks Jazeen fe pass a message that him back and Jazeen pick up him pen and go, 'Yeah man you got a mobile?' And Zafar laugh and say, 'Where me go get a mobile up Feltham man? Me just reach init.' So Jazeen smile and go, 'Seen. No worry I'll tell him. Safe man. Later.' Then him step outside again.

Best thing about just walk around far as Zafar concern was the woman them. Listen like I say man been away four year init. Him head must a been turn every minute seen. And nuff woman walk around Cannon Street Road init and them woman aint just like people mum believe me. Nuff a them fat old woman and all fe true but Zafar no have eyes for them is it. Seem like every where him look him a go see some fit woman init. Plenty a student and them thing. Russian Polish you name it man. Then just as him step back around onto Bigland Street him bump into one girl what him fuck a couple a time. Like that Lisa from Norton House. She look a bit older now fe true but that Lisa was well fit back then man. Nuff man around here is fuck Lisa init. And Zafar would definitely check her number and promise fe ring up and maybe see her later init. Believe me after four year of no woman that Zafar was prime and ready fe some action and him feel like he on a winner with this one. Him never need fe spin no lyrics that Lisa was all over him init. She was like touch him arm and look in him eye. Shit man. Easy now.

Him tuck her number in him pocket and as him stride off he just looking forward fe give that girl a fuck she aint go forget. If Lisa no change him know say she aint got no time fe make up is it but Zafar miss out on four years a woman and this one too good fe pass up. Believe me Zafar would be just walk around and think about how some pussy a go feel wrap around him cock init. Some nice tight pussy man.

When Zafar pass that Golden Lion again on the way back up the E-Z Call him hear man whistle init and call him name and as him turn around fe check it he seen that Jazeen is stand in the door way there and wave at him so Zafar cross and shake hand again.

'Shabbaz phone init. Him well please you back man and say fe meet him down the arch. He a go reach around six thirty.'

'Nice one man,' say Zafar touching fist with Jazeen. 'Later yeah.'

So this was where him a go now init. Now him leave E-Z Call after Foxy-T and Ruji-Babes let him stop another couple a night. Nuff man know that Shabbaz dad is got this arch down under the railway on Chapman Street where him sell like fabric and shit. Nuff time them use to spend in that arch back in the day init. They was there all the time man. When Shabbaz was at school him have a Saturday job a clean up the arch fe him pocket money. Him also have the key – so him and him spar would just go down there fe chill. Just a think about that arch and Zafar remember how it smell in there from all them big roll a fabric and all them big spliff. If you was walk down there on a Saturday afternoon back then you see them all a play football outside there and just from the way them laughing man know they well mash up.

The door was open when him reach the arch init and Zafar hear some man voice in there what is talk upon him phone like, 'I don't fucking believe it man. What did I tell you eh? What about the other one? Did you get the other one? Fuck man I can't rely on you is it. Listen don't bother fucking call me back guy is it not till you get that other one.'

Then him hung up so Zafar knock and say, 'Easy now. Zafar in the area!'

Someone inside go, 'No way man! Zafar? I thought you was inside man! Shit I don't believe it.' As he step inside him see Ranky and them shake hand and just laugh man. Ranky pass him a spliff and it only take one toke before Zafar mash up and pretty soon him start fe spin some story about Feltham what have Ranky hold him side and saying 'Stop it man.' It aint that him couldnt get no weed up Feltham but it was usually hash init and Zafar prefer him home smokes with spar from him own yard. Also him probaly spent so much time down the arch in him youth init that just fe smell them roll a fabric make him feel wreck. He hand the spliff back and Ranky take it then walk over to where Shabbaz dad is put in like a kitchen unit up the back a the arch there and him open the fridge and throw Zafar a beer.

'Shabbaz know you back eh?'

'Seen,' say Zafar as he split that can. 'Him say fe meet him here init. Six thirty.'

'Soon come,' say Ranky. 'Cunt never told me you was back is it.'

'Was keep it for a surprise probaly man.'

'Yeah init,' say Ranky laughing.

The two a them is just chill now init and finish that spliff and chat upon the old times but before he can finish him beer Zafar hear a car pull up outside. The door slam and it drive off then Shabbaz appear.

Zafar stand up an embrace Shabbaz init then shake him hand.

As them greet Zafar say, 'Shit man you is look good Shabs.'

And fe true Zafar probaly feel a bit shabby init. Both him spar looking well sharp but him just wear same as he was a wear four year ago. Plus some woman T-shirt. It fit him and that and it was just a plain Gap init but Zafar felt like he was still at school compare to them other two. Shabbaz was look well crisp. He was wear like some khaki jean and big black boot then over that some black polo neck. Also him have the kind a hair style that dont happen by pure accident. Zafar know them kind a hair style take nuff dollar fe keep up. Also both a them both Shabbaz and Ranky is also got little like beard and that. Not serious beard cause them two aint all that religious is it. Both of them is wear them type of beard what is make them white man look gay like George Michael or whatever but look well cool on them Asian youth.

'When you reach?' aks Shabbaz.

'Last night man.'

'Where you a go stay?'

'Me sort that out init,' say Zafar. 'Just up the road there.'

'Seen.' Shabbaz sit down on a office chair init and drop him bag then stroke him chin and look at Zafar then him laugh and shake him head and just go, 'Shit man.'

'Good init,' say Zafar.

'You got work eh star?' Shabbaz aks him.

'Give me a chance man,' Zafar laugh. 'Me pick up a giro when me get out init. But man know that no last long!'

'True,' say Ranky. 'True.'

'How much you got?'

'Fifty,' Zafar say quickly though him got a bit more.

'Listen man. Since I get you message off Jaz I been thinking about thing. We a go sort you out init.'

Shabbaz have a plan seen. Him figure that man look after him spar init so him propose that if Zafar give him that fifty as downpayment on a couple ounce a weed at cost then Shabbaz is lend him the rest till he sell it. Then him can buy a little more. While him talking Ranky go down the back a the arch and him come back with a bag what is full a eighth deals. 'That way you keep you giro fe live and rent and make some dollar fe yourself besides. Pay me back in a week init.'

Zafar well chuff init and go, 'Shit man you sure?' but Shabbaz just go, 'Listen is what man do init. Look after him own. Beside what else you go do tell me that?'

Ranky hand him that bag and Shabbaz undo it and count the deal them before hand it to Zafar. Is been a while since Zafar hold that much weed in him hand believe me. Him just lean down and smell them bag init.

'Is good man,' Shabbaz say. 'Listen, where people gonna check you now?'

'E-Z Call,' say Zafar.

'Serious? That where you a stay?' Shabbaz turn and look at Ranky init and him raise him eyebrow but Zafar just say, 'Seen. Thats me grandad old place init. I'm a just rest up there while me sister away.'

Ranky is laugh and make him hand like Foxy-T massive tits init and them other two laugh.

'Fe true fe true,' say Zafar. 'She well fit init. Me no kick her out a bed is it.'

'You be lucky star,' say Shabbaz.

'For real man,' say Ranky and nod him head, 'but Zafar speak the truth init she well fit that girl.'

Zafar is only just met Ruji-Babes and Foxy-T init so him dont know them two girl that well is it. But also Zafar aint stupid and him know them well enough just in one day fe figure that them two girl would be vex if them knowed he was selling weed. Kick him out straight away fe true. But also him figure that long as him keep it quiet they never gonna know is it. Aint gonna take him long fe sell a couple ounce.

'You got a mobile?'

Zafar look up and don't even have fe say nothing till Shabbaz just laugh and shake him head and go 'Seen seen. Sorry man. I aint thinking is it.' Then him turn a Ranky and say 'Where that Anwar put him old mobile man?'

Ranky go and check it init and toss it to Shabbaz and him switch it on fe check it a go work. Then him pass it to Zafar. 'Pay as you go init. Man left some credit. Aks them up T&T for charger. Tell them I go pay.'

'Safe man. Thanks,' say Zafar as him put that phone in him pocket. 'I owe you man.'

'For real!'

'How much this weed go for now then?'

'Twenty five dollar a eighth so give me another three back on this init – nuff man round here chasing weed. You aint gonna have to work too hard man.' Then him think a second and say, 'Anyway enough about that star. I keep forget you just got out! You got your eye on any woman except them two up E-Z Call?'

Zafar laugh then Shabbaz see what him a find so funny and him laugh and all init.

'I aint gonna fix you up with a woman and all man! You have fe do that on you own init!'

Ranky hand him another spliff then Zafar take a draw an remember that him bump into Lisa earlier and him tell Shabbaz that he plan fe check her later.

'You want my advice man dont go near that bitch is it.'

'Serious?'

'I know say we all been there init but nuff things change around here man and that girl a right slag now believe me,' says Shabbaz. 'Got a kid init. Shit you is about the only guy what aint in the frame for that init. You have a alibi star! No but listen man last time I seen her she begging 10ps off man in the street.'

Ranky look at him watch init and Shabbaz say, 'Anyway star is good fe see you back man. We is have fe run now. Call you yeah.'

Zafar figure that him spar have runnings fe attend so he place that weed in him jacket pocket and pass the spliff to Shabbaz.

'Yeah listen I got to run and all init. Respect.' He pat him jacket pocket and then touch fist with Shabbaz and Ranky. 'Later yeah.'

'Seen. Take it easy man. Good to have you back init.'

As him walk back up a E-Z Call that Zafar feel well please and satisfy init since him spar check for him. A couple a fit girl like maybe student them is wait at the bus stop there and Zafar smile at them init cause him feel a man now.

There nice music come out the door a Cannon Video and Zafar make a plan fe go in there later and check some a them CD but right now he go back in to E-Z Call and him see nuff customer in there when him open the door. But him sense something a go on while him down the road. Ruji-Babes is stand there and saying, 'I tell you man you turn you back init,' and Foxy-T say, 'I was just try fe sort them phone init.'

'Aint your fault man,' say Ruji-Babes. 'I tell you T. Fucking thief them! I could fucking kill them man.'

Zafar aks what happen init and them tell him some rude boy a run in when them back turn and jack three box a BT-Cellnet. 'Three box man,' say Ruji-Babes and she almost a scream init. 'Three box! Them thing cost we three hundred dollar man.'

'Is it?' him aks pure surprise. 'Shit man. Three hundred!'

'Fe true! And just from sell them we is go make six init! But now instead a that we lose six cause we have fe buy another three box. Shit man I tell you it aint worth it man.'

Ruji-Babes so cross she almost crying init.

But them thing she say make sense to Zafar seen. Him never think about them kind of thing before is it. Him never have no reason fe think about them thing. And believe me him jack nuff thing in him time and just figure them thing in shop for free init. Never cross him mind them shopkeeper a pay fe them stock out a there own money is it. But now cause him pocket full a weed and him only have like thirty dollar in him pocket cause him give Shabbaz that fifty and because him already a start plan how him a go deal with that and how him a go spend the dollar him make it make sense what Ruji-Babes a say init and him know say how he would a feel if someone jack that weed init. Zafar knowed he would kill them thief for try something like that. Cause believe me as him walk back up Cannon Street Road him head full a them sharp clothes him a go buy init even though him no fool and he knowed you aint go make a fortune out a deal some few eighth a weed. More like you is just go cover you own smokes init. But that aint stop him a dream is it. But also he been try fe figure out how him a go sell that weed init cause him sharp that Zafar and just then he put them two thing together in him mind yeah and them piece fit seen.

'Plenty thief round here init,' say Zafar.

'Believe it,' say Ruji-Babes. 'You is got you door open and they a go come in init. Seem like most day init T?'

Foxy-T was just look vex and no say nothing. She well upset init cause that thief a come in when Ruji-Babes a go upstair fe make a coffee init. And Foxy-T aint keep a eye on the counter so some rude boy just run behind that and do him thing. Wasnt till some customer a shout she knowed anything about it is it.

'You is need some security init man,' him say. 'You have fe do you work init. Cant keep you eye open all the time man.'

'Eh listen to this,' say Ruji-Babes. 'You got that right man. Only thing is you ever seen bouncer outside a phone and internet? Them man aint stand there cause they feel like it is it. Fe true we need security man but where we a go make enough dollar fe pay them camera and thing. You a think me a Stelios?'

Zafar stand him ground. Him knowed that Ruji-Babes aint be sarcastic at him is just cause she angry init. 'No I know that man,' him say, 'but listen if me sister away like another week init then I aint got nothing fe do is it. You know say none a them rude boy a go come in if they seen a man about the place is it.'

But Zafar knowed that Ruji-Babes well upset and aint really listen a what him say is it. So him just go, 'Sorry man I dont know is it. But think about it like I say. Maybe it a go work.'

Later when they finish lock up and go upstair and eat some roast fish and chapati Ruji-Babes seem a bit more relax init. She just been do them thing in the kitchen and have some cassette there and Zafar just been sit at the table an chat and listen to them music. Him no like them old film cassette normally is it but now him a bit mash up he get well into it believe me and just tap him foot to them drum init and read them cassette box. And fe true even though they is just met both a them feel well relax in each other company init. Ruji-Babes enjoy have someone fe chat with init and that Zafar aint have him nose bury in a book is it so Ruji-Babes find him easy fe get along.

Foxy-T no come upstair till them dinner ready is it cause she have fe check them computer and that. But when she come up and they eating Ruji-Babes just look over at him and say, 'Well Zafar you sister be back soon init and you fe go home. But I been think about what you say init and maybe you right man. Lets see what happen over the next couple a day init maybe them thief a go think twice when them see you.'

Cause Ruji-Babes a think through them business side of thing init and she probaly figure aint gonna cost her nothing for few days is it and since Zafar happy fe help out he might as well be do something init.

Foxy-T just sit there and eat and she no say nothing is it but for once that Zafar too busy to notice what Foxy-T a do. Him well chuff by what Ruji-Babes a say and him just go, 'Wicked man. Them thiefs gonna be well vex init – them no try them trick with me around. Thanks man.' And trust me that Zafar also relieve cause in fact him no try call him sister yet is it. Him just make that up cause him still consider this him yard init and he rather spend some time down this way before him go up Dagenham. And stopping with them two girl him see that him gonna live a well comfy life for a few days init. And believe me anything would be comfy after Feltham. Just fe know man can step out the door when him want or not have fe worry about what toilet is the best chance a not get box up by them cunts what run thing down there. Just fe go and piss on him own feel like a luxury to that Zafar. But even then is true this a go be comfier still init.

Once them a finish there dinner Ruji-Babes aks Zafar if him want fe take a bath. She dont have fe aks him twice is it and him still feel mellow from them couple a spliff him smoke with Shabbaz and Ranky. You no need me fe tell you how much him would a enjoy that bath is it. Just fe slide that little bolt on that bathroom door there and sink down in some like bubble bath or whatever. Shit you know how good that would a feel init. So think how good that sound and times that by like ten or whatever and thats how much Zafar enjoy himself just lay there and soak away him vex and strain. He just be lay there and hear the sound a them two girl voice in the next room init but not listen a what them say cause him just day dream. While him lay there like that with him eye close Zafar almost feel he gonna see him grandad when he get out the bath but then him open him eye and see how the bathroom a change since him last have a bath there and him see all them shampoo and stuff what woman have in there bathroom and see how clean it all is now and him feel like well nuff thing change init only still when him reach out fe some shampoo him reach automatic fe where him grandad use to keep it. And that keep happen over the next few days init cause him hold how that flat use to look in him head and also cause a habit init. Stuff him never even think about when him up Feltham. And this is like whether him want fe get a cup and have like a coffee or whatever first Zafar would reach beneath the sink where him grandad use fe keep them cup and that and then him remember where them two girl keep them now and stop himself only then the same thing a go happen when him reach up on the windowsill for the coffee jar init and it aint there no more cause them two is keep it by the kettle. But apart from them type a thing him no really miss him grandad is it just sometime him reflect upon them thing. And believe me when him get out a that bath is only cause the water a get cold. Then by that time them two girl is gone to bed init and just that bed make up for him on the sofa.

Before him rest Zafar roll up a little spliff though init and lean out the window fe smoke. And this what Zafar always done when him live here before init. Him smoke him spliff out the window when him grandad a gone upstairs. Only now him grandad gone init and him back. And trust me man Zafar just enjoy smoke that spliff init even though it start fe rain but aside from feel them raindrop on him arm him no care is it cause him just soak up them sight init. After that believe me him no have no trouble a sleep.

Next morning him wake up when them two girl is chat in the

kitchen, then once him dress he open the curtain and that then go next door fe fix up some breakfast.

Foxy-T already gone downstairs by this time init fe switch on them computer and shit like she done every day. But Ruji-Babes just a clear up them breakfast thing and say like 'Morning' and aks him if he want toast or cornflakes then when him say she go, 'Listen Zafar man I aint get at you is it but you should a clean out that bath when you through. Guess you is out of the habit init.'

Zafar all embarrass now cause him figure that he probaly left it in a state. Him start fe stand up and go, 'Shit sorry man . . .' but Ruji-Babes say, 'No stress yourself man. Eat your breakfast init. I done it already.'

'Thanks man,' say Zafar but Ruji-Babes go, 'Is cool Zafar I'm just tell you for next time init.' Then she go downstairs and leave him to him breakfast and once him eat Zafar wash up him bowl under the tap and thing cause him a feel guilty through not wash out him bath before.

By the time him get downstair them two girl is open the shop and couple a customer a sit there and doing there email or whatever. Zafar figure him a go take the day easy init cause now he doing security him plan fe pull up a chair and pure relax but that aint the way him plan work out cause Ruji-Babes have a couple a job line up for that boy init. First of all she aks him fe empty the bin them and put the bags out by the lamp post and thats all the bin init upstairs one and all. Then once him done that Ruji-Babes aks him fe wash the window. And believe me that Zafar never wash no window before in him life is it and it take him ages man and by the time him finish him sleeve all wet. But Ruji-Babes aint stupid is it and she know how many thing she a go get away with aksing him and she bring him a coffee init once him finish them window. And once him put that bucket away it seem like Ruji-Babes aint got no more job so now him pull up a chair init and sit by the doorstep fe drink him coffee.

Cannon Street Road well busy by this time init and Zafar just pure enjoy sit there and check the runnings. Nuff man was come back from the mosque. Them old man always make Zafar laugh way them all look the same init with them white cap and raincoat and each of them have like walking stick. Some a them old man was chat and walk along in group while other a them was just walk on them own and loss in them thought. Them type a man remind Zafar a him grandad init. And how like in old time Zafar stand fe wait outside the Cannon Street Car with a coffee from the machine and wait for him grandad and he always use fe recognise him init and check him when him turn the corner off Commercial Road and him head always bow init and him just thinking about him faith or whatever. And since time Zafar always figure them old man cool and each to him own only them seem like they is come from a older time init when life a simple and them old time men live simple life of put bread in them family belly and long as them can do that and smoke them cigarette and pray them is well sorted init. And him could never figure how them old man bring them simple old time country way with them cause far as him knowed life in London far from simple init and respect to them man what can live the simple life and make time fe pray in a place like this with all them stress and strain. And maybe him never even think about thing might be the other way around is it and pure because a them faith that them life more simple but still Zafar never feel like them religion for him and him no believe. But nuff respect him think as him watch them all come down the road there even though him no understand.

One or two rude boy was a walk down the road and all init and when them check Zafar a sit there outside the E-Z Call there one of them nod him head and go, 'Later yeah,' as him walk past. Zafar no reckonise him is it but figure is weed him after and that Shabbaz is probaly tell nuff man where them can check it so when him think this him nod back init and say, 'Safe man.'

Aint seem like long him a sit there when Ruji-Babes aks him fe nip over the Nagina Sweet House fe buy a few samosa. She and Foxy-T well hungry since them a get up ages before Zafar. One thing about both a them is them get all feisty if them skip lunch init so them figure another job for that Zafar. Also they aint say nothing is it but them both feel like when that Zafar a sat there aint no young fool a try fe nick whatever and even if they never say this they is both in like a good mood init and them figure get some nice lunch instead of just have sandwich like usual and also them feel like that Zafar earn it for clean them windows what was well filthy init.

It no take him long fe cross the road and fetch them lunch. Them two aks fe cold vegetable samosa but Zafar like them meat one and he like them hot init so him cross back with one bag in him hand and one in him face and him a try fe blow that samosa and take a bite at the same time init. Since him have a few dollar left in him pocket and him figure that business soon be good Zafar was also carry some small box init cause him buy them two girl some piece of kulfi. He never knowed jelabi there favourite is it but Ruji-Babes well chuff even still cause though she no like kulfi that much she one a them type a girl what think is the thought that count init.

Is only when him look up that Zafar see Foxy-T a stand in the middle a the E-Z Call on one foot with her hand clasp on her head init. Him no say nothing but look at Ruji-Babes what just go like 'shush' then say like, 'T a concentrate init.' Him check a couple a them customer what is look round at Foxy-T instead of there computer them so he knowed that them PC must a crash init cause if you paid like dollar fifty fe spend one hour on them PC you aint go waste it by just sit there and look at the shop keeper seen. Even when that shop keeper is well fit like this girl. But Foxy-T in her own world init and probaly never notice them customer all stare or if she had of notice probaly she dont care is it cause that girl was just stand there like that and she well concentrating so Zafar look at Ruji-Babes and then him point back outside and return to him seat and eat them samosa what is cool down now.

That afternoon pass quick init. Nuff runnings fe Zafar a check all them coming and going. Couple a youth check him too init. And Zafar still have a gut feeling for them type a runnings seen and since time a pass him figure that other rude boy what stop earlier on would be plan fe reach in a bit when he still knowed where Zafar a go be. So to them other youth him say fe meet him down the Eastern Fried Chicken in a hour. And sure enough when him say to Ruji-Babes that him a take a break and go nip down the Eastern Fried Chicken down by the One Stop there and start fe cross the road him look down toward Bigland and see that rude boy a walk past the One Stop there. So by the time him reach at Eastern Fried Chicken all him customer a reach and all and him sell like four eighth to them youth and half a ounce to that other rude boy, and them youth all get them can a coke and like one portion a chip between them and man all sit and chat init except that guy what buyed half a ounce. Still Zafar no got all day is it so after five minutes him stand up and go 'Later seen' then him stroll back up a E-Z Call and him well please init cause now him only have a ounce left fe sell.

Zafar a pop him head round fe let them two girl know him back then sit back down outside. Easy now him think and fold him arm and stretch out him leg. Man you know it feel good to that Zafar fe know him back init.

It take him a while fe realise that the phone him a hear ring is him own and by the time him take it out him pocket it done stop ring init. Zafar cuss under him breath then check call register and since this Anwar phone it come up and say like Shabs call so him return init.

Shabbaz pick up straight away and go, 'Seen Zafar listen man you aint do nothing tonight is it.'

Zafar just laugh and say, 'You know it man. What a go on?'

Shabbaz tell him them a plan fe go down the Glass House init and Zafar aks what that is.

'Is a club man what you think?,' say Shabbaz. 'Ranky a go check you about nine init. Listen man you have any weed left?'

'Seen,' say Zafar. 'About a ounce init.'

'Safe man,' say Shabbaz. 'No sell it now seen. Cause I just check Red-Eye and them and tell them you is go sort them out init.'

When him hang up Zafar just sit back and pure enjoy the music what pump out a Cannon Video init. When him up Feltham them just have fe listen to station like Capital init and

Capital Gold and like Five Live when them a run football or whatever cause them white man is control the radio them seen. Them cunt would never listen to that type a music what Zafar and him spar is into is it. Believe me Zafar just smoke a Silk Cut and tap him foot and watch them thing hanging by the £1 shop there. Nuff like blow-up tennis and bucket is hang off there canopy and all get toss around in the breeze.

That £1 shop new init was fashion place before but most a them shop the same as when him stop at him grandad except like Ekota stationer and T&T Mobile and Mohamedia them what is new just them and that £1 shop only all them other shop is the same except for Tiffin Restaurant what have like new window and that. But even though him only reach a couple a day Zafar feel like him never go away init and them few thing what is change is start fe seem like they was always there. A couple of customer nod when them go in the E-Z Call and Zafar nod back init. When they gone in him smile and just relax. Trust me with each minute him back in him yard that boy no help it him just have fe smile init. And also when him not just sit and think about them two girl him keep try fe remember why him knowed the name Glass House. That club sound familiar even though him never been init. Then him look over the road there and check them poster what is stick on the wall two door down from the £1 shop and him see the poster what he been stare at all day without bother fe read it. Top of that poster say Underground Explosion init and under that it read UK Garage R&B Old Skool then it say the Glass House Puddledock Blackfriars but what catch him eye is at the bottom where it say Ladies Free B4 11PM. And Zafar smile again init cause him knowed that when them club say ladies free there be nuff ladies a turn up seen.

That took him mind off them two girl inside init cause Zafar was day dream and think about the place a go be ram with them ladies init and believe me Feltham seem like another life as him just sit there and plan what lyrics he a go give them girl.

Time Ranky pull up outside the E-Z Call Zafar knowed that Ruji-Babes and Foxy-T a start fe tidy up inside init and get ready fe lock up. Them last customer finish already init and them a take care a them thing like clean up and log off and put them top up and them phone card in the safe with there cash. Zafar take him chair back inside fe let them two know him a go out now. Ruji-Babes look up at him and smile init but him notice that she tired cause she have ring round her eye and that.

'No thief today is it,' him say.

'Fe true man,' say Ruji-Babes. 'That cause we got security init.'

She was laugh init but him pretend fe took her serious and go, 'Seen seen. Me put them off man!'

'Is you eat with us now Zafar?' Ruji-Babes aks him and Zafar go, 'No man me go out init. Me spar them just reach.'

Ruji-Babes nod and go, 'Cool. You have you key there now init?' and him tap him pocket fe check that spare key what Ruji-Babes give him and go, 'Safe. Later man.'

'Yeah later init.'

Him no see Foxy-T now is it cause she just tidy up them booth like wipe them window and them phone. Them two girl is do that every night init cause them like fe keep thing look nice and with air fresheners and that cause them figure man aint go want fe use no dirty phone is it. But still that Zafar a stand there for like a couple a second init looking down the back a that shop as if she a go suddenly appear only him no see her is it so him smile at Ruji-Babes and go, 'Easy now seen.'

As him step outside Ranky lean over fe open him passenger door and them touch fist init.

'Safe man,' say Zafar. 'Where this Glass House then eh? Blackfriar me never hear a that.'

'Down by the river there,' say Ranky only as him drive off him no go down Cable Street way is it what lead to the river there him turn down Bigland and that little car park by Surma Town Cash and Carry.

Shabbaz Sierra Cosworth a park up already init and him sound system turn up to the max. Man like Red-Eye and Shah is stand around the car and laugh init so Zafar open him door then stand up fe greet cause him no seen Red-Eye and that for year like since before Feltham is it. Them all shake him hand and go Respect init then Zafar see man like Ifty sit in the back a Shabbaz car there. Ifty pass Zafar a bottle a Bacardi Breezer out the window then after them touch fist him aks, 'Listen man Shabbaz say is you we a deal with then?'

'Seen,' say Zafar as him take a drink then check up the street fe check no police about before reach in him pocket fe some bag a weed. 'What you need man?' him aks.

It aint take long till him sell all them last bag is it. Ifty buy a eighth and Red-Eye buy a quarter then Shah check fe another quarter so by the time DK a turn up in him car and take another quarter Zafar just left with a eighth for his self init.

Zafar and him spar making nuff noise init and Red-Eye point up at them flat with him spliff and laugh and when Zafar check what him on about is some man lean on him balcony and smoke a cigarette and check them.

Red-Eye laugh and go, 'Hey is Elvis man,' and that Zafar is right pissing himself init cause Red-Eye right that man have like a quiff and sideburn and that.

Red-Eye shout up like, 'Alright Elvis!' only man no laugh is it him just look embarass and step back in him flat.

Shabbaz a get out him car and dust down him trouser then him check fe Zafar and nod him head over by them flat there. Zafar follow him over init and them two is have a quick chat in that stairwell.

'You have me money star?' Shabbaz aks him so Zafar put him drink down on the step init and spit down on top a the bin them before start fe count him takings init and when him done him end up peel off nuff a them bill init then him remember that eighth him a go keep and put one back with the rest what him roll up and give to him spar. Shabbaz say, 'No offence man,' and start fe count it and all seen but once him done that Shabbaz go, 'Safe,' then him take out a pen and place him tag upon the wall there above the rubbish chute then pass him pen to Zafar. One thing Zafar have plenty a time fe practice up Feltham was him tag init so him take him time and put it up next to where Shabbaz done his then him write Bigland Massive and the date and give Shabbaz back him pen.

'Come down me arch about eleven man,' say Shabbaz as them walk down the stairs. 'And we fix you up with some more init.'

Ranky already have him car start init and when them reach Red-Eye take him bottle and chuck it over the playground there and it smash upon the climbing frame. Ifty lean and open up the back door a Shabbaz Sierra but before Zafar get in him finish him Breezer and chuck it and all only when him get in

Shabbaz already turn up him music init so Zafar never hear that bottle smash.

Since them all mash up is like them all talk at once in that car so aint take long till them reach at the Glass House is it and by the time them inside the place ram up believe me. Couple a well fit girl make straight over where Shabbaz and Ranky is wait at the bar. Them two was dress up init and Zafar find him cant take him eye off them behind and how them G-string show through them white trousers. Them G-string is disappear right up there arse. Easy now Zafar. Shit man them two girl was lean over and say something in him spar ear and touch them arm and laugh init but Zafar just watch them behind like he never seen a girl before. Shabbaz put him hand upon that girl waist though init so Zafar figure aint do him no good fe check him spar girl is it and him better check fe some other girl a him own but him cant resist have one last look at that girl behind init and think how she well fit.

Zafar mind wander while them stand there and him try fe imagine Foxy-T dress like that but him cant is it. Man the way that girl dress have him vex. Him no figure how some fit woman like Foxy-T aint make the most a herself is it and just wear them trackie bottom and polo shirt.

When Red-Eye and them is go to the bar Zafar walk over there and like try fe chat with Shabbaz and Ranky init but them two is just want fe chat with them girl seen and them girl aint even notice Zafar.

But listen after four year up Feltham just fe be in some club feel good init. Nuff tunes them a spin believe me and it seem like that Glass House ram with pure woman and Red-Eye and them is already check some other girl and is all like laugh and that. Zafar step over the bar though fe buy some drink of his own but is when him wait fe get serve him spot some girl what is just wait there and all. And this girl alright init. She aint all that but I mean she alright. And she aint maybe dress up like them other girl and maybe look like a student or whatever but still even inspite of that she aint wear nothing special she still look well fit to Zafar but trust me any girl a go look fit to him. Zafar check her tits and all init and they aint as big as Foxy-T fe true but still she have nice tits so he like smile at her init and she smile at him and all only by now she have her drinks init so when she smile she is already turn away from that bar. Zafar consider run after her but tell the truth him already wait long time fe get serve and it nearly him turn seen. Any way him figure Glass House aint massive so him bound fe check her again later but though him keep him eye open while him drink that beer he never seen her is it and he never seen her when him visit the bar again neither. Every time him a go there Zafar think him must check her only she aint. And when him and Ifty go and check that rare groove room she aint there. Trust me that Zafar buy nuff beer through look for that girl and since him no drink since before Feltham aint long till him well piss up init.

That Zafar have nuff story about Feltham init cause out of all him spar Zafar the only one is been inside and them man all curious about it seen. So Zafar have them crease up init with some a them story and him pure enjoy just be the centre of attention cause is true that all him spar take them turn fe chat with him. And is cool only him never come out just fe chat with him spar is it. Was pussy him after tonight but time move on and nuff dollar is spent and in spite of him drunk there come a time when Zafar still sober enough in him mind fe figure that he is miss him chance now init cause fe true none a them other girl is come over and check him neither is it even though a couple a them is look over at him and then say something in them friend ear or whatever and laugh. But none a them is come over and none a them is even smile. So that Zafar try fe talk and joke with him spar init and smoke a couple of spliff and make out he well into them tune which he was only not that much but he still just keep look around fe check that girl only he never seen her.

Aint long till Shabbaz and them is come over and all and say them a go split. Them two fit girl is all over Shabbaz and Ranky init and Zafar well jealous believe me and if them girl look fit before man knowed they look even fitter now.

Even though him drunk that Zafar aint stupid is it and him start fe notice that is man like Shabbaz and Ranky and DK what is got them girl while man like Ifty and Shah and Zafar isnt and he knowed that is because them three have no car. Even that girl what Red-Eye have him eye on is split init and Red-Eye well vex believe me.

'Bitch aks where me a go drive her init,' him say. 'And me buy her nuff Breezer init shit man I aint go waste me time seen I a go split.'

'Is it?' say Zafar but him still try and look around fe check that girl only she definitely aint there. 'Shit man,' he say, 'nuff fit girl was eye me up but she aint here now is it. Me a come too init. Wasted nuff money already.'

But also since he aint even have him own place what is Zafar a go do anyway is it. Some fit girl no fe impress with him sofa.

Is well late when him reach E-Z Call. Man aint go waste him last dollar through pay for a cab is it so them three smoke a spliff by the river there and then is just walk home init. What else they a go do? Take them about a hour and them three broke now believe me and nothing fe prove what they a spend. Though fe true next morning Zafar knowed it.

'You look like you have a good night man,' say Ruji-Babes when him wake and find she still in the kitchen.

'Fe true man,' say Zafar and him smile in spite of him sore head cause he aint go admit how many dollar him waste. 'Place was ram believe me man.'

'So you is go back tonight then eh?' Ruji-Babes aks

'Maybe next week you never know is it. Some wicked tune and everything. Them type a club aint on every night though man'

'Is it?' say Ruji-Babes. 'Man them place just pure noise to me init,' then she look up at the clock and go, 'Listen me better go open up init. Do me a favour and make two coffee when that kettle boil man?'

'Safe man how you have it eh?'

'Black for me init and T have milk and sugar.'

Even if she no tell him Zafar figure him would a guess which girl have which coffee. As him sit there a nurse him sore head just fe think about black coffee no sugar make him feel sick to him stomach init. Nuff milk and nuff sugar is the way fe drink coffee is how him see thing and tell the truth him no feel that hungry neither so him put them cornflake away and get them mug out.

When him take down the coffee them Ruji-Babes aks him fe hoover and Zafar no feel him have no choice is it even though him have a wicked hangover. Took him ages fe hoover up that E-Z Call init cause him have fe move them chair and thing and also a couple a them regular customer already come and they in the way so that Zafar well vex by the time him come fe do the booth and all. Every now and then he a check Ruji-Babes what is sit at the counter and drink her black coffee and write something.

Foxy-T no say nothing to Zafar yet neither cause she just sit next to Ruji-Babes and concentrate upon that server or whatever but to that Zafar it seem like she a do this on purpose cause he remember how him feel when she catch him eye before init. Man practicly jump out him skin seen and he knowed Foxy-T a the same init. And Zafar cant help think Ruji-Babes just make him hoover cause she knowed he have a hangover and the fact she drink coffee black no sugar make nuff sense to that boy.

Them two is talk while they work init and Ruji-Babes a go 'Listen T you want me fe take it?'

'No man I'm done init.'

Then Ruji-Babes go, 'Thanks man I got loads left. They be here in a minute.'

Zafar no hear none of this though cause him stuck in them booth and finish hoover so him no see Ruji-Babes cousin beemer a pull up outside is it. That man come in the shop and say, 'You ready Rooj?' but Ruji-Babes go, 'No man I aint coming. Look at this. Nuff accounts fe do. T a go come init.'

'Seen seen,' say Ruji-Babes cousin. 'You ready T?'

Foxy-T go, 'Yeah man just have fe get them thing init.'

So Zafar never see Foxy-T grab them thing and drive up the bank is it but him notice that she gone when he finish hoover init.

'Foxy-T upstairs then?' him say when he come back in the shop.

'No man she gone up the bank init.'

'You have something you want me fe do now?' Zafar aks her but Ruji-Babes concentrate upon her accounts init and try fe get them thing done while they aint many customer so she no have time fe think about Zafar now is it and she just go, 'No man. Just let me do this init.'

Zafar take him coffee and him cigarette and sit outside the E-Z Call fe drink it since it no rain and aint that cold. Though what nag at him mind is just think about Foxy-T init. He cant get that girl out of him head is it and keep a think about when them eye lock and him feel like him gonna jump out him skin. And he forget him headache for a bit init but still him well vex through him no get no pussy down Glass House but even when him think about that girl what him try fe check last night but what must have left cause him no find her again and think about her tits and how she smile at him also Zafar thought keep go back to that Foxy-T and how she fitter than that other girl and also him think how Foxy-T a act when him around. But also now him start feel hungry init so take him chair back in and go up the kitchen fe fix some cornflake or whatever.

When him come back down stair Foxy-T already reach with Ruji-Babes cousin init and be stand there and chat. Only Ruji-Babes still aint finish her work is it so when them aks her something she just go, 'You want fe make me lose count man?'

Ruji-Babes cousin just raise him eyebrow at Foxy-T init and go, 'Easy now Rooj. Later yeah.' As him turn fe leave though him check Zafar stand down the back a the shop init and say to Ruji-Babes like, 'That him then?' and Ruji-Babes go, 'Yeah. Zafar this my cousin man.'

Zafar come over init and shake him hand. Is obvious through

the way him dress that Ruji-Babes cousin like a business man cause him wear nuff smart clothes init and like proper shoe what is polish aint no trainers. Zafar just check him leather coat init and he knowed it would a cost plenty a dollar like them definitely cost more than Shabbaz clothes or whatever. Man know Ruji-Babes cousin aint go be so impress with Zafar clothes is it but he aint say nothing just, 'Zafar. Cool man. Later yeah.' Then him gone.

And that couple a day become like a week init and time pass quick enough with Zafar keep sleep on there sofa up in the flat above the E-Z Call. Every day him enjoy there comfort and eat them food and every day him tell them him sister no reach yet but spin them some lyrics and make up some new thing what he hear off him cousin up Birmingham.

Shabbaz and Ranky was sort him out again and him selling a few small bag a weed only him never done that in front of the shop is it cause Zafar knowed them two would notice but nuff man check him and seem like he always chat with someone outside the E-Z Call there. But just through be careful him always arrange fe check them man later init and maybe go down the Eastern Fried Chicken fe sort him business. Or one a them stair well where them customer can make a spliff and pass half a hour just chat and smoke like that without be disturb. Ruji-Babes was well chuff and just enjoy have him around and fe true when him there them two no get rob is it. And man cant tell if this because a Zafar or whatever is it cause is only been like a few day and like too soon fe tell init only them two is feel like is cause a Zafar them no get rob.

Trust me that Zafar aint stupid and always on him best behaviour around them two girl init and always like quiet and polite and do them washing up after dinner or whatever and then them three would sit in there living room and maybe watch telly and like chat init except normally this was Ruji-Babes and Zafar what is do the talking cause Foxy-T generally read them like software manual when them two watch telly. Aint take him long fe realise that all him bragging about them kind of runnings him and his mates use fe get up to and what kind of shit went on up Feltham wasnt exackly what them two girl want to hear so Zafar save them type a story for him spar init.

So when him a talk with Ruji-Babes or maybe both a them girl when they eat there dinner or whatever then him tend fe aks them more type of question about say what them two want fe talk about and all question about the E-Z Call and business generally. He seem like a good listener and seem like whatever them two have fe say him find it funny in that piss-takey way of his. Also if they need stuff doing around the E-Z Call or whatever he tend to chip in with the work. This boy Zafar wasnt afraid of hard work or getting him hand dirty believe me and when him stand by the door like I say is no young thief is go rob them two girl and they is well please about that init.

And like that was what he mostly done just stand by the door and watch the runnings. And probaly them rude boy knowed him just reach from Feltham or else man knowed that Shabbaz him spar cause with Zafar a stand in the doorway like that it seem like them thief stop away. And this kind of job seem to suit him most because he like just fe stand there and watch the runnings them in Cannon Street Road and it aint like Zafar some big bouncer or nothing just that him there and him watch and probaly thats enough fe put off them casual thief.

But also him enjoy watch Foxy-T believe me. He couldnt figure that girl out at all is it. He like the way she look with them big tits of hers and all them curves in all the right place even if the way she wear all them boy type a clothes would tend to play heavy on him mind. Fe true when man cant get what him want then him tend to play for what them think them can get init but what nagging away in Zafar mind is that him click with this girl from the first init. Believe me them big tits of hers and her big dark eyes really turn that boy on but him try not fe let on that he fancy her cause by now him really fucking fancy her if you know what me say. So it feel better to this boy fe keep it as him secret. But them strange dreamy thing she tend to say and the way she stand there on one leg and a think about some problem or other with them PC and shake out that pony tail would make him laugh and that boy aint stupid cause him know that you aint find some girl what make you laugh every day is it. And him want fe aks her out or something and it was always on the tip of him tongue but say whenever him start fe think that him couldnt go another minute without aks her out he would just keep quiet and then take a stroll outside and have like a cigarette or whatever and concentrate on all the runnings up and down Cannon Street Road fe take him mind off it.

Then also if him spar was park up down Bigland or whatever sometime man like Ifty or DK is phone and aks him if he still have any weed and him take a break and go meet them init. So them time Zafar go down and sit in like DK car and smoke a couple spliff fe pass like half a hour or whatever. Or maybe Ifty is bring him football and them go in that yard there and play some quick game init. And them time is also get him away from E-Z Call and have fe think about Foxy-T. Cause believe me if she there he a go think about that girl init.

But is nuff graffiti on them wall round that yard seen and all paint up like massive. Man like Mash and FMZ and Sham and Monz and all them Norton Massive them. Plus Ranky and Shabbaz and Red-Eye and them is all have tag down there init. But when them play one time and Zafar is lean down fe pick up the ball when him in goal him notice down in the corner there is Foxy-T and Ruji-Babes. And these aint like massive tag or whatever is it them two name is just writ real small in a gap between the bricks them. When him see that Zafar must feel is no escape init but that boy cant help but laugh cause fe true them two girl is well serious now and run them business but is them what write this init back in the day. And Zafar is just lost in him thought for a second and reflect upon them kind of thing and imagine what type of runnings them two might a been into when they was like teenager or whatever and what they was into and why they was here where is only man play football. Only Zafar aint think about them thing for long is it cause Ifty is aks for that ball now so Zafar just shake him head and kick that ball over where him run.

But trust me seeing them two girl tag there like that play on him mind though and while him suppose fe like in goal and watch the game him just keep laugh fe think about them two girl and what type a thing them get up to in them youth.

Back up the E-Z Call most days if it aint rain or whatever Zafar would take him chair outside and just sit there watching and doing that security. Even if it like cold or whatever and this might have be because of him time up Feltham when him lock up inside and cant get no fresh air or whatever except when them say so and now him like make up for lost time. And most days he be sit outside and listen to that music out of Cannon Video and just a chat with whoever man. Like youth what him may know start fe stop and chat init. Pass the time. And maybe man like Shabbaz would come and park up down the road yeah and Zafar step over and sit in Shabbaz Sierra Cosworth and smoke some spliff and chat for like ten minutes and then when Shabbaz got business fe attend Zafar get out the car and be a bit mash up and he would be like happy fe just sit outside and listen to that music for a couple of hour and maybe nip over Nagina Sweet Centre fe buy some kulfi or a bag of pistachio if him get hungry.

One time Zafar phone ring when him just sit a front of E-Z Call and think about them two girl and drink him coffee and is DK aks him fe come down that car park in Bigland. Zafar expect DK to ring init since him plan fe buy half a ounce off Zafar plus them girl is pray on him mind so him glad DK a call only he aint sound cheerful is it him sound well vex over the phone so Zafar just go, 'Yeah me soon come,' then take him cup inside and tell Ruji-Babes that he have fe go meet him spar for like ten minute. And as him start fe walk down Cannon Street Road Zafar walk fast init cause of how DK a sound on the phone and Zafar is try fe imagine what make DK so vex only he never knowed. But once Zafar turn down Bigland Street and hold him breath as he walk past them old meat bin there and when him reach Surma Town Cash and Carry on the corner there all him hear is DK voice a shout. And Zafar start fe run init cause if you hear you spar a shout like that is only mean that something a go on init so Zafar start fe run so him reach sooner.

As he turn the corner Zafar is see that DK park him Vauxhall in that car park by them flat there and he is just stand there and like shout at two man. One a them look like a Arab and that other one what shout and all is got like a Russian accent init and DK is just stand there and shout at them two man only Zafar never knowed what him spar is shout about is it.

'What happening star?' him aks.

DK just turn and go, 'These cunts is clamp me car init. Them say me owe them eighty five fucking dollar fe unclamp.' Then him turn to one a them guy and go, 'I live here init where me go park if me no park here man. Unclamp me fucking car!'

And that Russian man there is just shake him head and go, 'No is eighty five quid you have fe pay now.'

Zafar take him mobile and dial Shabbaz number cause him figure that Shabbaz and Ranky is probaly down him arch what is just over behind them garage by the yard where them play football. Shabbaz pick up him phone init and go, 'Yes Zafar. What is it man?' So Zafar tell him and Shabbaz go, 'Keep them there man we coming.'

And fe true in like thirty second him see them two come run round the corner from the garage them. Ranky is talking in him mobile while him run and Shabbaz is got some like jack in him hand what he must a fe borrow from them taxi repair place next to him dad arch. When them reach he hold up that jack init and go, 'Unclamp the fucking car man! Unfuckingclamp the car!'

But then Zafar notice that the Arab him have some like hammer in him hand and for all Zafar knowed this might be what him use fe lock up that clamp on DK back wheel but man have that hammer clench in him fist behind him back init so Zafar go, 'Cunt have a hammer init.' And Shabbaz is hold up that like jack and going, 'Unclamp the fucking car now!' but them two clamper is just stand there and go, 'No thats eighty five quid init.'

Zafar is stand behind them man and they is look at Shabbaz and aint pay attention to Zafar and Shabbaz check this and look at Zafar over them guy shoulder and and like raise him eye brow so Zafar knowed what Shabbaz a say like that and him run and grab that Arab guy by him arm and Shabbaz is hold up that jack and him grab the guy jaw and like push up him chin and go, 'Do it man. Unclamp the fucking car. Do it now man and you no get hurt.' But that guy just go, 'Dont hit me man I just do me job init.'

Is all happen quick after that init but Zafar notice that Shabbaz is raise up that jack as if him a go strike the man so him kick the Arab in the back a him leg so him fall then soon as him down Zafar kick him in him stomach there cause him figure aint do so much damage as if him get that jack in him face and Shabbaz is just kick the bit what is nearest init and this is that guy leg. Except that guy dont stay down is it and somehow him manage fe roll and scramble up on him feet and he just a step backward and looking at Shabbaz and wave that hammer around like as if him saying, 'You no come near me is it.'

Shabbaz is follow him and try fe parry him with that jack init and the guy swinging him hammer and Zafar cant get no nearer is it cause a them other car them what is park there. DK is see all this go on init so when that Russian guy him talk with a turn fe check him mate DK box him upon the side of him head and dash him down on that bit of grass there and just start blazing man. DK is reach over and grab him shirt then start kick and punch him about him head but that guy is try fe get away init and reach up fe fend him off and and when DK make fe like stamp him that guy is use that split second fe like roll over then turn and run like him a sprinter init and run up by Surma Town Cash and Carry and leave him van there where is park next to DK car. That Arab guy what is still keep Shabbaz at bay with him hammer is check this and cause him check him mate when he swing him hammer it go through the windscreen a one a them car there. It take him a second fe pull him hammer out the glass though init through it got stuck and Shabbaz bring that jack down where the guy arm is but him get away init and Shabbaz is just smash that car bonnet. Then them two guy is gone init. Them run for them life man believe me.

'Eh DK guy unclamp it yet?' Shabbaz aks cause he wasnt like pay attention to that Russian man is it since him have the Arab fe deal with. DK is just walk over and dust down him arm and go, 'No they aint is it. Shit man. Eighty five dollar! And look at me shirt man him rip a fucking button init. Is fucking Ralph Lauren man. Man I would a box him more if I seen that.' Then him look around and go, 'Cunts left there van though init.'

Is like some little Bedford van them clamper was drive. That van have is window open init and one a them guy is left a walkman on the dashboard so Shabbaz put it in him pocket and it aint a bad one neither.

Zafar seen man like Shifty and Red-Eye a reach now init plus some a them kid from the Bigland what was play football on the grass there before. Red-Eye is try fe check what happen and looking over where them stand so Zafar nod him head and go fe meet him spar. When him reach is down by the playground there and them all greet and go, 'Whats happen star?'

Zafar tell them init and Red-Eye laughing and go like, 'Fe true?' and while him say this them turn cause them three hear some like siren just go on and them see some police through that entrance way there come drive up Cannon Street Road.

Red-Eye look over where Shabbaz is stand and go, 'Eh Shabs is the Feds man.'

Shabbaz lift him head and go, 'Safe.'

When them police turn down pass the Surma Town Cash and Carry them turn off them siren init and man can see the two clamper them is walk down beside them car. Now is safe init cause them two clamper is probaly figure they aint get box up now.

A couple a police get out the car init and one a them is like speak into him radio what is fix upon him shoulder. The other one is come over and go, 'Whats all this about then eh.'

DK is shout at them police and go, 'Cunts clamp me car init. Where me go park you tell me that man. I fucking live here init and them say me have fe pay them eighty five dollar. But there no space up there is it nor up there. Where me go park! There thief man pure thief.' When him see the clamper is come back now the police is arrive DK a run over and try fe grab that Arab guy init cause him no carry no hammer now is it only Shabbaz step in and hold him and through Shabbaz a bigger man DK no reach that Arab. Shabbaz just go, 'Easy now man. Be cool init.' And DK is struggle but he knowed that he aint as strong as Shabbaz and him stop init. And believe me is nuff rude boy stand around and watch now init. Nuff man hear the siren and come down fe check what a go on. Other people is watch from them balcony. Them police is try fe calm thing down and all init and one a them is talk to them clamper and the clamper that Arab one is point up at the flat where is the sign about clamping. But DK is see this and go, 'Yeah but it wasnt there last week is it you fucking thief. I been park here since time init and now you cunt come and try fe clamp me!' Him turn to one a them Police and go, 'Cunts just put the sign up init and me never notice. I been park here since time man they cant clamp me for fuck sake.'

Then that Fed check the windscreen init and go, 'Who done this then eh,' and him look at Shabbaz and go, 'Was it you?'

Shabbaz go, 'No was him man him have a hammer init. Wheres your fucking hammer man?' but the Arab guy is just shrug him shoulder and shake him head like him no understand. That Russian guy is go like, 'We just do are fucking job man. Theres a fucking sign init. Is big enough.' Then him point at the car windscreen and go, 'That was already like that man.'

Zafar and Red-Eye and them is stand back in the crowd init and though him concern about him spar him more concern that he no get pick out and arrested through him throw the first punch. But Zafar also feel him have fe go speak up for him spar but before he step forward Red-Eye is put him hand on him shoulder and go, 'More police man,' and them must a radio cause another car is pull up behind with is light flash init. 'Stay there man,' him tell Zafar then him walk over on the other side a where them clamper is park there van. The Arab guy is see him there and go, 'Stop looking at me man,' then turn to them police and go, 'Cunts threatening me! Get him man! Look the cunts threatening me!' But Red-Eye dont care is it him just look over the top a them little van and stare at that Arab guy. And when him say, 'Stop looking at me man,' again Red-Eye is laugh and shrug him shoulder and talk to them rudeboy what is stand around and go, 'Is a fucking free country man I look where I fucking want init. Who a go stop me man. Is a fucking free country!' Nuff a them rude boy is laugh init so Red-Eye is like big himself up and go, 'I thought this was a free country guy. Man can look where him want init!' And one a them police is point at Red-Eye and go, 'You. Get back and shut up.' But Red-Eye is go, 'I wasnt doing nothing man. Fuck sake is them what done that.'

Then another one a them rude boy step forward and start shouting at one a them police so Red-Eye step back and walk over where Zafar is stand over the back there and say, 'Go on man piss off init.' But Zafar is just go, 'No man me a go see what happen init.' Red-Eye shake him head and go, 'Nothing a go happen except DK aint buy him ounce is it. Him have the money init through him plan fe buy that weed off you man. Cunt just have fe pay up init. Come me check you later.' Zafar shrug and go, 'Seen,' and Red-Eye go, 'And no worry about that weed is it. Is me a go take it now. I'll check you up Eastern Fried Chicken in about a hour init.'

Zafar see that them things a go take a while yet cause even now them rude boy is determine fe confuse them police init. Couple a guy is just bait them already so them cunts never knowed what happen. Seem like everyone tell them something different and them police is pure confused man. Zafar shrug and start walk round the back a Turner House there. Is a couple a old white woman stand and watch init. And one a them is go, 'Bloody pakis,' but Zafar aint say nothing is it and walk past them two and some white guy what was walk him dog with him son what is wear Man U kit but is stop fe check them old lady and they is all just stand there and shake them head. Zafar turn up by Miles Court then and down the back a Norton House. Then him double back down Bigland Street by the school there and start walk up where Cannon Street Road.

But when him go past Surma Town Zafar check down the car park and see DK stand there and count out him eighty five dollar. One a them police is stand next to that Arab and going, 'Just write the fucking receipt.' But Red-Eye still stare at him through him driver window init and the guy is go, 'The cunts threatening me man.' And the police looks up and goes, 'You! Stop it! And you just write that fucking receipt.'

Zafar see the funny side a thing now init and do up him jacket and go back over the E-Z Call. When him reach Ruji-Babes look up and go, 'Easy man. How's it going Zafar? It no rain yet then.'

Fe true it seem strange come from that to this but Zafar aint say nothing cause him no want alarm Ruji-Babes and Foxy-T is it.

'No is safe man,' say Zafar. 'I miss anything?'

Ruji-Babes smile and look up from what she doing and point over where that old Somali guy is talk upon the phone and a couple a other customer is tap away upon them keyboard fe use up them one fifty and Foxy-T is just work on one a them other PC up the end what maybe crash when some guy was try fe paste some text on Hotmail. 'No man is cool,' say Ruji-Babes. 'You fancy make a coffee?'

Later it start fe piss down init and Zafar was just think about go down Eastern Fried Chicken fe check Red-Eye and sort him out with that weed what DK plan fe buy init. As him step out a E-Z Call Zafar check Ruji-Babes cousin beemer pull up init. Zafar think nothing of this is it but man wind down him window and go, 'Eh Zafar where you go man? You want a ride?'

Zafar go, 'Safe man no me just go down the Eastern Fried Chicken init have fe check me spar down there.'

But Ruji-Babes cousin shake him head and go, 'Listen man me want talk with you init. Come. Me drop you off in a minute seen.'

Zafar no feel him have no choice is it and him get in that car. And as him close the door him like whistle init cause believe me that man have him car well comfy inside init.

'Nice eh?' aks Ruji-Babes cousin and Zafar just shake him head and go, 'To the max man. Where we a go then?'

Him no get a answer though is it but them aint drive far cause him cut through by Roggs there and pull up in that yard down behind the Lahore Kebab where is all small business unit and fashion place. Is all rain beat down on the windscreen there. Zafar is wonder what this about init but Ruji-Babes cousin just go, 'Them tell me is your grandad use fe live there man. I remember him init.'

'Seen,' say Zafar. 'But him dead now init. I never knowed him die till Ruji-Babes tell me.'

'Yeah me sorry man. Is tough init.'

Zafar knowed that he aint come take this drive just fe talk about him grandad but him have fe hold him cheek back init through respect and in the same way him act all polite with Foxy-T and Ruji-Babes.

'Listen though Rooj tell me you is just stay a bit till you sister back star. She say you is OK init.'

Zafar go, 'Thats it man them let me stay a bit init so me do security try fe stop them thief man.'

'Seen,' say Ruji-Babes cousin just look out the window there but then him turn to Zafar and go, 'Man tell me that aint all you is doing though is it.'

Zafar is turn around quick init and go 'How you mean man?'

'You know what I mean Zafar. Listen me go tell you straight you aint go do them type of runnings from E-Z Call is it.'

Zafar is just look at him blank init and think how could he a knowed this. Fe true him still hope fe get out of this init.

'Listen man me a go back home on business for a couple a day init and if they is happy fe you stop there and do security is cool but you aint go sell weed you hear me star. Come now me know say you was just go fe check Red-Eye init. Give me that weed star.'

Zafar knowed he aint go get out of this init. Ruji-Babes cousin just hold out him hand and look him in the eye there and Zafar knowed that if he fuck up things a get serious.

'Give it me man.'

Zafar take it out of him jacket pocket init but go, 'But me have fe pay Shabbaz init. Me owe him man.'

'No vex yourself about Shabbaz is it. Is me him have fe deal with. I tell him already man. He aint go fuck with me is it.'

Till now Zafar no seen the way things run is it. Them type a running what Ruji-Babes uncle a deal with was invisible to that Zafar init and him never seen how thing connect. Fe true him scared now init and humiliated. Cause he knowed that him no control him life is it. Believe me is the same type a feeling like when him arrest back then. Them kind a moment when man know that them mix up with something bigger than them and have no say in them own life and from that moment things a go be different and man cant do nothing about it seen. Thats how Zafar feel as him hand over that bag of weed init.

'No fuck with me again is it. You hear me star?'

When Zafar get drop off back up the E-Z Call him pure

embarrass init. Man have diss him to Shabbaz and Red-Eye and make Zafar feel like a kid init. Like him get told off at school. Shit man Zafar well angry believe me and him just sit there and think about them thing and how him could a play thing different but even Zafar knowed is pure fantasy.

Him no say nothing to Foxy-T and Ruji-Babes is it and him no want to phone Shabbaz and them through him pure embarass. So Zafar is just pretend thing never happen init and is easy since Foxy-T and Ruji-Babes never even knowed her cousin come by.

And them three is all sit there in the E-Z Call like that init. Foxy-T do something with that printer cause it keep only print the first page what man send init. Ruji-Babes sit there behind the counter like usual and Zafar leaning on the counter there and like spinning some coin and hope fe catch Foxy-T look over at him only she aint is it cause she busy. And them last couple a customer gone home and aint seem like nobody a go come now fe send them email or whatever and it aint maybe even like six yet but nuff hail and thunder man. When them customer gone they was hold them carrier bag over there heads init and make a run for it.

'Aint nobody else a go come now is it,' say Zafar when them last customer is leaving.

'Seen,' say Ruji-Babes. 'Unless it stop raining.'

'I'm go upstairs and watch a bit a telly then init,' say Zafar. 'Lock the door man. No fool a go come in this is it. Give me a shout if it stop yeah.'

Him well angry still as he go upstairs init. Now that he on his own his hand start fe shake.

That Zafar put the telly on init but he aint watch it now. Just him figure them two aint go come upstairs for a bit is it cause fe log out and cash up and that and like clean up a bit take maybe a hour and normally he would of knowed that he have a hour fe watch what him want. Listen that man spend four year just watch what other man say init. But this time him no care about the telly. Him just sit there and speak to himself init. Like say them thing what him want fe say to Ruji-Babes cousin and imagine take out him knife and stab him and all them things him frustrate that he never done. So like the Simpsons be on but him no see it even though normally he would just be sit there and laughing init.

Cause normally when Ruji-Babes and Foxy-T is up in there sitting room then generally him have fe watch what them want and now Zafar back in him yard is just that he probaly want fe watch what him want. But what them watch is mainly what Ruji-Babes want fe watch init cause Foxy-T would be just like sit there and read most night. And Zafar just a fe sit there init cause is there front room and all aint just him bedroom. So he just have fe watch whatever init. And trust me maybe he would a gone out more only man cant go out every night is it. Them club cost nuff dollar just fe get in and once you in believe me them beers expensive and all. And it wind Zafar up believe me cause he would just be try and catch Foxy-T eye and she just look at that book till is time for bed and maybe sometime just stare at them poster upon the wall there like she a think about what she just read. And she aint a fast reader that Foxy-T is it so sometime she turn the page and Zafar swear that is maybe half a hour since she turn the last one. But Zafar aint know shit about software is it so for all he knowed is just a complicated book or whatever.

And this what happen later init and while Foxy-T is read that Ruji-Babes is just sit and watch like Newsnight or whatever and her eyes is all sore so she screw them up if she look around fe check what Zafar a do or fe look over and aks Foxy-T if she want like a coffee or whatever.

But even if Zafar no feel like a man outside a the E-Z Call fe true him still feel like a man when him here with them two init. Like he knowed that Foxy-T still act funny when him around so him try fe push it init and just enjoy test her like that only most night he aint even get the chance is it cause she aint even look at him and is just Ruji-Babes what is sit there and chat with him and that and aks him about him sister and if he have any like brother and why he come and live with him grandad but that Zafar a young man init and them kind of chat him just find boring. But is them type of thing what girl talk about init and is there place. Even though it still feel a bit like is still him grandad place. But still even if him a talk with Ruji-Babes you know Zafar mind aint on what them discuss is it cause him just mainly think about Foxy-T. So maybe like he be nodding and agree with what Ruji-Babes just say but you know that inside him blood boil just fe see her there and if he would have had the money man know him would a go out just fe escape init.

But seem like Foxy-T aint interest in nothing just her book and she just be sit there and maybe look at the last page she was reading fe check her place cause she nuff distract with that Zafar keep stare at her and believe me she a go do anything not fe catch him eye init and that girl aint concentrate upon her book is it that girl just think about Zafar and that thief and they is all mix up now fe true and is also true that Foxy-T never knowed what him a go do next so she just on tender hook init just wait fe Zafar next move..

But even though man could a cut the air in that room with a knife there something is make Zafar feel at home in there sitting room cause even though is well different now is still feel like home and still that same gas fire on the wall there even if everything else is change.

This one other night it was start fe rain again init and pretty dark by then and Zafar figure no rude boy a go come fe nick whatever now so him come in and they was just gonna lock up. So they pull down the shutter what they can lock now because Zafar borrow some big drill off the guy down the One Stop and match up them hole so they can slip a big padlock in there. And once they lock up and get all log out of them servers and that or whatever and total up and put the money and the cards in the safe then they all go upstairs and switch on the fire and its all cosy in that sitting room of theres and they probaly put on the heating and all.

So Zafar take off him jacket and shirt and he is wear one of them ghetto boy type string vest underneath init because him still young and like many young man them him no like the feel of a collar round him neck. And he just sit down in one of the armchair and maybe get him fags out him shirt pocket and just sit there and feel like a king. And Ruji-Babes and Foxy-T get in the kitchen and there chatting and there listening to the radio and Zafar is just sit there and start fe think that he wouldnt mind living here his self all the time since this was a well comfy flat and easy work. And then suddenly him think, 'Well if me marry that Foxy-T it would be mine,' or whatever.

And he was just sit there for a second pure shock by what

him a think. It took him a while fe catch up with his self believe me. This was well radical seen. But then he smile inside and kind of think well yeah what a fe go stop him is it. Fe true that Foxy-T was well fit even if she gay. Didnt even matter if she be like five years older than him or whatever. And another thing was that because she was maybe gay she wasnt exackly good with blokes. Zafar figure that him definitely knowed more about life and relationships than she done. It was like she was the younger one out of them two and him was the older one. And him just sit there for a bit init just a soak up that new dream and enjoy the way it feel fe think about. And it didnt seem like him doing anything wrong by think about marry Foxy-T and maybe this show like a different side to Zafar if he can think about just marrying someone like that. Just because him think say him found a good little number living in this flat up above the E-Z Call and just because he reckon that he can.

But I tell you he aint stupid this Zafar so he know that he better not come out with it for a while is it. Him know that he better not even think about it to himself hardly. He knowed that he better put that idea right to the back of his mind believe me. Because him no want fe wreck this nice little number is it. He knowed without even really think about it that him better play it by ear. Just like him knowed without even really thinking about it that if he a straight away go tell Foxy-T about this idea of his she would probaly just laugh in his face init. He werent stupid is it. In fact quite the opposite. That Zafar quite smart in him way seen and him definitely would a know that if him just went up to Foxy-T and say, 'Listen T. You and me is meant to be together init. I want fe marry you cause I love you,' he knowed that if he said that this Foxy-T would most likely cuss him and tell him he better fuck off and stop being such a arsehole init. Cause Foxy-T often make it plain she think like most man Zafar age was arseholes and she could well rip the piss out of some of them stupid boy what come in the E-Z Call. Zafar had a seen her do it. And he knowed that if him no careful she would well rip the piss out of him and all and her and Ruji-Babes would just tell him fe fuck off out the flat and everything init. So him figure like him grandad sometime use fe say – 'Softly, softly, catchee monkey.' Meaning that if you want fe catch a monkey you aint gonna just stand there in the jungle and aks the monkey fe come in this nice cosy little sack is it. You aint gonna talk about it at all is you. Cause the more you talk about it the more scared that monkey gonna get init. Then it just gonna fuck off init. Take a bit more skill than that fe catch a monkey init.

If him play chess Zafar might say it like a game of chess or whatever. Even if him didnt play chess and he didnt because he was even shit at draughts this Zafar and always losing him fags up Feltham but like I say even though him never play chess he think well its a bit like a game of chess init – you have fe plan your move careful.

And he was imagine this story like when his grandad or whatever would say it and think about what you need fe do if you is gonna catch a monkey or whatever. You have fe keep cool and together init. And go out early into them jungle or forest. When its all quiet and misty between them tree. And its all about you have fe feel it rather than think it yeah like playing pool or snooker where man just feel him way around the table and without even a think about it you just know that you can pot that ball. And he was good at snooker this Zafar. Well he had plenty of time fe practice up Feltham init. And him know that with snooker is like man destiny and the ball destiny or the monkey or whatever is all wrap up together. And you kind of hook on fe that monkey before you even seen it and its like a kind of magic even before that monkey has smell your human smell in the forest. And without even know it that monkey is probaly try and find a way fe escape just like you might say that snooker ball got all them different direction what it might take is somehow inside of it. And then it turns in to that kind of game of chess what is not finish until that ball is in the pocket or that monkey in the sack. And is like when they say some sportsmen or whatever is in the zone. You in the zone too whether you is hunt monkey or play snooker and you dont aim at that ball or whatever is it. You use the cue fe push it where it never think it want fe go cause even though it no think it want fe go there in fact there some little bit inside it which is also begging fe go there too. Same with that monkey init. You have fe make it go where it no think it want fe go. Like in your sack. Because thats where you want it fe go. And you dont do this through using all your skills of persuasion or through declare your love or even by get out your calculator and a work out all them angle through mathematic in the case of snooker because believe me that will fuck things up for you if you do that and that ball will bounce off the cushion or you will pot the white for sure init.

Zafar knowed that he couldnt get Foxy-T fe marry him as general dogsbody and security man up the E-Z Call is it. She would have fe marry him as a man what is the only man for her and he figure him have fe play things like with snooker or whatever and make her go where she no think she want fe go because Zafar figure him knowed how fe make her go there inspite of what she think she want. Or thats what him think. And if this was like a hunt for monkeys then him not even left the house yet is it. And if it was a game of snooker then him not even rack up them ball yet. So him decide fe stay cool because him no want fe fuck things up is it. And if he just chill then them two girl wouldnt notice nothing strange about Zafar. Far as they was concern he would just be that same Zafar what they took in because they felt sorry for him back when him come out of Feltham. Then he could play him game real slow. Like that long slow game of chess or snooker or whatever and that monkey is just jump straight in him bag.

So him a sit there in him string vest and feeling right pleased with himself and all him big idea and him cool seen. And Zafar sit there and just blow smoke ring like he learn off Deepak up Feltham.

Then he hear like Ruji-Babes in the kitchen go, 'Shit, T. We didnt get milk is it. I better go down the Quality Food.'

And she pop her head round the door and go, 'You want anything Zafar? I'm going up the shop.'

And hes like, 'No thanks man.'

So she says, 'Do you want to lay the table Zafar? Cause that tea gonna be ready in a minute yeah.'

So he finish up him fag then gets up and goes out the kitchen where Foxy-T is just check the rice and as she lift up the lid this big cloud a steam come out init and smell all of rice and bayleaf. Then she stir the little bit of dal left over from last night what there heating up for tea and she check under the grill that them lamb chops are cooking nice and she pour a bit more a that yogurt and spice over them. And she still all quiet around Zafar init because she cant really be near him without feel really out of it still and start fe think about how she feel when that thief looking right at her that time only now she think of Zafar like that thief. And with good reason as we just seen cause him plan fe steal her init.

So he just go quietly over to the draw and get out some knife and forks and put them on the table and she dont look at him at all while he done this. Then he run that cold tap a bit and fill up the jug and put out some glasses next to the knife and forks and she still dont look at him. Then him get like the ice tray out of the fridge freezer and put some ice in the jug and all and still she dont look at him or say nothing but he can feel that she know him there and that she try very hard not fe look at him. Then he get some hot lime pickle out the cupboard and a teaspoon out the draw. And he take a saucer out the other cupboard and put the pickle and the teaspoon on the saucer before him lay it upon the table. And when him a finish put this out on the table he stop and still he say nothing neither. Then he light the candle what is in the middle of the table like they always do when they have there tea because it make even beans on toast feel kind of special especially when you just finish like your long hard day at work or whatever. But when him stop all a this and wait for her to say something or do whatever she still dont say nothing is it just feel even more out of it.

And like a minute or so go by like this with both of them just stand there and him look over at her but she got her back to him at the cooker until he break the silence. Cause for all him think about how him a go catch that monkey Zafar pure busting with him plan init and what Zafar no learn yet is when man have a big idea like that man better think it through. Is why him shit at draught init cause him only plan one move ahead seen. Cause him young him no think about them consequence is it and thing may not go him way. Now he knowed that him a go aks her that question is like that aks him question become him goal init. Zafar no learn that when man know him have fe make a big move is better fe like stop and see what happen on is own and when is seem like no other way man better find one seen.

'Foxy-T,' he say quietly.

She look up from the cooker.

'Yeah?' she goes a bit sudden.

He look over at her and it feel like he cant see her properly over there by the cooker even though she a stand just there in front of him.

'No, nothing.'

'What?' she says again.

'Oh. I was just gonna aks you something,' he says.

'Yeah? Whats that then?' she aks. And she aks him this all quiet and slow but she just feel that empty fear and shaking inside of her like with the robber before. But she dont let on that she is feeling like this. 'What was you gonna aks me?' she says again.

And he get all shy himself init but that piss-takey side of him come out now and he goes, 'What do you think I'm gonna aks you?'

And his voice all quiet there in the kitchen but she could like feel it a vibrate inside her somehow.

'I dont know, is it.'

'No, go on,' him say. 'What you think I'm gonna aks you?'

'Don't know,' she say.

'Listen,' he say.

So she just turn right around there in front of the cooker and push some bit of hair behind her ear and dont say nothing just look at him.

'Listen,' he says. And she can feel his voice inside her or like its some gentle little animal against her skin instead of that Zafars voice aksing her a question. And through Zafar just wear him vest Foxy-T feel pure charge a come off him skin init.

Zafar feel like him a go bust now cause he knowed Foxy-T is go say yes init. 'Listen,' he say again. 'I was gonna aks you fe marry me.'

Foxy-T almost didnt hear what him say because she just think more and more about how him voice feel and how him skin charge the air and less and less about them chop under the grill. She was try fe turn back to the cooker and do something but she couldnt move not so much because she was surprise but more because she knowed now what that Zafars intentions are. And she just stand there for a bit sort of looking down at the sink and at the washing up liquid on the windowsill and thinking that splash back need a bit of a wipe and think about anything she can except what him just aks her.

Zafar was just leaning forward and looking at her and she could feel that him a smile that piss-takey smile of his what might just be him natural expression but she always took wrong.

Then she just snap out of it and goes, 'Fuck sake, dont be a arsehole Zafar! That dont wash with me is it.'

Zafar never expect that is it. He never seen Foxy-T shout before is it. Shit man that Zafar realise that him well blown it and him pure vex init and no understand how thing go so wrong so quick. That Foxy-T was in him hand and he knowed she want him too init. But he dont say this him just stand there and say nothing still. Just be cool. Then he think well I better say something else so he says all quiet, 'I'm not being a arsehole T. Why you think I is fucking about? I just aks you fe marry me man.'

Foxy-T was thinking he sound really upset init. And how the sound of him voice make her feel all out of it but kind of cool no matter what him talking about. She try to find something inside of her only that bit of her what just said 'Dont be a arsehole' seem to be lost for a minute and she felt right out of it believe me. But then she found it again and say, 'You talking so much shit Zafar I swear. Thats so fucking stupid man. You know I'm older than you for a start you is just a kid man. How can I even think about marry you? Stop fucking around man.'

'No,' he says. 'I aint talking shit and I aint pissing about neither. I'm being honest man. And I know for a fact that you aint that old. Even if you was it wouldnt matter is it. Age dont come into it and you know it. You could be whatever age and I could be like sixty it dont matter we can still get marry.'

Foxy-T feel like she gonna faint and feel behind her for the edge a the counter fe hold herself up. He was talking fast just blurting it out and she could feel him voice right inside her and there wasnt nothing she could do about it.

Zafar seen this init and it seem like thing aint go so bad after all seem like the way she shout at him make her weak init. Like she no use to it. He knowed is best fe keep talk now.

'I dont know man,' him say. 'You aint much older than me like a couple of years I dont know what five years or something. That dont matter and you know it. Thats just a excuse man.

Come on man you know me serious init. You know me check the way you act man. Come on man.'

The way he carry on like this make her feel unsteady on her feet and she didnt say nothing.

Zafar feel like him want fe go like 'YES!' like that monkey just jump into him sack or him pot that black fe win the game. So him try fe press it home now.

'You and me T! I want fe marry you and thats it man. Why not eh? Tell me that?' He stopped then and wait for her to say something else. He could see her just stand by the cooker and she look like she lit up inside but she didnt say nothing and she was looking down at the lino and he felt like she was his. But he think he better maybe just let it sink in and he didnt think he better touch her or kiss her or anything.

'Oh go on T,' he said. 'What do you reckon then. Come on man.'

He was like a dog with a bone now that him thought he won. He wasnt gonna let go until she say yes is it.

Far as Foxy-T concern his voice was definitely too close for comfort now and he come even closer still. 'Go on T! Say you gonna marry me.'

'No,' she says and she sound really weak and far away and she well upset at the way thing a turn out. 'Tell me now. How the fuck could I marry you Zafar?'

'Easy,' he says and he put his hand on her arm but she still looking over at the cupboard under the sink and well out of it. 'Just say yes init. Come on T! Course you can man.' Then him lean forward as if him gonna kiss her and she practicly jump out her skin with that electricity what is coming off him.

'Get away from me man,' she shout and move away then she

stop and look at him. 'What you on about Zafar. "No" I said. You no hear me man?' But she was out of breath init and couldnt say nothing else.

'Oh come on T! I aint joking man. I want fe marry you and you know it. I want us fe get marry. Come on. You know I aint joking man. You know I'm being serious man dont you?'

'Eh?' she said.

'You know I aint pissing about is it.'

'You say you aint pissing around Zafar. Thats what you say anyway.'

'And you know I aint dont you eh.'

'I dont know,' she says. 'I can hear you say that but I dont know do I.'

Then they hear the door shutting downstairs and footsteps on the stairs and its Ruji-Babes and it feels like she been gone for ages init but its probaly only been like five or ten minutes max. Them two aint say nothing is it and just listen when them stair creak as Ruji-Babes come upstairs and open the door. And believe me that Foxy-T pure relief init but no show it. 'You took your time,' she say.

'Yeah sorry I was chatting init,' says Ruji-Babes. 'Hows that tea coming on?'

'Its ready probaly,' says Foxy-T turning round and check them chops what have been a cook slow under the grill and what she pure forget in the past few minutes. They aint burn yet though and they is all spitting and sizzling as she pull the pan out and turn off the grill.

'What you two been talking about then?' Ruji-Babes aksed.

'Oh this and that,' says Foxy-T a dish up the rice. She put the hot pan containing that dal down onto a wooden chopping board on the table so they could help thereselves then she put them chop on a plate before sit down and them other two sit down and all.

Zafar feel safe now and like him win some small victory because he figure Foxy-T aint gonna blurt it all out to Ruji-Babes if she dont do it now. Which mean it something between him and Foxy-T. And that must mean that she put him first now init. Aint cross him mind is a other reason for Foxy-T no tell Ruji-Babes cause him think if she no tell Ruji-Babes now mean she a go say yes init.

'Wow,' says Ruji-Babes as she pour out some water. 'This a feast man.'

Them two both a bit surprise by her tone a voice init since them feel a bit space out by what they just been saying and Ruji-Babes is seem like some kid.

Ruji-Babes get up and turn out the main light then while she up she puts the milk in the fridge and then gets some folded breads out on another plate. But while she do this Ruji-Babes is look at Zafar a bit odd and she goes, 'Aint you cold Zafar?'

And he goes, 'No, its nice and warm in here Ruji. I'm fine man.'

Then him think for a second and realise him just a wear him ghetto boy string vest and no shirt like him at home or whatever and he says, 'Shit man is this OK?'

And Ruji-Babes goes, 'Oh no I dont mind.'

But both Zafar and Foxy-T can tell that she does mind.

'I'll go and get my shirt then shall I?'

But Foxy-T says, 'No if you is hot thats fine.'

He went like, 'Yeah I'm fine long as it aint rude init.'

'Well we'd normally think it was like bad manners for someone to just sit an eat in there vest or whatever . . .' say Ruji-Babes.

But Foxy-T interrupt and goes, 'What? You joking man? We never even think about stuff like that. We aint never said that.'

'Well,' says Ruji-Babes, 'you'd normally say it was bad manners T if some boy was eating in him vest.'

But Foxy-T go all quiet and sit there a pick at some piece of bread. And Zafar just look at them both. And think, 'Well I'll stop as I am init,' and then he get right stuck in to that tea. But Ruji-Babes was a bit put out because she suddenly see a cheeky side to this boy only fe true she never knowed how cheeky is it. Zafar hungry and him spoon out a big lump of lime pickle and eat it with him rice. He always eat him pickle first init cause it remind him of him grandad fe do this. His grandad always use to say the pickle a wake up your appetite and your taste buds init. Zafar remembered that most lunchtime his grandad would just have a bit of rice and pickle as a meal in itself. Like back home. Or just with a slice of mango. He could remember how him grandad would get out like this little wooden handle knife what he bring from back home and had since him a youth and cut off another slice a mango. 'That man could make a mango last a week,' he thought to his self. All them people what grew up back home was like that. Now you see people down like the Quality Food Store buying mango by the box and you know say them gonna chuck half a them out in a weeks time.

This was a different table now and the kitchen look well different and with tasteful wooden bread bin and that and none of it come from the £1 shop believe me but while he sit there eating him rice and pickle by the light of the candle and the lights of the east end outside with Canary Wharf and that all lit up he was still half expect to see him grandad sitting there in the dark and all outline against the night time sky through the window.

'Hey, dont forget this meat Zafar,' say Ruji-Babes breaking the spell. She was still put out man but she was like well mannered and it her house after all and him a guest of theres.

The pickle had sharpen up Zafar appetite though fe true and him go, 'No I aint. Pass it here Ruji-man.'

Then he stick him fork in one of them chop and carry it to his plate. Then he tore off a big piece of that bread and spoon out a ladel full of dal. 'You right man,' he say to Ruji-Babes. 'This a feast init.'

While he stuff him face he was going like, 'Mmmm,' without even meaning to.

Ruji-Babes was look over at him then nod and smile at Foxy-T because it remind her of her little brother again the way Zafar ate was just like a little boy.

Him like his food init. And him a mop up every bit of that dal and just tucking in like that conversation with Foxy-T and the thing with the bad manners never happen.

Like I say after tea Zafar would sometimes go out for a walk or whatever and check Red-Eye and them. But mainly him sit in that chair and watch the telly. And thats what he done init he just switch on the telly and sit there in his vest like a king in him castle believe me.

And although she didnt mind no one watching telly and couldnt exackly say what it was that he should of been doing Ruji-Babes think that this spoil her sitting room a bit. Because they done it out real nice init. With like that womanly touch or whatever. But then if this big youth is like sit there and watch some kind of stupid boy type of film with Jean Claude Van Damme it spoil it a bit. Though that was the kind of action movie that this boy like. Him cant get enough a them type a film is it.

Foxy-T sitting upon the sofa and read one a them big software manual. She got her usual dreamy expression and took her hair down not that it was very long but normally she wear it up like tie back. But she werent really concentrate on that book is it. She was half like day-dream as if she was listen to that thief whistling somewhere outside. It was almost as if she could hear it in the wind and the traffic noises outside. But every now and then she would still turn the page and carry on reading.

Ruji-Babes was going through them days figures or whatever just to make sure with that business brain of hers that them figure in her head and the picture of how the business was going down the E-Z Call was the same as what it was really doing. She knowed that otherwise man might have a different picture in him head and you might be doing much worse or much better than you think. And she like to be sure that any decision she might make was the right one and fully inform by the facts. But she felt a bit fidgety with them two in the room init and kept looking up secretly first at one a them then the other. Something about the way that Foxy-T was half read and a half dream was a bit annoying to Ruji-Babes that night.

'Shit man,' she say rubbing that dry skin around her eyes. 'I cant concentrate on these figures tonight my contacts is giving me hell init.'

Zafar look up and say nothing but Foxy-T goes, 'Yeah?'

Then Zafar turn back to that telly and Ruji-Babes try fe read them small line a numbers or whatever she keep in them books but she couldnt concentrate and so she look over at Foxy-T reading there and aks her a question with a funny look on her face.

'Dollar for your thoughts, T.'

And Foxy-T look up frighten cause she just been day dreaming about that thief or whatever as if he been sitting in the flat with them and that.

'Eh?' she says.

'Dollar for your thoughts I said,' say Ruji-Babes.

'Dont waste your money Rooj,' says Foxy-T.

'I aint wasting my money man,' says Ruji-Babes

'Yes you is,' says Foxy-T. 'Cause I was just like reading and listening to them fireworks go off outside init. Thats a quid man.'

'Yeah your right man. I have waste me money.'

'Keep your dollar then man,' says Foxy-T.

Zafar bust out laughing when he hear this and them two look over at where he sitting in his chair the telly forgotten for a second.

'You pay each other a dollar just fe tell you what you is thinking?' he aksed. 'For real?'

'Yeah,' says Ruji-Babes. 'Thats the point. Sometimes I give her like five pound a week init T.'

'Serious?' he aksed.

'Yeah if we aint got nothing else to do man. Aint you ever done that?'

'No way man,' he say laughing again. 'I aint never even hear about that! "Dollar for your thoughts!" Shit man.' Though fe true when him up Feltham man knowed him and him spar would a chat about what them a go do if them win the lottery or girl them fuck or whatever but he would a never aks them what them think.

'Well if you a work hard and live above the shop like we do then you might hear about something like that fe pass the time init,' says Ruji-Babes.

'What you get bored of the telly then or something?'

'Damn straight,' say Ruji-Babes laughing. 'Its just repeats and shit anway. Life can get boring man so you maybe play some game fe liven thing up a bit.'

'Life aint boring man. I feel sorry for you saying that.'

'Well you wasnt expecting a party every night was you?' Ruji-Babes aksed.

He look at her and think about it. 'Seen seen. I guess not, no, but if theres a good film on telly thats good enough for me man.'

'Good for you Zafar,' she says. 'Only you gonna get bored and all if you aint do nothing else every night init.'

And she look down at her figures again so Zafar could see them few grey hairs what was appearing even though she was not very old. And she never dye her hair or think about them kind of thing too much. Zafar hadnt yet gone back to the telly and he look over at Foxy-T who was still reading and day dreaming. He look closely at her face which seem like really pretty in this light and she was kind of looking around every now and then without really seeing anything like she was miles away. But she was listening out for that thief or whatever. From where he sat Zafar was just watching her man and Ruji-Babes was watching him watch her and fidget a bit while she read them figures.

Couple of hour a this is all Ruji-Babes can take init so them two girl tidy up the kitchen and went off to bed before Zafar film finish. Next day them all start work like normal only Shabbaz call fe check upon Zafar about eleven. Zafar no seen him since them scene with Ruji-Babes cousin and him well embarrass init only Shabbaz greet him like normal and go, 'Come we have fe talk init. No vex yourself Zafar is cool. Me and Ranky was just try and help init. Man give me back me weed. Should a known init. Man no fuck with them is it.'

Zafar pop him head in the door a the shop and see Ruji-Babes and say, 'Listen Rooj I'm just go for a drive with me spar init.'

And Ruji-Babes a bit taken back since him call her 'Rooj' like Foxy-T done but she just look up and go, 'When is you gonna be back man?'

Zafar just shrug him shoulder and say, 'Later. See you man.'

Shabbaz aint driving far is it. Him just pass down the road and pull up outside Eastern Fried Chicken and Kebab next to the One Stop there. The place empty and once them go in Zafar feel well hungry init since him only have like cornflake for him breakfast and that seem like hours ago. Shabbaz aks for like some piece a fry chicken and chip and two coke then them sit down at one a them table by the window.

'Figure you may want fe eat some chicken,' him say.

'Seen, seen,' say Zafar and reach in him pocket.

'Safe Zafar no fret. Me flush man.'

'You win the lottery then?'

'No me just done bit a work fe Rocky and them init.'

'Yeah?' aks Zafar. 'What you done then?'

Shabbaz tap the side a him nose and laugh init but fe true that Zafar no care how Shabbaz make him money and when them box a chicken ready him just tuck in and enjoy spend some time with him spar and forget about how Ruji-Babes cousin humiliate him seen. Also without him realise it them two woman and there ways was tax him and him glad fe be away from the E-Z Call. For a second while him drink him coke Zafar nearly chat to Shabbaz about him plan fe marry Foxy-T but him feel this aint the time and him probaly just get laugh at if him do that init.

Once they finish there lunch the two a them just get in the car and drive down Wapping. As them pass Cable Street them two is check some like photographer what is taking photo of some white guy stand against the wall there what is cover with tags. That guy is try fe look cool init so Shabbaz wind down him window and shout like, 'You fucking poof!' Zafar was pissing himself laughing init and that guy is look well embarrass. When them reach Wapping Shabbaz park up near the river then lead the way and soon they is stand by the water and a light some big spliff. It dont take long till they is feel well crisp is it.

'See that man,' Shabbaz say.

'What?' Zafar aks.

Shabbaz point at some piece a wood next to the river. Is like a tall L-shape thing made out a wood what stand there. 'That. Know what that is man?'

'I dunno like a crane or whatever?' Zafar say.

'Call a gibbet init.'

'Whats that then?'

'Man say they use fe hang them thief there init.'

'Serious?'

'Yeah pirates and that.'

Zafar laughing and him think like 'Pirates in London!' so Shabbaz is say, 'What man you no believe me. Is true man.

Back in the day them pirate and thief all wind up dead on that thing. Why you look at me like that you cunt! I aint bullshitting you man. Is true. We done it in history. You was probaly skiving that day init!'

'Shit man I'm glad things a change init,' say Zafar. 'Feltham was bad enough init without them hang you fe nick a car. Shit man. You winding me up?'

Back at E-Z Call things run like normal. There nuff customer init and Ruji-Babes a sit up the front a the shop and like scan them in the network or whatever while Foxy-T a tap away upon the keyboard and fix some like problem with the server. Only she aint concentrate on the job in hand is it. That Foxy-T still a day dream like last night. Seem like every noise is that thief and when she look out a the window she think she seen him Golf there only when she run fe check it that Golf aint nowhere. This go on all afternoon and she never notice like Shabbaz pull up outside and that Zafar get out him car. She never notice the door open either is it. And then Foxy-T look up from her day dream about that thief and see Zafar a stand there in front a there lock up cabinet and him look right at her and she practicly jump out of her skin believe me.

'Thief!' she shouts.

Ruji-Babes stop what she doing with them printout and stare at Foxy-T like she gone mad.

'What you on about T?' she aksed. 'Thats Zafar init.'

But Foxy-T is gone a bit red and looking over at them couple Russian man what was sitting around one a the PC them and she take no notice a Ruji-Babes.

'Why you a shout like that?' aks Ruji-Babes again. 'Only Zafar init. Aint no thief man!'

'Nothing man. I was just saying . . .'

'Yeah, seen, but what you was saying didnt make no sense T,' says Ruji-Babes.

'I know man I was day dreaming init.'

'You aint getting all jumpy again is you T? Was you talking about Zafar?'

'No course I wasnt,' says Foxy-T.

'Shit you give me a shock man,' says Ruji-Babes. 'Thats wound me right up for real.'

Zafar dont say nothing through all this partly because him well mash up from them spliff him smoke with him spar and it freak him out init and him a bit vex by what Foxy-T say. Fe true him never expect that is it. So him just take a chair and pull it up outside init and try relax only all him day dream was about pirates them and youth get hung down in Wapping fe nick like a loaf of bread and that.

None a them mention it after that is it. Even after they shut up the E-Z Call and gone upstair none a them say nothing. Even during them supper them no mention it. A bit later Foxy-T went out the kitchen and made some small cup of cocoa. They like a cup of cocoa before bed them two like they is old people. And they like it make with milk but not much sugar so is bitter. And Zafar enjoy that too because it remind him of his grandad who would sometime make it with water and just a tiny drop of milk and no sugar at all. Though you guess that Zafar would probaly like it with load of sugar and you be right. Ruji-Babes drink her cocoa down quick then yawn and stretch and say, 'Shit man. I'm knackered I'm going to bed. You coming T?'

And T says, 'Yeah in a minute I'll just clear up these cups init.'

'Dont be long man,' says Ruji-Babes. 'Goodnight Zafar you no forget fe turn off that fire is it.'

'Seen,' says Zafar.

Foxy-T took the cups out to the kitchen and put them in the sink where she like run cold water to fill them up then wash them up in the morning. When she come back in the sitting room she said, 'Dont forget that fire Zafar.' She was stand there half dreaming still init and she take out her pony tail and stand on one leg like she does when she thinking about them computer. And she looking over to the front window behind the telly and not look at Zafar at all. Him a watch her though. Every fucking move man.

He pat the arm of the chair. 'Sit down man.'

'No I'm going to bed,' she say. 'Ruji be waiting. She get upset if I take too long.'

'Hey T,' says Zafar. 'I was gonna aks you. Why you jump like that earlier on man?'

'What you talking about Zafar?' she aks.

'You know man earlier when I come in the shop and you say "Stop thief!" or whatever.'

Foxy-T say nothing is it.

'What was you a think about man?' him aks her again.

'I dont know its funny man,' she says. 'But for a second there I thought you was this robber what come in the shop before.' And she smile at him and like shrug as if to say 'init weird'.

'A robber!' he say. 'What you mean T?' Zafar was vex about this believe me cause him never hear about no robber since him doing security is it.

'Well,' she says. 'It was a few month ago now before you was here Zafar but I was sitting up the front of the shop and this thief come in and before he could do anything I saw him right and he just was stand there and a look right in my eyes man. Freak me out good I tell you.'

She turned back to the telly and stood there on one leg like she was before.

'You catch this robber or call the police or what?' aks Zafar.

'Shit man no he give me a fucking fright way him a look at me like that. Then when I seed him in the street after him run out the shop then he look back at me and kind of smile in this totally freaky way man.'

'Smiling?' says Zafar laughing. 'You was frighten?'

'Well not exackly frighten but he give me a shock man. Freak me out for a second thats all.'

'So you was thinking I was that thief is it.' Zafar laugh again.

'Just for a second yeah I must of been day dreaming init.'

'So do you think I've come fe nick them computer or something then? Or maybe I'm after them phone card.' He was still laughing.

She just look at him blank.

'I never been taken for a thief before,' he says. 'Except when me use to nick cars but thats different man. I never been taken for a thief by someone I knowed.' Zafar just shook him head and laugh init then look at Foxy-T and go, 'Come and sit down man.'

'I'm going upstairs Zafar,' she says. 'Rooj will be wondering where I got to init.' But she didnt move just stand there like that for a bit.

'So when you go answer me question man?'

'What question?'

'You know what question man. You aint that dumb. That question I aks you yesterday man. About us getting marry.'

'I aint answering that,' she says.

'Phone a friend?' he says laughing. 'Fifty fifty? What is it dont you know the answer or something.'

He was well laughing now init but Foxy-T say nothing and just stand there like before.

'Aks the audience then T.'

And she just say, 'No I aint answerin that question its stupid man. You aint got no right to aks me a question like that man. Sheer stupidness is what it is and you know it.'

'Is it because you think I am that thief from before?' he aks.

She look at him long and slow but dont say nothing.

'Dont put me down for that thief man,' he says then pats the arm of the chair again and aks her to sit down one more time. 'I aint come fe jack you man.'

Seem like that she wasnt gonna sit down though so him stand up instead init and him talk real quiet now like him whisper some big secret to her.

'Come on sit down a minute,' he says. 'Just for a minute man.' Then he touch her arm again and say, 'I aint that robber is it T. You dont really think I'm that robber do you?' And he put his hand on her upper arm and lightly pull her towards him and then he kiss Foxy-T on the neck. She just stand there like shes pretending it aint happening but then he kiss her on the neck again because she turn and looking over at the door and Zafar cant reach her face and her lips.

'Come on say yes man,' Zafar say and try fe pull Foxy-T a bit nearer so him can kiss her on the mouth but he just kiss her cheek instead.

Then they hear footstep upstairs and Ruji-Babes is going, 'What taking you so long man? Isnt you coming upstairs or what?'

'Shit man,' say Foxy-T turn back toward Zafar. 'Thats Rooj.' She kind of pull away and stand up straight. And as she does this he see an opportunity and reach over fe kiss her full on the mouth. Shit man him quick believe me. She feel like she been struck by lightning man and make a funny little noise through pure surprise.

'Come on man! Say yes init.'

'T!' calls Ruji-Babes from upstairs.

'Say yes.'

'T! What take you so long girl?'

'Say yes.'

'T!' shouts Ruji-Babes from upstairs in the dark. 'T!'

But Zafar not about fe let go man him a hold on tight and whisper, 'Say yes! Say yes!'

And Ruji-Babes is going 'T! T! What you doing?'

But she couldnt do nothing that Foxy-T and she couldnt cope with the both a them nagging at her like this so she just say like whatever she can think of init and its the wrong thing a course cause you always say like the wrong thing at them kind of time just fe get them other fucker off your back init and think that your words dont mean nothing but they do mean something seen and once you say them words or whatever you cant take them back which was a shame for Foxy-T because what she just blurt out then to get that Zafar off her case and out her face was, 'Yes! Yes! whatever. Just let me go to bed man.'

And she try fe wriggle out his grip like that but he got her tight just above the elbow init.

And him cant believe what he just heard. So him going, 'You said "Yes" man! You said "Yes". And thats a promise man so dont be with fucking me about now seen.'

And Foxy-T is going like, 'Just let me go. Yes. Yes, alright? Just let me fucking go now man.' Then she cry out like, 'I'm coming Rooj!'

So him shock and let go her arm and she was up that stairs like nobody business believe me.

Once she gone upstairs to bed that Zafar watch some more telly init. Only now Zafar all wound up and cant concentrate on that film is it since he just think over and over about what happen with Foxy-T and that she gonna marry him. Believe me for once him no sleep good.

Next day come breakfast they was all up and about and eating there toasts and drinking tea or whatever. His grandad like making tea the old way with all spice and boil milk but them two girl just use teabag like the eastenders that they is. And him sit around like he own the place and like they was the guests in him place. And when he put the kettle on for more tea he look over at Ruji-Babes and says, 'Listen Ruji-Babes you want fe know something?'

And Ruji-Babes was still a bit jumpy from last nights upset of Foxy-T not coming to bed when she want her to so she say, 'Yeah wassup man?'

Zafar look at Foxy-T sit there and eat her toast and he say, 'Shall I tell her man?'

And Foxy-T look up and she would a go red if she wasnt dark skin already believe me. She would of go so red that steam would a come off her.

'Whatever man,' she says. 'Tell Ruji-Babes only dont go spreading that nonsense around the street seen.' Then she took another bite of toast.

'What you say?' aks Ruji-Babes looking vex and tired. She

didnt have them contacts in yet so her eyes look all dry and a bit puffy like she was crying in the night. She look even thinner than usual man and that hair of hers look grey and all.

'Guess man,' say Zafar gloating and enjoy him moment a glory.

'Dont play game with me this time of day Zafar is it. Come on tell me man.'

'You aint figure it out yet then?' he aks her and him wink at Foxy-T while he is talking.

'No I aint is it. Like I say stop pissing about man. I aint guessing nothing this time of day.'

'We two is getting marry,' says Zafar.

Ruji-Babes stop what she was doing and look down at them pieces of toast on her plate as if she dont even know what they is or where they come from. They was like alien things there on that plate. She felt her stomach knot up inside like she could never eat nothing else ever again long as she live. She just sat there froze and staring with her tired eyes.

'What was that you say?' she aks eventually.

'We two is getting marry isnt it T.'

'Thats what you say man,' say Foxy-T. Then she blush that invisible blush of hers again till she fit to bust. She put that half-eaten slice of toast down on her plate too and feel like she not hungry no more.

Ruji-Babes look sick when she just a sit there and looking at Foxy-T. She look like some dying puppy on Animal Hospital. Or like that little dog in Geri Halliwell when she down Battersea Dogs Home with like George Michael and there that old frighten dog what is pine away for him old dead master init and you can see all that pain and worry in that little dog face and Geri just bust out crying remember? Thats what Ruji-Babes look like right then. Exackly.

'No!' says Ruji-Babes.

'For real man,' say Zafar grinning that sly grin of his. 'I aks her day before yesterday init and last night she say yes man!'

Ruji-Babes turn away like she couldnt be near the table no more. Like just the smell of that toast and Nutella was poison. Then she stands up slowly kind of feeling around for something to lean on whether its the table or the back of her chair or whatever.

'You must be fucking joking man!' She say quietly then getting louder. 'It aint gonna fucking happen man. You two is not getting marry and that is the end of it.'

Ruji-Babes was angry now believe me despite that pain what was eat up her stomach and feel like it a pull all the breath out her body. That anger was give her some kind of rush init. Like a new kind a energy.

'Why?' say Zafar. 'Why you no believe me man.'

Ruji-Babes was look at him the way she was looking at her toast a minute ago like him some kind a alien creature she never seen before.

'Boy,' she say, 'T would never be so stupid as to fall for such foolishness is it. Listen she got too much self respect fe marry some young rude boy like you Zafar. On my life you is such a stupid little boy init. She never gonna be so foolish and lose her independence like that. Shit man you is a fool if you think she gonna do that. She only know you like two weeks init. Fuck sake man you mad. T aint go marry some rude boy she hardly know.'

She was like squinting at him a bit with her screwed up eyes because of not having her contacts in yet.

He was getting cross now, and he goes, 'Listen man what you know eh? If me know she the one then thats it man. Whats your problem I dont get it man.'

She go, 'No exackly init.'

Zafar done nothing just sat with this angry look on his face. He look mean and well pissed off. Him no like being call stupid is it.

'Shit man! T dont know what she getting into if this a for real.'

'Aint none of your fucking business Ruji-Babes,' him snap at her.

'It fuckin is my business boy. More than it is yours and thats the truth.'

'Yeah, how you figure that out?' him aks. 'I dont know what you mean man.'

'Well yeah like I say. Thats what I mean init.'

'Whatever,' says Foxy-T who been a sit there quiet and listening to the two of them. 'Just shut up init. Both of you. You talking about me like I aint here. All this chat achieve nothing man.' Then she got up and roughly switch the kettle on then make herself busy with kitchen stuff.

Ruji-Babes didnt know what to make about this is it. She just sit down again and stop there for a second and rub her temples with her fingers and look at the table like she was try and focus on the table cloth. Then without saying nothing she pushed back her chair and went upstairs.

Zafar didnt move he just sit there fuming with a bad look on his face. If looks could kill man I tell you.

Foxy-T was clearing up the plates and stuff and chuck them uneaten slice of toast into the bin then run that water fe washing up but Zafar didnt move a muscle. Foxy-T seem to have forgot all about it and she just like humming to herself while she do them things in fact she look like her normal self. She would look over at him every now and then and think 'Shit you angry. You is just a big kid init. A big sulky kid.' In all of him anger and that he was as distant from her as he ever been. She watch that anger cross him face like the wind in a tree or like she would watch the traffic going by in Cannon Street Road when she was sat in the front a the shop and think about something else. Funny enough she feel no connection with Zafar at all is it.

Eventually Zafar get up and grab him jacket off the back of a chair and go down stairs a push past Ruji-Babes who is on her way down fe open up the shop. When she unlock the door him slip out and pull up the shutter on the front window. Ruji-Babes just stood there watching while he chuck the padlocks on the counter then he was off man and didnt say where he was going.

Shortly after that Foxy-T come downstairs and the two of them get on with the business of opening up the shop. Foxy-T switch on the server and take out the back ups. Then she log on the phones and check they is all working right and then starting up the back of the shop she switch on all them computer one at a time like she normally done. Them little routine was part of Foxy-T day init like breakfast and lunch. She logging in each of them PC now and check that they was all working which they was on this occasion. She didnt even look outside let alone aks Ruji-Babes where that Zafar gone. Ruji-Babes was going about the business of open up the safe and getting out all them phone card and top up and locking most of them in that big glass display counter. Then she take out the float and get the till working and check she got the right amount in there and stuff. Because unlike most of the shop around here where the assistants or whatever are on the fiddle and keep there till open all day and cream off some little tips or whatever they might call them Ruji-Babes was totally together with that money and she knowed what was come in and what was going out all the time and kept a close eye on them kind of things and she werent afraid fe see them thing like print down on paper is it.

Funny enough in spite of all that shit hitting various fan or whatever they was both feeling strangely relax and chill. Like them argument is clear the air. And this was obviously because Zafar not around. All together that day a shape up like a normal kind of morning like the ones they would of had before Zafar had even appeared at there back door and always be there in them face. They didnt talk about him at all and when Foxy-T went up and fix some coffee they went out and got some biscuits from the Mohamedia and just sit there chatting and giggling about whatever. Like one or two of them regular customer what they would make up stories about or bitch about them or whatever depending what kind of mood they was in. Just like in all shop or whatever when you only see one little glimpse of people life through them your customer but something in your brain join up all a them little moments and fill in the gaps like in between time them visiting your shop where you dont know where they are or what them a do is it. And your mind somehow turn it into a little story so that sometime if you aint careful you think you know about them people and is the same with them customer init like if you buy them thing in some shop regular then just cause you seen them shopkeeper man form idea about them init. But Foxy-T and Ruji-Babes wasnt stupid and for them is some little game or other fe pass the time when it werent that busy which was most of the time because when you run a phone and internet shop like the E-Z Call them customers aint come in fe chat with you is it. They come in fe chat to other people like there friends init so that actual eye to eye contact with your customer them aint happen that often in them kind of telephone and internet shop. Its just the giving people there cards and there change or telling them like Booth number ten man. Or saying 'Aint you got nothing smaller?' Or going like, 'No I only got Girls Talk in thirty pound I'm sorry.' Or take them money then bar code scan them log in number and give it them. Or saying, 'How long? One hour yeah? That's £1.50 man.' Or going, 'No sorry the printer a no work is it. You wanna send it again?' Or going, 'Yeah its 47p a minute to phone Islamabad yeah like it say on the sheet up there.' And thinking thats why the sheet is up there fool but just a smile and tell them customer what they want fe hear. Only every now and then them tariff would change like for whatever reason probaly because of like the economy or whatever and then it was a right pain fe get them step ladder out and take down all of them signs and adjust all the figures in the database where the phone stuff all got work out. But that Foxy-T man she is one clever bitch yeah when it come to like computer because she work out a way right of doing some kind of mail merge thing off the tariff database so that once it was all enter in the database she could just go to like merge in Word or whatever and open up a new thing and then go merge and all them tariff per minute and the country or the city or whatever would just merge into that new document. One on every page. So you got like a fifty page document or however many different place they got a tariff for but each of them page was a new like updated version of them A4 posters. So she didnt have to enter all them new figures by hand. Cause believe me once bitten twice shy init and ever since she had to do that whole job by hand one time she was try fe work out a way so she never have fe do it again. And in her way of seeming like she day dreaming and shake out her pony tail and stand there on one leg or whatever and check all the runnings out in the street thats when the idea come to her man. She well sharp init.

And the day pass quick enough like this. Like is old times again only they dont find it boring now believe me. Because they just feel relax and like they can stretch out and touch every little bit of this shop and its all theres and no one elses and wasnt no one else what done all the work to get this place going anyway just them two just Ruji-Babes and Foxy-T. And they feel like some eyelash what had got in there eye or whatever is suddenly been take out or something. That aint quite it though because its like a eyelash they forgotten was there or whatever until it been taken out and then man just think, 'Shit that was painful and I didnt realise it till now.' Ruji-Babes even went over the Nagina Sweet Centre and fetch some meat samosa and jelabi for lunch. And they was just drinking there coffees and eating all that crunchy and sticky jelabi and enjoying the feel of that cold sweet syrup flood them mouth when they crunch through them curly candy tube init. Jelabi was there favourite sweet from there like I say. It was like a real treat and they both deserve it was what Ruji-Babes say because normally she would never buy them kind of treats and they would just have a sandwich or something for lunch.

So the day pass in this way. Them both just enjoying there

work like they aint done for what seem like weeks. In the afternoon Foxy-T have fe go up the bank init. And normally Ruji-Babes cousin what take them init but just cause him away dont meant them no have fe still do them things. Them two is still need change for the till init and so them cash up a bit and put this in just like a normal carrier bag so it aint look like she is carry a load a money. Also cause the HSBC on Commercial Road is close down now she have fe walk up Whitechapel though is still only like ten fifteen minute walk. And one thing when Foxy-T a cross Commercial Road she see some graffiti on them traffic light there. And who ever writ it done it with one a them silver pen init like them sell up Ekota Stationer and it aint massive that tag is it but it say 'Zafar' on them traffic light by the crossing there.

Also this time when she go up Whitechapel and come out the back of the mosque on to the main road and cross over near the bank she hear some young rude boy shoutings init and when she look over where she hear it she see a group a youth all like running along the road from the Davenant Centre and a laugh too loud like they just done something them shouldnt and she well shock to see that one of them youth is that Zafar. Couple of them other rude boy she reckonise also but she dont know there names is it. She never knowed is Ifty and DK and Red-Eye him run with.

Fe true Foxy-T never think about where him go when Zafar nip out or whatever but even though she never really think about them kind of thing is still a shock yeah. She is sometimes forget that him have runnings outside of E-Z Call and she dont often think of Zafar as still be just a rude boy.

Zafar never seen her is it cause she just outside the HSBC

and him and him spar is cut down that side street by the small park there with them flower tie to the railing there where that youth get stab. Even if he had of seen her he probaly would of pretend he never init.

By the time Foxy-T get back down the E-Z Call is getting dark outside again. She dont say nothing to Ruji-Babes about she seen Zafar and him spar them up to no good up Whitechapel cause if she told Ruji-Babes this she knowed exackly what Ruji-Babes a go say init and Foxy-T figure she can do without them type a lecture. But they got stuff to do in the shop init and that take her mind off it any way.

Some of them fashion shop down there is shutting up and other ones like the Cannon Video is put its lights on and turn up the music and theres all the traffic going past and all kind of people wandering around and they can hear the sound a that guy and him basketball upstairs over the road and they both thinking that they like it round here and this E-Z Call was a good little move of Ruji-Babes uncle only they wasnt say it out loud they was just kind of feel it yeah through pure enjoyment but not like put into words.

But Ruji-Babes look a bit wreck soon cause all that night of crying is make her eyes all puffy init and her contacts was hurt her and she feel knackered man. So she look around at there shop what is almost empty and say 'What you think we should close up a bit early T?'

This was like about eight so it aint that early but still earlier than usual.

And T goes, 'Yeah good idea man.'

So they turn the lock on the door and turn off some of them light and whatever so it dont look completely open. Then when them few people left chatting in the booth or using there email or whatever finish up they could let them out then lock the door behind them again so no other customer can come in or nothing. Just like any shop would do. Like Woolworth up Bethnal Green Road does when they a close up. And pretty soon all them customer is gone and they cash up and log out and switch off and put whatever in the safe and then its just that shutter left to do. So they both go out and do that and all cause there like a little door in that bit of the shutter what is over the door so Zafar could still get in by unlock that and it open outwards then him would be able fe reach in and open that proper front door and let himself in like that. Which is what they would normally do and all init.

And actually it aint long till he come back and he got a carrier bag with some take out from up Tayyabs. And this was good timing because they was well starving by this time so they all finish locking up then go up the flat and get them plate out and whatever. Only Ruji-Babes dont turn off the main light and light the candle tonight is it. Cause she fucked off with Zafar and she want him to know him take out dont make everything alright. And anyway even though he brought back some nice take out including some lassi like sweet one for Foxy-T and salty one for Ruji-Babes the way them like him still in a right bad mood and all and dont really say nothing is it. And the fact that Ruji-Babes was effectively say this meal aint nothing special man only probaly make him even more pissed off. So him hardly say a word all through that meal is it and when he does Ruji-Babes just turn and look at him like him a piece of dog shit on her new shoes. He still try and be polite or whatever but them two could tell it wasnt easy.

Foxy-T was a bit out of it like usual but she seem to not notice that you could a cut the air in that kitchen with a knife. She just sat there like it was there business what they was fucked off about Zafar and Ruji-Babes and nothing to do with her. And it was like she was alright eating her karahi chicken or whatever so she didnt care that much what they was doing. Just sit there eating and then reading a bit of her big software book.

Later when him try fe sleep on the couch Zafar could hear them two talking upstairs. In a way that he didnt normally hear them. Cause hard as him try normally he always used to lay there and a try fe listen out at what they might be doing but never usually hear nothing. Every creaky floorboard or whatever or everytime he could hear the mattress squeaking the noise seem to be something to do with sex normally to his ear init. But he never heard nothing even though normally he just be laying there under the duvet with his hand on him cock and listen out for any kind of noise that might tell him they was licking each other pussy or whatever gay thing him imagine they done in bed. But he never heard nothing like that. But that didnt stop him imagining them doing it. He had a particular way of thinking about them going to bed what was guarantee fe get him cock hard man. He would imagine that underneath them trackie bottom and polo shirt or boyish kind of clothes that Foxy-T wore she would be wearing some serious stocking and suspender type shit. All lacy G-string tight up between the cheek of her arse and imagining the way the flesh on her legs would be slightly fatter over the top of them stockings and with suspender belt and the works. And he would imagine that Ruji-Babes would just maybe wear some kind of simple nightie on her skinny little body. And even though she was really flat chested her nipples would be stick right out through that like black satin nightie or whatever. And probaly not wearing any nickers either. He kind of imagine sometime that Ruji-Babes would have just some little wisp of pubes init but that Foxy-T would have thick black pubes what all spill out the side of her G-string. And sometime he imagine it the other way round so Ruji-Babes nightie would be stick out slightly where her pubes was and you could see this big bush through that thin satin nightie but that Foxy-T just had hardly any pubes or probaly shave her pussy a bit like them girl in Club or whatever what they use to put up on the wall up Feltham. And the way him generally imagine them going to bed would be Ruji-Babes just sitting there on the bed with her nightie lift up a bit so that you could get a good view of her pussy and just stroke her tits through the satin nightie or whatever and getting her nipple them really hard. And she just be sitting there and watch Foxy-T get undress real slow and probaly just stroking her clit and her pussy while she watching and maybe just laying back a bit against some big pillow with her legs apart and just wanking her clit like that so Foxy-T could see how wet her pussy getting. Then Foxy-T would take off her Reebok Classics and them socks but thered be stockings on her feet under the socks. Then she would stand up and slip her thumbs inside that elastic waist band on her trackie bottoms and slip them down over her hips man so you could see them suspenders against her skin. And sometime they be white suspenders or sometimes they be black ones. And white ones was Zafar favourite colour init because him think they probaly look best against her brown skin. Then Foxy-T would turn around so Ruji-Babes could see that G-string a disappear up between her big arse cheeks. And bend right over fe push down them trackie bottoms but also fe show Ruji-Babes her pussy swelling up inside that white like lacy G-string. Then last of all she would lift up her polo shirt and just be wearing some matching bra. Some really lacy one but her nipples might be poking out the top of that bra and it would make her tits look even bigger init. And she probaly got either really massive dark nipples or she got really tight small light nipples what are hardly darker than the skin of her tits. And sometime it might vex him that he dont know for sure init. But she then just chuck that polo shirt on the chair or whatever and then reach behind her head and take out her pony tail so her hair would fall down all black and shiny and half cover her face. Then she would just look at Ruji-Babes who still a sit on the bed and wanking like that. And it would make Foxy-T pussy wet and all but just stripping off in front of Ruji-Babes would already of got her pussy pretty wet. Then Foxy-T would get on the bed and crawl over where Ruji-Babes a sit and kiss her tits through that satin nightie then slip one hand up her nightie and start finger fucking Ruji-Babes while Ruji-Babes is pinching and rubbing her clit. And they be kissing really wet long kisses while they doing this and try hard fe not make any noise. Then Ruji-Babes would touch Foxy-T tits and push her bra down a bit more and just the feel of them big tits spilling out her bra and looking at them big dark nipples would make Ruji-Babes practicly come init but she would control herself and let Foxy-T carry on wanking her off while she just take one tit in each hand and just suck and kiss and tease them big dark nipples till there really hard. Then probaly she reach down with one hand and run it down between Foxy-T arse cheeks behind the G-string so it pulls that G-string up against her pussy and open her cunt slightly so Foxy-T can feel that lace rubbing up against her clit or whatever. Then Ruji-Babes just stroke her arse and her thigh and come round the inside where that soft skin is in between her thigh and just run her fingers along the edge of that G-string and feel her pubes a bit. Still sucking her tits. Then she would pull that G-string to one side and slide her fingers inbetween Foxy-T cunt lips and start really wanking her off so they both be wanking each other off for ages and just sighing and moaning and sucking and wanking. Ruji-Babes with her legs apart and Foxy-T with her arse right up in the air and her tits hanging down in Ruji-Babes mouth. Then probaly Ruji-Babes would just push lightly against the inside of one of Foxy-T thigh as if to say turn around and Foxy-T would know what she mean without Ruji-Babes need to say nothing and turn around and Ruji-Babes would slide down a bit so she not sitting up any more and Foxy-T would position her pussy right above Ruji-Babes face. And Ruji-Babes would open her legs even more so Foxy-T can just get down and suck her hot pussy and they both be sucking each other pussy at the same time and Ruji-Babes would be pulling down Foxy-T G-string and Foxy-T would just lift up one leg so she could get it off. And Ruji-Babes would go, 'You got the best arse in the world Foxy-T,' and just be in heaven look at Foxy-T big arse and hairy pussy and them white stocking and suspender stretch over brown skin. Then Ruji-Babes would slip a finger in Foxy-T arse and finger fuck her arse while she licking her out and they both be wriggling around with it and try fe not come yet only they both know they gonna come and they get out some big vibrator and start teasing each other arsehole and clit and slipping them inside there cunts and both saying, 'I'm gonna come I'm gonna come,' and both just feel this shuddering deep inside them like some big tidal wave battering down some secret door inside there bodies what aint go hold for long cause that wave be getting stronger all the time and they both just be shaking there heads from side to side and going, 'I'm gonna come I'm gonna come I'm gonna come.' Then they both come and its even sexier seen cause they still a try fe not make no noise and they got gritted teeth and cant help crying out and shaking and clawing and jamming them big vibrator deep inside there cunts or arses or whatever and they both just come like they never come before and it last for ages and they practicly pissing thereselves with come and sweating and shaking and then getting quieter and quieter and then just laying there like they cant believe what they just done and they just all wet with sweat and there legs and thighs is all juicy and soaking and they just go, 'I love you Ruji-Babes,' 'I love you Foxy-T.'

And normally that would be enough to make this Zafar come too just think about that type of thing they would be doing. Then other times when they is sixty nining he would come in to the bedroom in just like his shorts or whatever with a big hard on and Foxy-T would look over her shoulder at him and go like, 'Come on what took you so long man?' Then go back to sucking Ruji-Babes pussy and Ruji-Babes would like pull Foxy-T arse apart so he could get a good view of her licking Foxy-T clit and show him how wet Foxy-T pussy is and he just get on the bed and kneel behind Foxy-T with his balls over Ruji-Babes face and Ruji-Babes would just pull his cock down and start licking him head and using it to rub against Foxy-T clit and Foxy-T would look up and go, 'I want your cock Zafar man stop fucking about and give me your cock.' An Ruji-Babes would just take him cock out of her mouth and slide it in to Foxy-T hot tight wet pussy and he would just be fucking Foxy-T cunt while Ruji-Babes lick him balls or him arse or whatever and he just be holding on to Foxy-T hips and banging her man and just looking down at him cock the way it pump in to her cunt then maybe slip him finger into her arse while he was fucking her and Foxy-T would just be crying out for him to fuck her harder through mouthfuls of Ruji-Babes wet cunt and she'd be fuckin Ruji-Babes arse with a vibrator at the same time and theyd all just be banging away like that for ages and him get harder and harder and them two cunts getting hotter and hotter and wetter and wetter and tighter and tighter until it just felt like one big cock and one big cunt and they couldnt tell where one a them started and the other one a stop cause it was all just hot and wet and one big fuck and then he go, 'I'm gonna come in a minute I cant help it man!' And he might want to just pump all that spunk deep into Foxy-T pussy or he might just hold on till they start to come and all and just keep cool while they thrashing about and shouting and shaking underneath him init. Then when they stop coming they would disentangle there selves slowly and change around so he suddenly find himself fucking Ruji-Babes bony little arse an Foxy-T is just kneeling next to him pulling on Ruji-Babes tits with one hand and sticking a finger up him arse or stroking him balls with the other and a kiss him at the same time. And he just be playing with Foxy-T tits while him a fuck Ruji-Babes and he be getting harder and harder and Ruji-Babes would feel him cock deep inside her get even bigger and start fe twitch like she know he gonna come any second so she get off him cock and turn around. Then they both get down on there knees and both start sucking him cock so its like there half kissing each other and half sucking him big shiny cock and they taking turns to take his like big shiny head in there mouths and trying to get him to come in there mouths and one of them would be playing with his balls and he would just be watching them sucking him off init and looking down at there arses up in the air and he just reach down and stick a finger up both of there arses at the same time as he push his cock deep inside Foxy-T mouth so she gagging on him cock and then he just give one big push and shoot off loads of spunk in her mouth so she cant believe how much spunk he can be shooting in her mouth and throat and she all wide eyed and loving it. Then they would both be licking up all that spunk and kissing each other and going, 'Zafar your so fucking horny man. Lets do that again.'

Only it never happen like that. But Zafar is a young man right and all that spunk have fe go somewhere init. So when Zafar was lay there on the duvet listening out for like gay sex upstairs and try fe sleep he be laying there with his hand on him cock and thinking them kind of things.

But then he realise that he can hear them two voice kind a muffle through the floor or whatever but he maybe aint close the door properly so he just get out of bed or off the sofa real quiet and he just standing there in him shorts and goes and stands next to the door and he can hear them voices a little bit better from where he standing now. And that sitting room door is right squeaky or whatever only the squeaky bit is just before it click shut and because he aint shut it properly in the first place he realises that it aint gonna squeak if he just open it right up. So he does this and he can see out in the corridor and the orange street light coming in the kitchen window and he can hear them voices a bit better but he still cant hear what they is saying. So he step out onto the landing and start creeping up them stairs really slow and try to feel his way up there so them stair wont creak and he creep right up there till he is right outside that door there what is left from when there was like two flat up here init and what is closed. He was try and not even hardly breathe probaly standing there like that. And he put his ear to that door and he could hear Ruji-Babes talking.

And she was going, 'You aint marryin that Zafar, T. Hes a damn fool man. I dont think I could bear it if you was married to him. I would die man. And thats what the damn fool want I reckon. He want me dead and out of the way. And I tell you if you did marry him if you was stupid enough fe do that with some boy what you hardly know then you have fe go man you aint living here with that boy believe me. I hate him being here man. This is are place and it just dont feel right having some young fool all making eyes at you all over the place. I feel stupid man fe never notice them thing before. Shit man theres me say him like me little brother but all the time him scheme init. I wish we just turn him out that first night man. Wasnt are problem is it. We just feel sorry for him with that story about him grandad. Just go fe show I mean you do some fool a favour and they spit in your face init. Aint no one hate you so much as the one you do a favour is it. Since you know them weakness them always a go end up hate you init.'

'Well we just tell him he have fe leave in like a couple a days time, Rooj,' say Foxy-T.

'You mean it T?' Ruji-Babes aks.

'Yeah man. I dont care,' says Foxy-T.

'OK yeah. We aks him fe leave by like Friday or whatever.

Wicked. Then the fool will be gone for good man. I hate him being here now init. Way him a sit in that chair like he king of the castle. And you know he only after what he can get. He think we can support him. Damn fool. I tell you though man I aint gonna support him none. If he was OK he would never of end up in Feltham is it. You have fe tell him that you aint go marry him T. He just gonna make a fool out a you in it. Marry! Fuck sake him just wanna fuck you init. Him too stupid to go and get himself a girl. He couldnt look after hisself let alone a wife and all. He come over like he already catch you and you his wife man it makes me sick I tell you. You is already taken init.'

'He aint caught me man I aint his wife,' says Foxy-T.

'Try telling him that T. He probaly think he can run thing around here. Like he some big boss man at the E-Z Call. I tell you something for nothing man I aint slave and work my fingers to no bone just so that boy can come and take it from you and me. We never should a let him stay man. And believe me once we tell him he have fe go then he can go back over Dagenham where him come from and he forget all about this place. So you better hadnt marry him is it or you be left here like you never met the fool. And like you and me is nothing and we aint worth fighting for. Its you and me man. You and me is in this together.'

'Well he be gone by Friday Rooj,' say Foxy-T. 'So no fret is it. We tell him in the morning yeah.'

'Damn straight I'm gonna tell him man. I gonna give that boy some advice man,' says Ruji-Babes. 'He aint go turn up and run thing round here. I tell you man that little boy would make a fool a you if you let him. He aint after a wife he dont know the meaning of the word is it. Once a thief always a thief. Shit man you know no one get four years just for nick cars is it. I dont even want fe know what him must have done man and why him really up Feltham. You aint stupid T you know what a go happen once that boy a got what him think him want. Man I wouldnt want be you and let him get away with none a that shit I tell you.'

'He aint so bad as that,' says Foxy-T. 'He aint a thief no more.'

'So he say because him a try impress you init. But thief cant change him spots for real. Dont let the little fool hurt you T. You know I couldnt be dealing with them things.'

'Its me what would be dealing with it Rooj,' says Foxy-T. 'Aint you what would get hurt man.'

'What you say T?' aksed Ruji-Babes. 'Boy hurt me enough already. I dont need that shit man.'

Then Zafar hear Ruji-Babes start to cry, and him hear Foxy-T speaking to her real soft so him cant hear what she is saying. But he knowed she was comforting Ruji-Babes init. He aint that stupid. He crept back down stairs slowly. But when he try and sleep man him head was spinning. He shouldnt have heard what they was talking about but now he had and that was it. He couldnt pretend him never hear it is it. So him just lay there under that duvet on the sofa and stare at the ceiling. He could just about still hear them low voice from upstairs but then they stop and he couldnt hear them no more. But he could remember what they was saying before and them things was just run around in him head and keep him awake. And it wasnt no use him wanking now believe me.

After a hour or so he think, 'Shit man me never gonna sleep is it.' And as them voices upstairs had stop completely long time since he figure Ruji-Babes and Foxy-T must asleep now.

So him get out of bed and it was good to be standing up in the cool air instead of under that hot duvet what had been getting all tangle round him feet and make him sweat. He reach over and grab him shirt and trouser then his sock and trainers and in a minute he was dress. He crept back out into the landing but he wasnt going upstairs this time. There was nothing more to hear he knowed that. Beside he heard enough already. He crept across to the kitchen and flick on the kettle then quietly make himself a cup of coffee like stirring that sugar real slow and gently lay down the teaspoon on that dishcloth by the sink there. There was enough light coming in the back window that he didnt need fe switch no light on. Out the window he could see the roofs of the Mulberry and then them flats on Bigland and Norton House was catching the moon on all them windows and the floodlights on the roof was all lit up orange and there light was spilling down the sides of the building. Off in the distance he could see the roof a Shadwell station what he knowed is all close up now for the night and even further away he could see the top of Canary Wharf and its one single flashing light what was right on the top of that pyramid thing. He stir that coffee real silent and then he walk over where him jacket was drape over the back of the chair and he reach in the pocket fe check something or other is in there. Then he take the jacket off the chair and put it on. Grabbing him coffee he go out of the kitchen and creep slowly downstairs. Silently he open the door in to the back yard. He put the lock on the catch so it wouldnt completely shut behind him but it fit well snug and it look shut and dont let in that cold night air.

Zafar sit down on the step and put that coffee on the concrete beside him gently so it wouldnt make no noise. Reaching in the inside of him pocket he pull out a packet of Silk Cut. Tuck in the back was a pack of slim blue Kingsize Rizla. He slip it out and put it down next to his mug. Then he reach in the pack next to his cigarette with two finger and pull out a big cling film wrap. He put this down then pick up the Rizla and pull out a skin. He pull up his trouser so there was a kind of crease across his leg then he lay the skin along the groove. Picking up the Silk Cut he pull out a tailor and turn it upside down above the paper and just like twist the end like roll it back and forth between him finger and thumb so some little flake a tobacco fall out on the Rizla. He just twist like this till there is a sprinkle of tobacco along the Rizla. Then he twist up the end a whats left and put it back in the packet. Picking up him twist he open it carefully and choose a nice bud what snap off nice and easy. Then with both hand he crumble this bud up over the Rizla too. He never use the whole bud this time since he aint gonna share him spliff with like Shabbaz and you dont need so much weed when you is smoke on your own and what he dont use he put back in the wrap. Then he like rub his finger and thumbs together to get off all that oily dust what stuck to him finger. Then he poke that tobacco and that bud about till it well mix. Using both hand he roll up the spliff using him little finger fe stop any mix spilling out the end then he lick along the paper and stick it and quickly twist one end. Pulling a box of match out his pocket he pick a match and pack the mix down in that open end of the spliff before lay it back down in that fold on his trousers. He quickly tear off half the flap on him Rizla and roll it tight till its well springy then he slide this in the spliff. It open up through being springy and he dont need fe patch it with another Rizla. Skill he think to himself. Pure skill.

Him always build a nice neat spliff since time seen. Then he pop the spliff in him mouth and clear up that wrap and his Rizla and cigarette before light the spliff. He strike a match and burn the twist. The end of the spliff start flame for a second so he can see the wall at the end of the yard then he blow the flame out and him take a long toke.

Picking up that coffee he take a drink then pull more smoke. The weed sharpen up him sense and yet relax him at the same time.

Them conversation upstairs was forgotten and he look around the night time yard. It was well cold and them stars was all out in the sky. The moon was high up in the south. He could see the tree tops what lay between the next yard and the back of the Cash and Carry. Beyond that yard was the Mulberry. It seem like every leaf on the trees was pick out by the moonlight. He pull again on his spliff and hold that smoke in for a few second before he exhale in a big cloud of smoke. The weed was crisp and he was well chill as him sat there in the moonlight. It was cold sure enough as he sat there but it didnt vex him one bit. He feel like he could a be anywhere in the world right then. Far away he could hear some car burning up and skidding then burning up and skidding again and a police siren what echoed off the buildings down Commercial Road. Nuff police about init. He watched the lights off a plane what was taking off from probaly City Airport then saw the lights off another plane but this one was much higher and he guess it was like cruising high up on its way from Europe or somewhere to maybe the States. Or maybe from further away like India to the States. Then he hear another siren way down by the river there like it was speeding down the Highway. And for a second he think that

England is a well small place. With all them police speeding down the roads to where ever them a go. For a second he think about them pictures he seen of English fields and hedges and how all small and cramp it is and no room for a young Asian man like him like he always go come up against hedge and fence in this little country and it feel like the whole a England is like that map what use to be in Cannon Street Car where every place have is own price and you aint go be there without you have fe pay up that price man. And for a second he wish him on that plane man going off New York or somewhere. The States was massive thats one thing he remember off geography in school. And for a second he feel like England and all them fences and all them police car and all them laws that is just wait fe get broke by anyone who aint right and dont fit in and all a that come crowding in on him like them cell wall up Feltham and for a second he felt trap man. But then he sit back and laugh to himself real soft. He aint trap is it. He just enjoying a spliff and a cup of coffee and the night belong to him man. And Foxy-T a go belong to him and all. Shit man. He pull once more on the spliff and hear a seed popping in there. Man that weed Shabbaz supply was well crisp.

Then he hear something what make him sit up. It sound like someone knocking over a pile of milk crate. And he know where it come from because back when he first come out of Feltham he put them crate there himself init. That was how he climb over from the Mulberry into the carpark of the Cash and Carry. He stand up and listen then feel like he best take no chance so he slip inside quick and grab the baseball bat what is kept in the corridor outside the toilet. Then he creep back outside and pull the door to. And just fe be on the safe side him lock that door as quiet as he can. Then he slip them key in his pocket and throw down the roach and grind it out neath him trainer. Then he remember him coffee so he pick that up and put it down beside the step in the shadow there and he listen. And cause a that weed he feel crisp man init. Sharp and tense like nothing a go escape him notice.

Theres nothing for a second or two is it. Then he hear someone stacking them crate back up. One after the other. Then the sound of someone trainer hit the ground. Zafar tense up and slip into the shadow next to the old air raid shelter what is up against the wall on one side of the yard. The moon is light up the rest of the yard but where Zafar stand is well hidden and he just stand there with that baseball bat at the ready and keep him wits about him. After a bit he hear another noise in the back of the Cash and Carry then like the sound of someone climbing over into the next yard. Not the one behind the next house in the street but over the back wall. Because this yard is out the back of some dress place call Razzy Fashion Warehouse what is one a them big type a like sixties warehouse and full of all East European woman what operate them sewing machine. And they always got a notice on the door say 'Experience Presser Required' init and they keep all them old empty rolls of fabric out the back seen and while Zafar listen him hear someone like swear under him breath as he pick him way over them big cardboard tube and bin bag full a scraps. For a second Zafar aint sure and he wonder if they is gonna try and broke in Razzy Fashion Warehouse and if he gonna hear a smashing window over there. But he dont. What he does hear is someone going like 'hup' as if they suddenly making a big effort and he hear someone trainers scrabbling on the other side of the back wall as they try and get a foot hold so they can climb over. Then he see a pair of arm lay on top the wall like its someone a try fe climb out a swiming pool then he see the outline of a head and some trainer and a leg appears and that person pull themself up and swing there leg over and just before he swing over that other leg Zafar see the guy face pick out in the moonlight and he get a good look at that guy face but he never seen him before so figure well he aint from round here and he aint from Dagenham. Then the thief jump quickly down in to the yard. He only be about six foot from where Zafar is hid in the shadow next to that air raid shelter. And he quickly look up at the windows of the flat and the next door places fe double check no one a watch. Zafar dont look too because him no want take him eyes off the thief now and he dont want fe risk being seen or making no noise at all. So he just watch and wait. That thief get to the top of the stair and try turning the door handle. He so quiet that it dont make no noise but that door dont shift at all is it since Zafar lock it. Then he catch sight of the toilet window next to the back door and Zafar can barely stop himself from swear out loud because him see that the little window in the top of that damn toilet window is open. It aint a big window but some thief dont need no big window is it. A little window like that is well big enough. That thief reach up with him right hand and grab the bottom of that open window then swing himself up so he like kneeling on that stone windowsill at the bottom. With his other hand he undo the catch and open that window right up then begin the business of worm him way through it by reaching one arm right through fe brace himself against the windowsill on the inside. Seeing that the thief attention was elsewhere Zafar step quick and quiet out of the shadow where he been hiding. In three steps him standing so close to the thief that he could reach out and touch him trainer as it scrabbling on the wall and try fe get up on the windowsill.

Zafar swing that bat round behind his head init and bide him time for a second before bring it down with full force on the guy ankle. Theres a howl of pain in the toilet and that guy head crash up against the top of the window as he start try fe pull himself out. Zafar dont give him no time to do this and bring the bat down on the guy other knee what is still kneeling on the windowsill. As Zafar done this the thief lose him balance init and crash out through the window and down on the floor. Him holding his ankle and Zafar reach down with one hand and grab the collar of him jacket. That thief turn round like he cant believe what a go on and him look at Zafar what is stand there with the bat above him head and that thief go, 'No man dont hit me man.' And Zafar try fe pull him up by him collar but when he does this he step back and crash into a old Calor Gas cylinder what was left up against the wall there and he begin to fall back. That thief just take the advantage and spring up and end up knocking Zafar back. Zafar got hold of the man collar still but he wriggle out him jacket and run for the back wall and before Zafar can get him balance again fe like turn and chase him that man tumbling over the wall into the next yard and crashing through them cardboard tube and bag of scrap and cussing and swearing and then few second later Zafar hear them crate again and he know that the thief him got away. He just stand there with that jacket in one hand and the bat in the other and he take a deep breath and then he hear the window opening upstairs and Foxy-T is leaning out and she going, 'Whose there?'

And Zafar step out into the light and go, 'Is me man.' And he hold up the thief coat and say, 'I just catch a thief but him got away. Him was trying a broke in the shop man. But I catch the fucker init.'

'Thank fuck for that man,' says Foxy-T. 'We was shitting ourselves.'

'Sorry,' says Zafar.

'Why was you up anyway?' Foxy-T aksed him.

'I dunno man I couldnt sleep is it and then I heard some noise over the Cash and Carry so I hid down there and wait.'

Zafar lift up the coat. 'Man left him coat init. Him wriggle out of it and run because him know I would a bust him up. He gonna be limping for a week now man believe me. I catch him good with this here bat a yours I tell you man.'

Zafar held up the leather jacket like a trophy.

'Is a good coat man,' he say. 'Look. Fit you I reckon.'

'You never catch me wear that,' says Foxy-T. 'I think we have fe burn it tomorrow man.'

'Seen,' says Zafar.

'You coming back in now then,' says Foxy-T.

'Yeah me soon come,' says Zafar. 'Go back to bed him gone now. He aint coming back. I give him the fright of him life believe me. Hey what time you got there T?'

Foxy-T leaned back in the bedroom for a second then say, 'About four man.'

'Yeah me come in in a minute man. Go back to sleep yeah. You safe init.'

And Zafar fetch him coffee what is well cold now and him sit back on the step with that bat across him lap. He take a sip of coffee and then reach in him pocket for that pack a cigarette. Taking it out him build another spliff. Strong one this time because him buzzing now init and he realise otherwise him never gonna sleep now. Then he just sit there and smoke and him get well mash up on that crisp weed init but just sit there with that baseball bat on him lap as if to say, 'Come on then all you thief what think you hard. You aint no match for me man.'

And he keep guard for a while and relive that moment when him brung the bat and dash it down on that thief knee and the fool come crash out the window. Zafar start fe think about that thief damn lucky that Calor Gas cylinder was there. Fuck sake that man would a been dead if him no fell over init. Then he just gaze up at them star and watch a couple of plane fly over on there way to wherever. When he finish smoke the spliff and sit a while him start feel the cold init so he drain him cup and stand up then let himself in the back door and once him a lock up and check the window no broke him go straight to bed. Him well mash now and sleep come quick once he laying upon that sofa. He go out like a light believe me.

Foxy-T no sleep so good though is it. What with the thief and thing she well tense believe me even though Zafar catch him. And even when she did sleep she have a well bad dream she dream that Ruji-Babes dead init. Foxy-T was like cry in her dream and she have fe bury Ruji-Babes in some coffin. Only it aint no ordinary coffin because for some reason it make out of fruit box. Like them mango box down outside the Mohamedia grocer. All nail together fe make some kind of cheap coffin what still fill with crumple tissue and polystyrene like fe protect them mango. And Ruji-Babes body just cold and lay in that coffin made out of mango box and Foxy-T was look everywhere init for some lid only she couldnt find one and there was no more mango box even what she could a make one with and the only thing she can find was that thief coat. And she have fe tuck Ruji–Babes body up with this coat what is too small fe cover and in her dream Foxy-T was just cry her eyes out and try fe cover Ruji–Babes with just this thief coat. Then she woke up and was crying still.

First thing when they got up and dress Ruji–Babes and Foxy-T even before they had breakfast they was down in the back yard looking at that coat. Zafar had hang it up on the door knob of the air raid shelter. It was a well cool black leather jacket and man knowed is worth a lot of money. Good thick leather and gold fittings. And the lining say like Gucci. It must of cost that thief a whole heap a money.

'He gonna be sick man thats a expensive jacket for real,' say Ruji–Babes. 'If him wasnt some thief you feel sorry for him init.'

Foxy-T keep quiet and just stand there look a bit distracted. She reach out her hand and feel that leather. She could practicly smell it though them two could easy tell it aint exackly new. It still have that strong smell of thick leather init.

Zafar come outside and all. Him look a bit red around the eye since him only catch a couple hour sleep. When she hear him footstep on the back steps Ruji–Babes turn around and walk past him back into the flat.

'Wicked jacket man,' says Zafar.

'Yeah,' says Foxy-T. 'I wonder how many house him have fe rob fe buy this init.'

Zafar thought for a sec.

'Eh T. You recognise it man? You think him that same thief what you seen before that time. Remember?'

Foxy-T thought the jacket look familiar but without the man in it was hard to tell.

'Probaly,' she say.

Zafar watch her but him cant tell what she thinking. That Foxy-T confuse this boy init because she so quiet and not use to men ways but also kind of hard like a man herself. It seem like what she think and what she speak was two different people and him cant figure her out is it.

'You a go keep it?' she aks him.

'Dunno. Lets think about it after breakfast init.'

'Got that strong leather smell init,' says Foxy-T. 'Someone tell me once that a sign of cheap leather. Smell like them leather shop up Brick Lane. All a them cheap jacket there.'

She could still smell it on her hand just from stroke it.

'No. I reckon its real Gucci man,' says Zafar. 'Its quality init. Thats a good bit a leather that. Maybe get it clean or whatever though I reckon. Him may have flea init.'

'Ugh,' says Foxy-T.

'Never know is it,' says Zafar.

Later on she see that Zafar have brung the jacket in and hang it from a wire coat hanger in the hallway. Seem like that smell a leather is get in her head.

Zafar was well fucked off all day. Perhaps from him late night or perhaps from what him hear them talk in the night. Or both init. Whatever. Or perhaps cause him no really get the respect him due fe catch a thief. Maybe him think that through catch that thief them two girl would change there minds from what they was saying the night before init. Man if he hadn't a been there theyd a been rob. And they aint give him no credit for it. Him face look like a donkey arse. But spite a this him still polite and that. He didnt say nothing about them getting marry and just keep well clear a Foxy-T all day. Much a the time him sit out front and read him paper. Except he get up every now and then and shake some brother by the hand and chat. Man like DK and Ifty is drop by init cause him call fe tell them about him catch a thief. Or other time some car would pull up and him get in there and chat for a bit or smoke some little spliff. But most a the time him be sit outside the E-Z Call. Doing him security thing. And probaly feeling well please and satisfy on account of that thief what him catch. And him well bragging init. To all them spar what him chat with. Man knowed Zafar would a tell that story over and over and it getting better every time him tell it. A couple of them guy him bring through the shop and show them the jacket fe see if them know who it belong to. Man like Red-Eye and Shifty a come by init. But them all shake them head and go, 'No I never seen no one wearing that, man. I'd a recognise it init.'

And Zafar laugh and go, 'Listen man. If you see some guy who limp real bad and stand there shivering with no jacket then give me a bell init. You got my mobile.'

And them guy them friend of his like Ranky and Shabbaz laugh and all when they walking back through the shop init. And them nod at Ruji-Babes behind the counter as if fe say, 'Hello.' And she manage to nod back even though she dont really trust them neither if there friend of Zafar and when Zafar go past she be concentrate upon sort out them top ups or something and dont say nothing to him. And believe me that Zafar is act like he angry with her and all so him dont even try fe say nothing to Ruji-Babes.

Come the evening and they was having there supper yeah.

Ruji-Babes didnt want that Zafar eat with them two which was fine with him init cause him prefer eating on him lap. Before them dish up Ruji-Babes tell that Zafar that him have fe move out at the weekend init. Zafar knowed this was coming init but him pretend fe shock even though he aint. But him no mind not have fe eat with them neither cause Zafar well fucked off with Ruji-Babes and just enjoy eat his bit of channa dal and rice with plenty a pickle and some cucumber on him lap in front of the telly. This never bother him much like I say since he usually done this since time init. But Ruji-Babes and Foxy-T eat there tea on the kitchen table like normal they even light the candle like usual and he could hear them chatting while he ate though he couldnt really hear what they was saying cause of the telly. After that they just sit quiet for a couple of hours and all watch the telly together though neither Ruji-Babes nor Foxy-T said nothing to him. Ruji-Babes had some of them accounts on her lap and was reading through the figure and thing. While Foxy-T wasnt reading her software manual like normal she was reading some woman magazine what she nip over the road to Ruposhi Novelties and Sari Shop and got earlier on. With all kinds of dress in it. Like fashion shoot. Only all Asian style. With all How to Marry a Millionaire type thing in it. All them dress and that was mainly traditional stuff but also some like western stuff.

Zafar was play with him mobile. Playing snake or sending text or whatever them couldnt tell just see him concentrate and push them button with him thumbs.

Every now and then Ruji-Babes would look up because it hurt her eye just focus on them row of small numbers. She see Zafar hunch over him mobile.

'How you go get to Dagenham man?' she aks him.

He finish something then look up. 'Dunno man tube or whatever I dunno. District Line go there or number 15 bus. Either way. Aint got much fe carry is it.'

'So Saturday morning yeah?' she aks.

'Seen,' him say.

'OK,' she say looking down at them book spread out on her lap. But then she look up again and aks. 'What is it you gonna do then eh? If you dont mind me aksing you Zafar.'

'Do?' him say. 'What you mean "Do"?' This had piss him right off.

'You know what I mean init. You and T. What you gonna do about all this getting marry and shit? You sort out the dates already eh? Send out them invite?'

Ruji-Babes was right taking the piss man believe me and Zafar no say nothing yet is it just wait till she play out.

'Been over Tiffin fe plan you catering yet Zafar?'

'Oh that,' him say. 'I dont know init.'

'You aint know much is it?' she aks him. 'So come Saturday nothing a go change is it. Still dont know?'

'What of it man,' says Zafar waving his mobile around. 'I can phone init. Or email. Whats the difference?'

'Seen,' says Ruji-Babes. 'You can probaly get marry by email and all these days init. But it matter to me on account of E-Z Call since T and me is like business partner. I need to know them date and shit so me can get some new staff in. I got to advertise and interview and all that init.'

'Foxy-T could still do them thing,' Zafar says. 'Just because we was marry wouldnt mean she couldnt do them thing she does. Why you have fe find someone else Rooj?'

He was playing a bit stupid here init and also try fe annoy her through call her Rooj instead of Ruji-Babes. Because him well know what Ruji-Babes a go say next.

'Obvious init eh?' says Ruji-Babes. 'This flat and this shop and that aint no place for some marry couple. Is only a one bedroom flat for real. Aint hardly enough money for the two of us let alone for a marry couple. And there aint no real work for you here init. If you two was marry you a go have fe check you own place and new job and everything init. Think about it man.'

She was tapping the side of her head when she say this.

'Think about it Zafar. No way man.'

'Me know say I have fe move out man,' says Zafar.

'Seen. Glad you see thing my way,' says Ruji-Babes. 'Thats what I say init. But aint just you is it is T and all. When she gonna move out thats what I need to know man.'

Foxy-T look up but she say nothing then look down at her magazine again init while them two just sit and stare for a second or two. Zafar stare at Ruji-Babes and Ruji-Babes stare at Zafar.

'Ah,' say Zafar eventually. 'I dont know.'

Ruji-Babes was enjoy this.

'What? You tell me you no think about this yet is that it? You is suppose to be getting marry yet you aint think about when you is gonna take your wife? Is you think about anything else man or was that idea just a joke of some kind? Was you joking when you aks her fe marry you?'

'Course I wasnt joking man,' say Zafar. 'But I'm going back over Dagenham init.'

'What just you?' aks Ruji-Babes. 'Or was you thinking of take your wife up Dagenham and all?'

'Course man.'

'You listening T?' says Ruji-Babes looking over at where Foxy-T is sit with her head in that magazine. 'Zafar say you moving out Dagenham on Saturday and all? You pack yet man?'

Foxy-T look up a bit quick as if she about to laugh but with a odd expression on her face.

'News to me Rooj,' she say.

'Good news though man,' says Zafar.

'Maybe,' Foxy-T say and look back at her magazine.

'Is you ready fe move out Dagenham way,' aks Ruji-Babes.

'Depend what type a place init. I aint go sleep on him sister sofa and thats a fact.'

Zafar look at her and smile.

'You think I should go first and like scope it out?' he aksed.

'Aint no alternative man,' says Foxy-T.

'Smart girl,' says Ruji-Babes. 'See what kind a move him make and then you can decide if you is going or not. Anything else is pure foolishness init.'

'I reckon we should get marry before I go init,' he say. 'And then take it from there man.'

'See what I say? Listen to the boy T. Pure foolishness. How is you gonna get marry between now and Saturday Zafar? Getting marry cost money you know,' say Ruji-Babes.

Zafar wasnt listening to Ruji-Babes though is it. Him look at Foxy-T and wait for her to speak.

'What about you T?' he aks.

She look over at the telly.

'Dont aks me man,' she say.

'What you mean?' him aks.

'What you mean?' She repeat back at him. She was laughing

now. 'I dont know what I mean. I aint thought about it yet is it.'

'What you need fe think about then T?' he aks.

'I got nuff thing to think about and that should be obvious to you of all people init,' she say.

He look at her like I dont know what. Like she just join up with Ruji-Babes against him. It seem like whatever him say she would take the piss out of him. Mood she was in or whatever.

'Up to you man,' he say eventually. 'Your decision init. You can move over when you is ready T.'

'The boy see sense at last,' say Ruji-Babes turning to Foxy-T fe share her victory then turn back and watch the telly confident in she win this argument.

Come midnight or so Ruji-Babes say, 'You tired T?'

'Not really man,' says Foxy-T. 'But if you is ready for bed I'll come and all man.'

They both get up and go out the room without saying nothing to Zafar. Him just sit there and watch the telly like he never notice what they is doing. Later him hear Foxy-T shouting down like, 'Goodnight Zafar. Turn out the kitchen light yeah.' Like him nothing more than some guest or other. And he wish then he should of gone out and run with him spar or whatever. Go for a drive and smoke some weed down the Bigland near the playground but him no feel like it is it and also him no tell them none a this is it and Zafar knowed that him spar would take the piss if he did init merciless. Worse than Ruji-Babes fe true and he was still angry from the way she bait him tonight init. What the fuck is it have fe do with her him think. Bitch just have fe get use to it. And Zafar was just sit there and run them thing she say through him mind and all them thing what he should a said init. Even when he turn off them light and the fire and that and him settle down on the couch he was feel restless and none of them thoughts about what Ruji-Babes and Foxy-T might be get up to upstairs was enough fe like settle him down and he took ages to get to sleep and there was none of that weed left neither so him couldnt just get wreck and sleep like that. And laying on that sofa under there spare duvet with them orange street light shine in the window through the curtain him feel like he really waste him life here if he not careful. What he hanging around here for anyway. Shit them two lezzers aint worth it man him think to himself. But then eventually him remember about Foxy-T on her own or at least the way she act when he is around and the way she think him a thief that one time and how she dont know if she coming or going sometime and he was think to himself like 'Well why shouldnt I want to marry her?' and he almost forget and totally fool himself and all with them ideas and feel like maybe he really did love her. Cause why would he want to marry some lesbian if he no love her anyway. Must do init. He aksed her for real. Him Zafar Iqbal had aksed Foxy-T fe marry him init. And he believe it then and feel right pissed off at the way them treating him. Like he just some guest or other when he aint nothing like that cause him and Foxy-T is gonna get marry. They is engage init. Then he lay there with his hand on him cock and just think about Foxy-T and getting her on her own and all kind of thing they would do or whatever. And him get to sleep eventually.

Next morning Zafar was in a right bad mood. He look really distract because him thinking. Him thinking about how much him want Foxy-T fe marry him and move up Dagenham. He figured it was signed and sealed till last night. He still never knowed why him want fe get marry. He was a bit young for that fe true. None of him friend was marry. Like maybe one or two older cousin. Maybe people back home. But not in London. Him mind made up though now man. Him want to marry Foxy-T. Yet thing dont seem to be going his way no more. Thing not working out is it and Ruji-Babes just make it worse. Man if it just down to Foxy-T and him there be none a this is it. This is what was piss him off. As Zafar got up and eat or whatever him nuff angry through think about them things. And also because he really didnt know what fe do about it. He never face them kind of thing before. But he reason bide him time and play it cool. Foxy-T may start figure well why not marry Zafar. She no want just Ruji-Babes is it. Zafar still think about that if Foxy-T no want fe marry then she would a tell Ruji-Babes direct init soon as him aks and the fact she never mean thing aint all that between them two and that give him courage init. Foxy-T a go come round and realise that Ruji-Babes just in her way init. Zafar figure that probaly the way thing would happen so he just have fe keep quiet and be cool. Now him plant that idea in her head its only a matter of time till she see that life would be better with Zafar than with Ruji-Babes.

Still also there was no need fe argue with Ruji-Babes since she went out after they open up the E-Z Call. She never tell Zafar where she going and Zafar never want fe aks Foxy-T is it. Even though Foxy-T probaly know. So Zafar just pull up him chair outside and watch some kids them pulling all piece a wood and old broke up pallet out of that skip down by Savera Sweet Centre where them a go build like some new flat and drag them down the road. Then before long some of him spar from like Norton Massive or whatever come around and them all chat there for a while and big it up. Then maybe Ranky pull up in him Escort GTI and so Zafar stand up yeah and pull him chair back in the shop and go get in the car and drive down like Bigland down by the Surma Town Cash and Carry there and maybe a bit of money change hand and Zafar got himself some nice eighth anyway. So them just cranking up the music and chat and chill and watch them kid build that bonfire there in that yard where them play football. And one or two other of him spar turn up and all init. Man like Red-Eye and DK. So this way him spend a cool couple of hour and roll a couple of spliff.

'Shit man,' say Zafar as him chuck the roach out the window. 'This shit nuff strong init. Fucking laughing gas man believe me.'

And its true cause them was all get well raucous and shout and laugh and maybe go get some Bacardi Breezer up the newsagent. And Red-Eye got some big like box a fireworks init so they all get out a the car and start light them firework with them spliff then either chuck them, or if they was like air bombs or whatever they would hold them out and fire them thing up into the trees or whatever. They was having a wicked time believe me. DK was put them firework in empty bottle init and them things blow up like a grenade man. They was pissing themselves laughing init. And cause a this him forget some of them trouble what was weighing heavy on him mind back in the morning and him still never told him spar about getting marry neither cause him figure them no understand.

When him walk back up Cannon Street Road he cross over again and as him walk past T&T Mobile he see Ruji-Babes cousin car pulling away up the road and see Ruji-Babes standing and wave on the pavement. Zafar knowed that Ruji-Babes cousin still away init and when him check is just her cousin driver is sit in front of the car. Something make Zafar stop init and hang back there. He just stop for a second and light up a Silk Cut and watch Ruji-Babes pick up some bag or whatever and start try fe carry them up towards the E-Z Call since they was park down the road outside the Mohamedia. Some kids was let off a load more fireworks over the road down toward the laundrette where theres that little park. Ruji-Babes look tiny from this distance init and as he watch her struggle with her bag and shit he think how much he hate the bitch. And believe me man if looks could kill I tell you. Zafar was feel a bit stoned again now because of the cigarette init but he was start fe see Ruji-Babes in a new light init. Way she a bait him was get under him skin init and he was just talk under him breath and saying 'You fucking bitch I hate you. I wish you was dead and then you wouldnt get in the way of me and Foxy-T init. I wish you was dead you lezzer bitch.'

And he was thinking that he wouldnt piss on that bitch if she was on fucking fire believe me. Thats how much him hate Ruji-Babes at that time. And he see Foxy-T come out of the shop all cheerful and hurry fe take one of them bag and help that little bitch Ruji-Babes. And he see Ruji-Babes stop and let Foxy-T take all the bag except some bunch of flower what Ruji-Babes was carrying. And he was just think that no way Foxy-T should help the bitch is it. Him sick a the way Foxy-T creep around and do whatever Ruji-Babes a say.

Zafar was thinking how much him like to ram them flower down the bitch throat. See how she like that eh.

He walk a bit closer until he could hear them talk. Ruji-

Babes was going, 'Come on T let me carry some of them thing yeah. Aint fair you carry all that man.'

Foxy-T was going, 'No way man. I hate see you struggling with all them big box man. You is the brains init.'

'I just hate it man though,' says Ruji-Babes. 'Cause you is always think of me too much and deep inside you is thinking "What about me? Who thinking about me?" init.'

'When do I think them kind of thing?' aks Foxy-T.

'You is always think them kind of thing. And now you is think them thing over that Zafar and why I dont want him come live with us for good init.'

'No way man,' say Foxy-T.

'I know you is. You gonna be right pissed off when him gone up Dagenham init.'

'You reckon? I aint so sure man,' was Foxy-T reply. 'Time will tell init.'

'Yes time tell alright,' says Ruji-Babes. 'Problem is you letting him treat you like a slag aint it. I dont know what you is thinking of man. You is set your sights pretty damn low if you let him treat you that way.'

'I aint set my sights low man,' says Foxy-T.

'Yes you is. What else? Him just a boy init. Some little gangster him think. He taking you for a ride init. I know him say you the one man but I tell you him no respect you if you get marry. Boy dont know how is it. Him just want some kind of mother init. And him think you it. Cheeky fucker. I wouldnt want to be in your shoe man if you get marry.'

Foxy-T look down at her Reebok Classic and laugh and go, 'Seen Rooj. They is too big for you for real.'

'Us woman have fe stick together init,' says Ruji-Babes and

seem not to notice Foxy-T joke at first. 'That youth,' she go tut tut and shook her head. 'He too big for him boot and thats for sure. Remember how him turn up like he own the place?'

'We aks him fe stay in the first place though Rooj init,' says Foxy-T.

'We didnt have no choice the way I seen it. I tell you man that Zafar really wind me up. Why you let him treat you this way?'

'I dont let him treat me no way man. Dont fret yourself about that little boy. Neither him nor you is gonna treat me no way.'

Foxy-T was speaking soft but there was a sharpness to what she say.

'Oh I see,' says Ruji-Babes. 'Its my fault. I might a guess init. Is you try fe hurt me with all this foolishness? Is that it?'

Zafar catch him breath when him hear this init. All this time Zafar was stand outside T&T Mobile and listen but them never once look him way. Just Ruji-Babes and Foxy-T standing outside the E-Z Call. The light from the window was shining on there faces and Ruji-Babes pull open the door fe let Foxy-T carry all them box in the shop.

Well believe me after him hear all that he see thing clearer now. Zafar always been a good listener and a bit quiet most of the time. And now him well curious fe check how Foxy-T was like bait Ruji-Babes. This give him a edge he reckon init and when you add it to the way Foxy-T never tell Ruji-Babes when him aks her fe marry. She no want fe share them thing with Ruji-Babes is it. But even see Foxy-T bait Ruji-Babes it dont make him feel no different about her is it him still hate that bitch way he seen it. But boy let me tell you him feel more than ever that him want that Foxy-T. Him want her real bad man. Like she and him got some special link and feel like they was maybe marry already only in secret. Zafar feel this with a big rush in him gut man like him just smoke some extra wicked spliff.

Shit man Zafar was near to praying that Foxy-T would take him up on him offer. Like they could get marry in like January or something. Couple of month. Not long man. And this show a bit how Zafar was maybe a bit young for him age. Fe true him could probaly get some girl down the Mulberry or whatever. Few of them girls on the Bigland was easy man everybody fuck like Lisa and shit. They was right slags and nuff brother fuck them in the past and he still have Lisa number init. But Zafar feel him grown out a them type a girl now because him just feel the need fe marry Foxy-T quick then fuck her later. Perhaps because Foxy-T gay or whatever him feel they couldnt just fuck. Fe true she was too old fe come on him type of runnings just she always would be wait for him back home. Whereas other girl maybe Zafar fuck in the past was generally slags what you would just fuck then fuck off home init. So he was thinking marry her quick then fuck her slow then worry about everything else another time. Or perhaps he should just play it cool and maybe she would like stay up tonight and not go upstairs just because like Ruji-Babes want fe go up to bed or whatever. Maybe Foxy-T would like stay up with him just fe spite Ruji-Babes. He just wanted to get her tits out man and stick him hand down her knicker. Feel how wet him make her pussy. Zafar was getting hard man just think about it. He want to get her out of them trackie bottom and polo shirt or fleece or whatever. Them boyish clothes init. And see her like a woman.

Shit man Foxy-T got beautiful tits. Not like Ruji-Babes little sharp tits that is barely there at all. Her tits like little stones or something init. Not like Foxy-T who would definitely have them big full heavy tits. He just wanted to put him cock between her big tits and see her suck him cock while him just squeeze them big tits like that. Believe me man Zafar blood a boil up with all them thought. Him well angry init and no want fe see them two yet so him go back down Bigland fe check him spar still there.

It was well cold now and he zip up him jacket and wish he was wear that thief jacket instead of this thin little jacket. That would be nuff warm that Gucci man. As he walk past the stairwell of them flat there he see some little youth a huddle around and when him pass one a them is hold up some massive three skin spliff and when this youth see Zafar check it him just laugh and say, 'Nice init!' Zafar dont usually have no time fe them schoolboy but him cant help but laugh too is it.

When him reach back at the car park there Shabbaz have him sound system on init and that sound system well loud believe me. The other car there was Rankys Escort and the two of them Shabbaz and Ranky is sit there inside Shabbaz car and smoke some spliff. When they see him come up Ranky reach back and open the back seat init. So Zafar get in that warm car and sit down. Things have mellow down since him leave half a hour ago init. Shabbaz pass him some little spliff. They was listening to some mellow tune man and just chilling there and Zafar skin up a couple more spliff while him sit there. Till they was well mash up. Then Ranky say him must split and get out the car and they is all, 'Laters'. And Zafar get out and just take a stroll nice and easy fe clear him head.

He walk along Shadwell and see a load of bright light around them boarded up blocks. There was like buses and vans and shit and a light on top a crane which was well massive man. Nuff people stand there too init. Some like posh white woman in a puffa jacket was stand with headphone on and drinking tea out of polystyrene cup and some white guy was there and all. Like maybe thirty forty people. Some guys was just chat on there mobiles. Other people with like them clipboards and that. Next to one of the buses was a load a people standing and smoking while inside the bus was like a cafe init not like a normal bus with seats and that this one just have table and chair inside. And then he see some like camera there and all. On like a little crane. And them boarded up flat was all lit up like it daytime init. Only nothing was happen. Perhaps they finish already or was just setting up fe do some filming or whatever him no know. There was plenty people watching from the footbridge up Watney Market and down the grass near the DLR and tube. There was also a couple a police stand there init but they aint pay attention to him and he stand and watch with everyone else for a bit. But nothing happening is it and him get bored a stand there in the cold and wait just in case they gonna do something so him figure walk on by. And him walk down neath the bridge pass the Crispy Cod and onto Cable Street. The cool night air was sweet and the streets was noisy with car sound system and plenty people just chilling and them bus like the D3 and the 100 going pass with all them lights on and Zafar feel well easy and refresh. Him ready fe go back up E-Z Call now.

When Zafar walk up them stair and open the door in to the flat there him get the shock of him life. Man could see him well mash up from the way him eyes was shine and because him stroll out in the cool evening air him cheek them red and all. He walk in and stand there for a second and because him a bit stoned him feel him stand there a bit too long init. He still have that jacket on and he feel like a total stranger like him no belong in this place no more. So he look at them two girl a sit round the kitchen table and for a second him feel well out of it believe me. What give him this shock was that Foxy-T a change. Them fleece and trackie bottom gone and instead she a wearing like some shiny T-shirt got tiger stripe on it and a pair of well tight jeans. Not even that she was wear them kind a jean like you see what have got the waist band cut off so they is like all fray and well low down upon her hips. With like some loose belt slung round her pussy. She look well wicked. He just stand there for a bit longer now with him mouth open practicly. He wouldnt have been more surprise if she growed a beard or something. Fe true she only a change her clothes init but to Zafar she seem like a different woman like she totally change inside and all.

'Shit man you look wicked T,' he say. 'You dress up man. Me never expect.'

Foxy-T look up a bit embarassed then smile and say 'What you think I should wear Zafar?'

'Them usual trackie bottom and a fleece or whatever. Usual stuff man.'

'Thats my work clothes init.'

'I thought you wear that kind of thing all the time man. Aint that just cause you feel comfy in it or whatever. I just never think I see you in this type a thing is it. Suits you man.'

'I dont like fe wear them kind of thing after work Zafar.'

She was well embarass though he could tell from the way she pour him a glass of water out the jug and he notice that she had her nail done and all. So where her finger nail was normally short now they was long and all paint up or whatever with glitter and that. He sat down at the table now but he couldnt stop look at Foxy-T. He just check her once then check her again then check her again still man.

Ruji-Babes was just sit there quiet and poke her dinner with her fork. But Zafar never even seen her man. Like she was not even in the room init. Even while him break off a piece of bread and eat it man he never took him eyes of Foxy-T. Him never even drink him glass of water.

'Shit man you is well different,' he said eventually.

'Fucks sake man,' Foxy-T say well embarassed. 'Anyone would think I change into a pig or something.' And with that she get up and walk over to the oven. Then she open the door and like squat down to look at them foods in there. Him could see the shape of her hip and leg or whatever the way them jean a cling to her body. He could see that seam pull tight up her arse and the top a some like lacy G-string poke up over the top of her jeans. Shit man that Zafar really couldnt believe him eyes now. She look really like a woman even though she was a woman he knowed that already for real but he never see her look quite so much like a woman as she did then is it. But when she stand up and say, 'No they aint quite ready is it,' he nearly choke upon him bread. He could like see her tits and everything and believe me him never look so close at a woman body through her clothes like he did now.

It was like she land from outer space or something. This wasnt the Foxy-T that Zafar knowed. This wasnt the Foxy-T that he saw earlier on in her usual trackie bottom and polo shirt and fleece and Reebok Classics. It was like even in him wildest fantasy he never really figure that she really look like this under them normal clothes she wear. It was like even all them time he wank over Foxy-T he never really guess what she look like. Then it just hit him like that that this is what a woman is yeah. Like soft and with a gorgeous arse and hip and just some few clothes between you and there pussy. Like he could just slip them jeans off and all she got to do is open her legs and she can give herself to him. He never thought of woman in that way before. Even ones he like got off with or fucked in the past.

The fact that she only would have to slip off them jeans for him to fuck her and knowing that she want fe do exackly that suddenly make Zafar feel well strange. It was like she make the runnings now and like she after him not the other way round like before. Zafar feel like him fucking her was what she expect of him now.

'Its like a funeral in here man aint no one gonna say nothing?' aksed Ruji-Babes finally. Zafar turn and look at her like he just notice she was there. The way he look at her make Ruji-Babes hate him even more than she already did.

'What you talking about a funeral Rooj? What kind of thing is that to say man? I was just day dreaming init.'

But when Foxy-T say this she remember her dream from a couple a nights back about Ruji-Babes in a coffin made out of mango crate.

'Let me guess,' says Ruji-Babes. 'You wasnt dreaming of a wedding by any chance?'

'Maybe.'

'Was you dreaming of are wedding?' aksed Zafar.

'Dunno Zafar. Maybe I was. I dunno.'

Foxy-T was feeling a bit shy now for real. There was something about wearing them clothes and shit that make her feel a bit quiet anyway. But also it make her feel like she totally naked. Perhaps just because she wasnt use to it I dont know. But right then Foxy-T a feel like she not wearing no clothes at all. Like she was being a bit forward or something.

This was Friday night init which mean next day was Saturday when Zafar was going up Dagenham. And for a bit once Foxy-T dish up there dinners and they had a bit of food inside them they talk about them things. Arrangement like what time him leaving and all that. And them small matters take all a there minds off what they really thinking about. For a bit it feel like all them trouble of the past weeks was disappear. Like they was just good friend chatting quietly about this and that. Ruji-Babes didnt say much is it but she seem cool or maybe she just pure relief. Perhaps this was because she knowed that Zafar was going in the morning. Like she see the light at the end of the tunnel.

When Foxy-T clear up the dishes and start washing up they all help wipe up and whatever and Ruji-Babes was making a bit of a effort to be nice because in spite of everything and hating Zafar for what he done she still feel like sorry for him.

Zafar all this time was just wait till Ruji-Babes go to bed and get out of him hair but he was polite enough and all cause now him feel she nothing init. And they all took there drinks in the sitting room fe sit and watch TV but there was no sign of her going to bed yet. None of them a talk much now either them all just watching telly. But probaly none of them could a tell you what programme they was watching. It was like they was just watching the pictures and hear the sound but not putting them together into nothing and all just alone with there thought or whatever.

After what feel like hours Foxy-T look up and aks Ruji-Babes what time it is.

Ruji-Babes look at her watch and say, 'Twelvish.'

Zafar look up from the telly but dont say nothing.

'Bed time init,' say Foxy-T.

'You said it girl,' say Ruji-Babes.

'I'm freezing man,' says Foxy-T. 'Shall we have a hotty? I'll put the kettle on.'

'Nice one T,' say Ruji-Babes.

In a bit Foxy-T fill up the hot water bottle and take it upstairs. She probaly plumping up them pillow and that Zafar thinks. Ruji-Babes dont move but just sit there listening to Foxy-T moving around upstairs. She was probaly do the same thing Zafar was init. Probaly imagine what Foxy-T doing up there.

Zafar think maybe she a go say something but she never and after a couple of minutes with Ruji-Babes sit there like that Foxy-T come back down again and say, 'You coming then.'

'Yeah in a minute man,' say Ruji-Babes. But she sit there for like ten minute and not move at all. Foxy-T give up wait in the doorway like that and she come back in and sit down again.

Zafar was sit there in front of the telly still but he wasnt even pretend to watch it now. He just look at them two and see that something have fe give and he figure he might as well make some kind of move init. Since he going tomorrow he aint got nothing fe lose now is it.

'I'm just gonna check the yard,' he say. 'Get some fresh air. You go come T?'

Foxy-T look up like she never hear someone say her name before. 'You aksing me?' she say.

'Yeah man come on it be good to get some fresh air init. Aint too cold neither.' The sound of him voice have different effect on them two girl believe me. To Foxy-T it sound close and exciting like she can almost feel it upon her skin. To Ruji-Babes though it sound like the teacher scrape him finger nail down a blackboard in school. 'Go on T,' he say again. 'Just for a minute man.'

He was standing up now and she was looking up at him from where she'd sat back down.

She couldnt do nothing but get up as if he reached out his hand and pull her up.

'You cant go out now T,' Ruji-Babes protested. 'I thought we was going to bed man.'

Zafar think well you should a gone upstairs init if you gone upstairs Foxy-T never would a come back down is it so him pay her no mind and him never give T a second to answer he just look around and say, 'We wont be long is it.'

Foxy-T just stop for a second and look at first one a them and then the other one. Like she didnt know who to go with. Ruji-Babes stand up now and all.

'Its too cold man you gonna freeze in them thin clothes. I aint gonna let you catch cold.'

No one said nothing for a bit. Ruji-Babes was puff up her chest like a little boy what is corner in the playground.

'No vex yourself Rooj,' say Zafar. 'Bit of fresh air never hurt no one. She can borrow my jacket init. Come on man.'

He was talk real sharp and angry even though him words not really vicious. And the fact he called Ruji-Babes 'Rooj' catch her off balance so she couldnt do nothing. Yet when him say

'Come on man' to Foxy-T he say it so quiet and nice that she got no choice but go with him.

And thats what she does init. She turn and walk towards the door where Zafar is now standing.

Ruji-Babes feel like she played all her card now and none of them is work. She feel them tears well up inside and she start fe shake and then bust out crying.

Foxy-T look round and start fe go comfort her like she done so many time before but Zafar have her hand now and he keep a tight hold and she cant move because deep inside whether she know it or not she dont want to move and go comfort Ruji-Babes.

'Leave her init,' say Zafar. 'If she dont cry tonight she gonna cry some other time. Might as well be now init. Get it over with. Crying will make her feel better. Thats what she need man.'

And gently he pull Foxy-T after him out onto the hallway and she look back and see Ruji-Babes still stand there crying and not even really notice that she gone. Dont make no difference now if I go or not thinks Foxy-T. She gonna cry whatever.

When they get to the bottom of the stair Foxy-T just know what he gonna do but she still cant quite believe it. What him do is he start fe take off him jacket, but then stop and look up where the thief jacket hanging. He take it off the hanger init and drape it upon her shoulder. The smell of that leather swamp her for a second believe me. She feel suddenly light headed and completely took over by the smell of that thief jacket. Like she drowning or like she in someone else body with her new outfit on and all. It all feel totally different on her skin and she feel like she gonna faint for a second and like her head all clog up with that leather smell and she got that buzzing fuzzy feeling in her head. But then Zafar unlock the door and she get a shot of cold air in the face that wake her up and he keep walking and leading her outside and down them steps in to the yard. And as she walk down the step they can still hear Ruji-Babes how she cry upstairs and she stop and say, 'Listen Zafar this is stupid man I got to go back and sort her out man.'

He let go her hand for a second and she turn and start walk back up the stairs. But then he reach up and stop her. He catch her arm and hold her fast.

'Yeah T I know you is going back but you can just wait a bit.'

'Let go of me,' she say. 'Ruji need me init. We broke her heart man. I got to go in.'

'Why is you always do what that bitch want? I seen the way you do that init. What about your feelings T?' him aks.

'What?'

'Your feelings is just as important as hers init. And my feelings.'

'Your feelings?'

'Yeah what you think you and me dont matter? No point wreck us and all man is it.'

And he took her hand and place it upon him cock as him stand there in front of her. Foxy-T like flinch for a second and cant believe he done this is it but she aint try fe move her hand now. She just cup her fingers under him balls and stroke them init. Feel her finger nail extensions scratch against the denim.

'Listen man there more important thing in life than just run around and try fe upset Ruji-Babes.'

She could feel Zafar cock get harder through him trousers now and feel him pulse in it and it seem like it flick a light switch in Foxy-T brain and also in her pussy init and it was only then she realise that him really mean what he say. This boy really want her init and he offering her him body. Foxy-T just catch her breath now init and she couldnt move at all then. And she forget about Ruji-Babes and all. Only thing she could think about was Zafar cock what she can feel all hot through him trousers and how much she want that cock right now.

Zafar never knowed this though is it and him broke the spell by putting his arm around her then and lead her back down into the yard. 'Come on man we need to talk init. Tomorrow I gonna be back up Dagenham and we need to talk now before I go. And it nothing to do with her seen.'

He pull the door shut behind them so they couldnt hear Ruji-Babes sobbing and wailing upstairs and they went and sat down on the bottom stair like that.

Zafar took her hand and felt like he didnt want to let that go. Like he could just hold her hand and play with her fingers all night.

'Lets get marry soon,' he say.

But like I say soon as Zafar took her hand off him cock he broke the spell now init. Fe true this boy never knowed how to impress a woman is it. And she pull her hand away for a second and say, 'We is being foolish Zafar and you know it man.'

She make as if fe look back up the steps and maybe was thinking of standing up then for a second and going inside to where she knowed Ruji-Babes was still cry even though they couldnt hear her no more. Zafar pick up on this and speak again to take her mind off thing.

'Nothing foolish about this T,' he say. 'We could live out Dagenham and both get a job easy. You is wasting your life here init. I could get some like security job and you and your computer. Shit man theres always them type of job anywhere and you know it. We could find a nice like flat or whatever. Whats wrong with that T? Why is you think we foolish fe marry? I figure that you and me belong together init. I never think till now but I like the idea of someone be there for me all the time.'

'If is just someone you after you know say you always find another girl init. Might be some girl whose into them same kind of runnings as you.'

'Seen man I know init. But me wouldnt want them kind of girl. You is the only girl I ever met who I think them kind of thing about. We talking about are whole life now man. Them other girls aint even interested in that type of thing. They is too young and foolish not us T.'

'You dont think them girls would want fe marry? Is that what you telling me Zafar?'

'I dunno man. Maybe they would I dunno. But see listen when I think of my life ahead or whatever I want you in it man. Is you and me that belong together not just some girl or whatever.'

'What if we dont belong together?' Foxy-T was look at him in that quiet way of hers.

'Yeah man but I think we do and I reckon you do and all.'

They sat there for a second. It was a cloudy night and there was no moon so just the orange lights of the city reflecting on them cloud above there heads. But up above them Zafar knowed was all the star and the lights of all them plane going this way and that. Some full of people go back home or go a holiday or start new life somewhere else and him feel strongly with them who was start new life elsewhere. And Zafar knowed that him and Foxy-T was also need to do that themselves. They was still holding hands and Zafar know say that a couple of days ago him would have try to fuck Foxy-T but something about the way she sat there in her new clothes and being a proper woman who want him too make him feel like him no better blow it now. For all that she was now sitting next to him like a proper woman who just trembling fe pick up him hand and put it on her hot pussy he really feel a bit afraid or not really afraid but like it too important or something and that stop him reach across and put him hand on her tit or whatever. Him feel like there plenty time for them things now and no rush. Is also true fe say that him feel responsible for the way she suddenly become a proper woman and him better respect that now stead a take advantage like him might of done before. And in think them type a things he feel like perhaps him a man now himself and not a boy no more. Only him wrong init like I say cause him broke the spell.

Instead him pull out him pack of Silk Cut from him jacket pocket and just build a little spliff while they sit and talk. Him no make a strong number is it just a little single skinner fe top up what he smoke earlier on. Foxy-T aint smoke since she and Ruji-Babes was into them kind of runnings but she guess from long time that Zafar was into them thing and she no mind at all. It part of him youth and she like it. It make her feel like she had got a bit too old before her time in this kind of life she lead with Ruji-Babes. They is living like them parents she know now and they too young fe them kind of life. But in spite of them thing she was think she feel like they being honest now and so she say what she feel. And she still not sure if she ready fe trade that old life with Ruji-Babes fe the same type of life with Zafar.

'Is you gonna tell you sister about us when you back in Dagenham, Zafar?' Foxy-T aksed him.

'No man me figure just play it cool. She no need fe know is it. Not yet man. I'll just make out like I just got out of Feltham in it. She never know when me release due or nothing. Far as she know me just got out init. Then later maybe I'll tell her after we is marry.'

'No Zafar we is being foolish. We too young fe marry and thats a fact man you know it.'

'Why is we being foolish?' he aks. 'You know we both want each other man.'

'I dont know this whole thing.'

'What cause its me is that what you saying? It foolish fe marry me?'

'No is me who is being foolish,' she say.

'Dont you want fe get marry?' him aks and light that little spliff.

'I dunno man. That the problem seen. I dont think I feel strong enough either way. Nothing to do with me liking you thats just me I'm a talk about.'

Zafar take another toke and look at her. Him feel well out of his depth now and dont really understand what she mean at all. Foxy-T reach and take the spliff out of him hand and take a little toke herself then blow it out straight away.

'You know say you happy fe sit here with me now though init?' he aks.

'Fe true Zafar I dunno man. Part of me maybe but then another part of me want fe go upstairs to Ruji-Babes. Yet another part of me want nothing to do with the both of you.'

'I dont believe you man. You been looking for a way a split up with Ruji-Babes for a while now init. I seen you man. Even when you never knowed me watch. If you wasnt then you wouldnt have come out here with me and you know it. You no want fe go back up there and sleep with Ruji-Babes now is it? You want put you hand back on my cock and you know it man. Answer me true T.'

Foxy-T took another toke and hold it in for a bit longer this time. Then she look up at Norton House and think for a bit. They could hear a siren speeding pass down Cannon Street Road. Eventually she speak.

'No I dont you right man. I dont want a sleep with Ruji-Babes tonight. You right about that.'

'So that mean you dont really want to be with her init. You no want fe grow old together is it?'

Foxy-T felt that these was big thing them discuss but she feel some kind of relief now too because she had been think them thing for a while now but not even admit it to herself probaly.

'No you right there and all man,' she say. 'We cant spend are whole life like this. I dont want fe grow old with her.'

'And what about me? Can you imagine me and you be together when we old?'

'Not like this Zafar no. Can I? No. I cant man.' She thought about him youth and thing and realise that it partly him foolishness that she like about Zafar.

'No,' she say eventually. 'I wouldnt want you to be old at all.'

'Nothing wrong with getting old T,' he say. 'Is gonna happen whether we like it or not believe me. And I reckon say them thing easier if you is got someone a grow old with you init.'

'Going down Shadwell on Monday morning fe collect are pension together and that. Stop it man you making me laugh.'

Zafar wasnt laughing. He never know how fe take her jokes is it. Way she talk make him think about two old people waiting in line at the post office and him lost for words. Eventually he say, 'No I didnt mean that.'

'Anyway I dont know what the difference between me and them other girl you keep talk about. I aint that much older than them or you is it. I aint even twenty five man. That aint old.'

'I never said it was but you is different to them kind of girl.'

Zafar take another toke upon the spliff now but it nearly burn down and the smoke taste bitter. Is just the roach a burn. He grind it out under him trainer.

'I aint though is it. You talking like I'm your mother.'

'Dont take the piss,' said Zafar.

'I aint man.'

'Good because these things I say is serious. And I aint joking man. We need to talk about these things serious too init.'

'What so I cant laugh when I want to is that what you is saying?'

'Kind of man. I dont know. I just know that when I say something serious then it kind of upset me if you take the piss. I dont mind a joke but I dont like being laugh at.'

Foxy-T let this sink in then say, 'No Zafar I aint laugh at you.'

Zafar get a bit of a rush maybe from the spliff or maybe from what Foxy-T say to him. He look up and say, 'You know I aint pissing about though init.'

'Yeah I guess,' say Foxy-T but she sound bored init and like she was just agree with him fe get a bit of peace. Fe true she was get bored a this conversation now and also she knowed that Zafar miss him chance. Him could a have her a few minutes back but him show that him just a foolish boy through not give himself to her when him had the chance and just talk about the future instead of the present.

All this was lost on Zafar though init and him no care about her tone of voice neither.

'So we maybe get marry in like January or whatever?'

'Yeah whatever man.'

He sat back and smile triumphant.

'Wicked man. That's it then. Sorted yeah.'

Then he sat there and say nothing just feel that triumph in every vein and every muscle and feel strong as the city all around them. It was like he was waking up or something. And he suddenly feel cold and realise that Foxy-T maybe cold and all. He stood up and shook himself off a bit. Dusted them bits of grit off the seat of him pants. Taking her hand he help Foxy-T up then turn and lead her back inside. Only before they went in the door he says, 'Kiss me then init. Now we agreed you better kiss me.'

Then they kiss quick and nervous. And there nervousness make them both feel young and like they kissing for the first time. And there mouths are like cold there lips and that. It was late though now and they was both a bit tired.

Once they got back upstair to the flat Ruji-Babes was sit there on the sofa with the curtains open and no light on so the living room was all lit up orange from the street lights and she look around with her tired swollen eyes but say nothing. And him think that Ruji-Babes look like she hate them both but she also look like she broken and got no pride left or something.

To Ruji-Babes they both look well different. She couldnt put her finger on it but he seem alive in a way like she never seen before. While Foxy-T for all that she was standing there in front of her and was the same Foxy-T as ever but for all that she seem like she was far away and like she was hiding from Ruji-Babes. And Ruji-Babes maybe felt that Foxy-T was hide something from her or make herself distant and not be giving herself to Ruji-Babes no more.

'I didnt think you was coming back in,' says Ruji-Babes.

'Course we a go come,' say Zafar. 'Where was we gonna go?'

'I didnt know,' says Ruji-Babes. 'Anything could have happen init.'

'Seen,' say Zafar. 'Thats true enough man. A lot has happen. For one thing we is gonna get marry in January. We sorted everything out.'

'Oh well I'm so fucking please for you two. I'm so fucking glad you sort things out,' Ruji-Babes spit out the words like they taste bitter.

'Yeah we is glad too init,' say Zafar and choose to ignore Ruji-Babes sarcasm.

'You ready fe bed T?' aks Ruji-Babes.

'You serious man? I'm exhausted init. Come on.'

Foxy-T look over at him after she say that and realise that she would rather stay down here with him even though she dont feel any more that they is really gonna get marry than she did before. For some reason it seem to Foxy-T that stuff she say to Zafar dont matter. Like she just say whatever in order fe get through the moment. But still she rather stay down and chat with Zafar than go upstair and have the row with Ruji-Babes that she know is coming. She feel like she wish it all already happen and they was marry and inspite of everything she feel like she happiest when they is together. So fe go upstair to bed and have to go through all the lie and game needed fe comfort

Ruji-Babes seem like a big waste of time. She look at Zafar and hope he gonna say something. She hope he gonna aks her to stay downstair with him tonight. Also she remember how him cock feel when he put her hand there. He pick up on this because he feel close to her and he feeling something the same like wishing she didnt have to go through them lie and sleep with Ruji-Babes. It feel like she is reject him again even though she just accept him a few minutes ago down there on the steps in the yard. And because of this he aint sure how far he can go now. He already went to the edge man and there wasnt nothing left to push thing that far again right now. So he just look at Foxy-T and miss the point again and say, 'Dont forget what we just promise each other T. You wont forget will you? Its sorted now init.'

As he look at her while saying this she feel him eyes fill her up until she feel full of him even if him never say what she want to hear. She smile at him and feel a bit sorry for him and him boyish manner and then she feel like just going upstair with Ruji-Babes this time was not so bad.

So it obvious that things aint gonna run so smooth as Zafar Iqbal think even though right now him feel like he score a six fe win the test.

Next day he phone the register office and see how much him need fe pay up in order to get marry. When him eventually speak to someone she go through them procedure and the various form they need to fill and whatever and what him need to bring in order fe do this. It seem pretty simple except he never had that much money at that time so they talk about it and decide they can do this in a week or so when him next giro come and maybe they go half each or whatever. Plus his birth certificate was definitely up his sister place so they couldnt do it that morning even if they did have the money up front. So they both agree that they maybe meet up in a couple of weeks and fix a date fe go up the register office and do them things. There was plenty of dates left in January when they could get marry so no rush. Then after that they could find a place or whatever and move in.

Zafar had never been able to save no money. He never work at anything for long enough or earn enough fe save and put money by. He never dealt more weed than he needed to cover the cost of his own smokes is it. And he never upgrade to brown or white like some of him spar.

'Time like this man I wish I got some savings,' he said to Foxy-T. 'Or like a car fe sell. Just fe get some little cash init.'

Then he pack his bag and the two of them walk up Whitechapel and Foxy-T buy a ticket and all so she can come stand on the platform with him then catch the East London back down to Shadwell. And the two of them stand there and wait for that train a few minutes. Zafar bought a bar of chocolate out of the machine and they sat on the seats there and share it and Foxy-T link her arm in his and the two of them leaning on each other like that. Then the train come and they kiss quickly and he get on and find a seat then turn and look through the window at her. And as she stand there watching him she was stand on one foot init like she does when she concentrating on stuff like when she try fe figure out some problem with the PC them and can see exackly where they is going wrong. And it feel a bit like that now init and also like a part of her was leaving on the train with him. And she want fe like smile and wave init but he just stand there and look and not make any kind of move just stand there and look at her. And the train doors shut and it pull away slowly and in a second he was out of sight and the train had gone under the footbridge and round the corner down towards the tunnel and on the few miles to Dagenham.

As the train disappeared she felt a bit out of it. And like she couldnt remember what it was like having him there and how that make her feel. She wondered if she could even remember what him face looked like. And felt like if he wasnt there then the part of her that exist when he was there is gone with him. But then she realise that she could remember him face. It was clear in her mind what Zafar look like. How he look a bit cheeky when he saying something fe try and provoke her and the way he laugh that laugh like him try fe act more cool than even him arrogance would allow. But that was all she could remember as she stood there on the platform and then turn to walk down the subway. Because without him there she couldnt think of how she was when he was around. Like she remember him but she forgot herself. Or at least that part of her what had gone on the train with him.

One thing Zafar did before him leave was also to open up a email account. Though he never use the thing and didnt really like write letters or things is it but just so they could keep in touch if they need to. But they never spoke except him leave a message one time to say he arrive. So they wasnt them kind of lover who speak on there mobile every five minutes and say 'Hi darling,' or whatever. Only he check his email in some little internet cafe on Stratford Broadway when he went shopping with him sister Radya on like Monday. There wasnt nothing in there that time. But then he found a internet cafe in Dagenham on like the Wednesday evening and he open up him emails and there was a email from Foxy-T.

He press print init so he can read it at home but also him sit there and read it upon the screen.

It say:

From: Foxy__T@hotmail.com
Sent: Monday 4 November 2002 22:37
To: zafariqbal1000@hotmail.com
Subject: Hi
Hi Zafar, I been thinking and running things through my mind about the two of us and what we was planning and the more I think about it the more it seems like pure foolishness. I never feel this way when you was here because in a funny way Zafar when your there I cant seem to think straight or do things for myself. But now you arent here in the flat anymore I can see how stupid we was being. Ruji-Babes and me is getting along like old times and I feel like I was all wrong about her and how for some reason because I aint thinking straight when your around I'm probaly treating you and Ruji both unfair. Like I must be leading you on in someway even though deep in my heart I know that I dont love you enough for the two of us to get married. I really dont. I know I said yes and everything but I cant believe that I meant it because I dont feel that way now. I was just like saying all that fe shut you up. All them thing people say about love and know when you meet the one for you and everything is just pure bullshit Zafar but even if it wasnt and it was true I wouldnt feel that about you. So I feel its important to be

straight with you now. I dont think theres any way we should still be thinking about getting married so I think we shouldnt meet up and do them things at the register office next week like we planned to do. I'm sorry to say that I dont love you and I hope you wont be hurt by this too much but I'm sure that in your heart of hearts Zafar you must feel the same way. I remember when I was in love with a couple of boys at school like head over heel man before Ruji and me was together and I can honestly say that I never feel that way with you. I dont think we know each other well enough really to even say we are friend let alone be man and wife like that. I can say that I feel like I dont know you at all hardly. So how can we get married Zafar answer me that questions.

   Me and Ruji is safe now and I feel that what I feel for her is like twenty times more than I feel for you. I'm not saying this to hurt you Zafar please dont think I would do that but I just trying to be honest with you like I say. Because thats the least you deserve Zafar. But I love Ruji and I know all them little things about her and I dont know what I would do if something I did cause her any more pain than I have already done. Ruji and me is gonna be together for a while yet I think and even if it dont last for ever it worth holding on to that. Who can say what is in the future. But I know she sickly and that sometime and I think we need each other in a way that you and me dont need each other. For myself Zafar I is getting by and muddling through the usual kind of days at E-Z Call you can imagine cant you. But I cant really even seem to remember much about you Zafar so this make me think that I must have been going a bit mad when you was around and putting a lot of burden on you just because you was there. And certainly not because we have anything in common the two of us. You and me is so different Zafar and you must know this too. I cant even think of why I would love you but I know why I love Ruji in a way that I cant even remember with you. And also I dont know why I said I'd move out to Dagenham with you and find a place. I dont know what I was thinking when I said I would do that. I must have been going mad because my life is here with Ruji-Babes and are work and everything which I love doing and thinking how easy I was talking myself into giving up all of this makes me think that I would do the same thing to you Zafar and just up and leave you without knowing what I was doing so it seems like I really dont want to do that to you or to myself by dropping everything and move out there with you. I'm just glad that I didnt completely fuck everything up with Ruji and she is still here for me because if she wasnt I dont know what I would do Zafar I really dont! Even when she is cross with me and upset like she was for a few days after you gone. So what I'm saying Zafar is that we should call it all off and not go through with this stupidness. I'm sorry if I led you on but I really dont think we can get married and thats the way I feel. I can only say that I'm really sorry because I dont mean to piss you about just that I dont think I really thought about what we was doing or saying and somehow we was leading each other on. So just get on with your life Zafar I know that you will make a go of it out there for yourself and maybe find some girl whose into the same kind of things that you are. Dont worry about replying to this email I mean it you should just forget about are moment of madness and thats what I will try to do as well. You forgot that jacket. You know the one that the robber left. I wore it a couple of times but I dont like it really so I will send it over in a parcel or something if you want. I got your sisters address written down here somewhere. Sorry I've been so stupid as to let you think we could get married. But lets forget all about it and get on with are lives. Are real lives not this foolishness. Ruji-Babes sends her love too and wish you luck for the future. Her uncle is coming over this week from back home. Sorry Zafar but it has to be this way.

Foxy-T

Believe me Zafar in a daze when him read this init. Him pure shock and just close down him email and just sit there for a bit. Then him get up and take them page off the printer and step outside. Man only use ten minutes of him time init but fe true him no feel like sit there now and him no feel like he can reply is it. Man have fe think sometime init so he just fold that up and put it in him pocket. When him reach at his sister place Zafar just smoke a couple spliff and think about them thing she say. Couple a time him start fe write a letter init but Zafar aint no writer is it and him just screw them thing up. He never knowed what type a letter fe write is it. None a them sound right is it.

'Dear darling Foxy-T.' Then what man?

What he done instead was he just read that email over and over init. Just sit there and ignore him sister and that and read–

ing that email till they gone to bed and him have the sofa fe sleep. Man hardly slept is it through just turn them thought round in him head. Even when him wake Zafar read this letter when he was eat his breakfast in front of the telly after him sister gone fe take her kids to school and gone to work. He put down the bowl of Weetabix and just sat there for a minute or two staring at the telly but not even watching it. He was mad believe me. Him just eat up inside through pure anger.

'Fuck!' he thinking. 'She fucking me around bad this time.' No way she can do that him think. Once you promise them thing you dont take them back. No way man. She was his. He was set on that it was his life now that they was gonna be together. She was everything to him and without her he would have fe start again init. He sat there all morning till the cereal was dry around the edge of the bowl just thinking over this and thinking how could she do this. She promised! She fucking promised! He was well angry and even forgot the telly was on init.

Somehow man come to himself around lunchtime init and if he hadnt been plot some way to get Foxy-T back he might have done something stupid probaly I dont know. If werent his sister place he might have smash things up and wreck the place. But Zafar aint totally stupid is it. So come lunchtime him make a coffee or whatever and roll up a nice spliff and sit out on the patio in the cold and think long and hard about thing.

Looking at the fence and the walls around him and hearing the noise of the roads and shit all around for a second him felt like he had felt that one time before when he was sitting in the yard out back of E-Z Call and think that about all England patchwork fields and that just a prison and the streets of the city no different. Like they is there only fe control youth like him and keep them lock up init.

But chilling like that on the patio him figure that if this is the case then even more reason for him to plot and scheme some way of get around what Foxy-T a say in that email. And the spliff done nothing fe cool him anger but it allow him some focus and a way fe think clearly about him situation. But funny thing was that what him thinking about while him a sat there was not Foxy-T. See the thing that rankle him mind that worry him like a loose filling and that him see no way past the thing him have fe remove like a bad tooth you understand was Ruji-Babes. No way round it. Man have bad tooth him have fe go the dentist seen. If him want Foxy-T him have fe get rid of Ruji-Babes for good. But how he a go do that? It seem impossible fe get her out the way. But man know him so angry that he knowed this the only way fe get Foxy-T back for himself. Because inspite of what she say in that email he knowed that she wasnt going mad when she say 'Yes.' Zafar knowed that she want it as much as he do just that evil bitch Ruji-Babes so fucking demanding and poisonous that she turn Foxy-T against him and try fe act so weak that Foxy-T have no choice but look after her and commit to there dead relationship for fear that Ruji-Babes do something stupid like kill herself or take a overdose or whatever. And he knowed this the way Ruji-Babes control Foxy-T init through act weak and keep aks Foxy-T fe prove herself. But he also knowed that Foxy-T no like it seen cause she told him init and even if she say things run smooth now is just through habit init and through Foxy-T try fe play safe. But fe true is a threat that Ruji-Babes use even if she would never say them thing out loud and both a them knowed it.

Well he reason if that the way she want it that the way she can have it init. And Zafar make up him mind at that point. He knowed damn well him cant talk Ruji–Babes out of it and reason with her because she beyond reason that one. And if she a go kill herself anyway at some point or other then him course is clear. She practily begging for it anyway.

Zafar sister Radya not about in the day like I say cause she at work init and Zafar got no cash fe go and get the tube over Whitechapel but him remember where she keep her cash and Child Benefit book and stuff in the back of the kitchen draw so he figure that him may have fe borrow it and see what him can scrape up in the way of change. The Child Benefit book is there alright but there aint no cash in the draw. But when him check it he see that the benefit due that week init and she no collect yet. Him figure if he cash it he can pay her back at the weekend even if him have fe nick something fe do it.

Zafar sister sent him fe collect the benefit once before init when him stay there like five year ago so him remember which post office he need to visit and he sit down there at the kitchen table and fill it out as if she signed it for him to collect. But that money aint no use fe tube fare him need that fe other things init so him start look in them cups on the shelf or whatever to see if he can find like a couple of dollar fe tube fare only there aint none there nor down the back of the sofa or anywhere. He know that him sister keep her change and then take it up the bank when she got twenty quid worth or so so perhaps she done that either way theres no cash to be seen anywhere. But Zafar that vex and wound up that he think fuck it man and decide fe walk it anyway. He decide fe the benefit first and then walk over Whitechapel init. So him fresh up and get on his clothes then slip on him jacket and trainer and set off.

Dont take him long a walk over the post office down Dagenham Road is it. Once he pick up that cash him feel a whole lot better man. And now him have near enough a hundred dollar tuck in him pocket give Zafar courage. And once he got that he set off toward Whitechapel. Since it only take a half hour on the tube him figure it be a couple of hour walk but him well wrong. Where him sister live is in them flats up Rush Green Road which is practicly in Hornchurch. So him step up the Dagenham Road and figure he follow the road back over Ilford way. And the best way him figure fe do that is turn back on Rush Green Road and follow that past the park and the school and whatever and over Wood Lane roundabout then he can follow Wood Lane up till Goodmayes and get on the High Road.

Listen man if you never been up that way let me tell you is a serious distance from Whitechapel. It took him upwards a half hour just fe reach Green Lane and him walk cross the railway bridge and up on the High Road and some serious walking take him along past the railway yard at Seven Kings. This was all his manor when him a young rude boy. Him and his spar from school would sneak in the yards with there cans and tag everything in sight believe me. The hole in the fence was still there now init down the side of Aldborough Road. And checking the graffiti upon them trains and shit he could see that nuff youth is found there paths a bring them down this way too. Anyway this take him upwards of one hour. Zafar had glance at him watch as he leave the post office and it like two or whatever and it was at least three before him even reach St Mary's church there. For a second him tempt fe broke into that hundred dollar and get like a tube ticket but something about this walk was focus him mind and allow Zafar fe meditate upon the things he have fe do.

Before him left Zafar had skin up a few little spliff fe keep him going init and him spark one up now as he step under the North Circular and past that sports ground there. Part of him want fe stop and take a seat there in that little park. But he been walking for ages now man and him figure that if he stop now he stop for good since him feet already get sore init. Funny thing is since him a kid he know this road like that from always drive up and down it with him family or whatever. But he never walk down this way is it and him find that he never knowed half a what is there. Everything look different and where ever he look is some shop or carpet warehouse or take away what he never seen before and fe true some a them shop may be new init but it also feel like he had somehow shorten the road in him mind so he think say one bit might just be pure houses and one bit might just be pure shop but when him walking along there he see that it aint like that at all.

By the time he get to Woodgrange Park though him feel that he better take a five minute break or else him no gonna make it so when him reach the cemetery gates he nip in there init and find a spot out of the wind fe smoke a quiet spliff. So him find a bench and while him smoke him watch the wind batter them trees and blowing the last of the leaves off.

But him no stop for long is it. And he walk back to the road feeling like a young kid in some ways because he crunch through them piles of dead leaf on the way init. His mum never let him do that when he was a real kid since she say there be dog shit or whatever under them but now he no care about that him just enjoy.

Once he get back on the road it all seem to pass a bit more quickly even though him well freezing by now. Romford Road is a long road but he know it lead to Stratford and then not far to Bow. And he figure take it a little bit at a time like that it gonna pass quicker. Because he feel him anger a bit more under control now init. He holding that back fe later. Now him a warrior who must bide him time and make him preparation fe battle. And he do that by plot him movements once he get over Whitechapel. First thing fe do is get down Shadwell and check fe Rocky and them. After that he not quite sure because a lot depend on what Rocky and them can do fe Zafar init but either way him begin to work out some plan.

So while him a walk down pass all them bank and shop there he well concentrating on what he have to do. And a couple of time he bump into people come the other way because him not really watch what him doing there. But when they shout and say whatever at him he decide fe play thing cool and keep an eye out since him no want fe get in any angry scene or fight since that would fuck him plan for real.

As him get near to Stratford him tempt fe buy some cool drink because even though it cold and him just wear him usual thin jacket with just like T-shirt an jumper underneath he still burning up and a sweat yeah from the pure physical exercise a walking. But all the while him aware that he mustnt spend the hundred dollar in him pocket. He gonna need that later. But listen because then him have a stroke a luck. Kind of thing that might happen to anybody walking down some busy street like that. Because as him step over the cross road at Stratford Broadway he see some like business guy come a rush out a that small business centre there and run fe catch the 25 bus what pull up there and while him doing this he pull probaly some bus pass business or whatever out of him pocket and some paper or whatever fall out of him pocket and all only that man no notice this and him just jump on the bus init. Zafar quickly check if anyone else notice this and him realise no they never so him swiftly bend down as if fe tie him trainer and that paper there next to him foot so he pick it up quick and hold it in him fist while he tie them shoe lace. Then standing up he stuff it straight in him pocket and carry on. He dont need fe check to see that this piece of paper like a pale purple colour because him know is a twenty.

Shit man him bust out and laugh as him walk down the road, and near the town hall him see place like Cafe Mondo which is some like cafe and takeway behind the Fish and Chip and him figure well no point go hungry at this stage is it so him step inside there and order up some big milky coffee and like chicken sandwich and chip. There was a nice table free near the heater and him slip off him jacket and unzip the collar of him jumper and just sit back and wait fe him food to appear.

Zafar look a bit out a place there fe true since all them other few customer is like white for one thing but most of them at this time of day is like student or whatever so him no stand out too much. And him figure well me spend a white guy money init! Which make him laugh again.

That coffee arrive first but him also get a glass a water which him drain in one go then wipe him chin on the back of him hand and take out a Silk Cut and enjoy himself. Him stretch out him feet neath the table init and pure relax and just think, 'This the life man fe true.'

One or two of them young student is pretty you know and

one of them girl turn around fe check him then she and her mate huddle up close and say something him no hear and laugh together. Shit man! If he wasnt on him way fe sort things out with Foxy-T he would a check one of them girl number before him leave this place init. Zafar felt like a king there eating that chicken sandwich and take him time over the coffee so by the time him come fe leave him feel well rested and ready fe whatever the evening might throw him way.

Mind you it take him another hour near enough fe reach like Bow tube there and by this time it start rain. Not serious just that shit English drizzle where you hardly see it in the air but it catch on your coat like mist and slowly soak its way through till the wind just need fe catch it and it send chill deep in your heart. Zafar hate this shit English weather but him no tempt fe catch the tube now. Him nearly there.

Last time him come down this way was the day he was up in court. Him go in the front door of the magistrate court there but him come out the back way fe true! Last bit of fresh air he had that day was a cigarette out the front where all them guys what is sent up have there last smokes before them hearing. The pavement done litter with them cigarette end and piece a gum and roach. Nothing change much round here and him shudder fe remember stand out here and smoke and wonder what them magistrate a go say. But this time him no need a last cigarette is it and Zafar reflect that him never going in there again fe true. One stretch in Feltham was all any man can take. Especially an Asian youth like him with all them racist boy up there. Zafar had kept him head down and through sheer luck never need fe share a cell with one a them cunts. Sheer luck man thats all it was. And Zafar smile to himself and think about find that money on the pavement and think about how him come across Foxy-T when him look for him grandad and how he get the better a that thief out in the back yard and I tell you man him figure that he is a lucky guy generally seen. Which is good because he a go need it later init.

By the time him approach Stepney Green it way past five like five thirty or so. And him reckon it now time fe give Rocky a call so he pull out him mobile and call up the number. Him no keep none of them kind of number in him phone book just remember them is safest. Him stop outside the cinema there and make him call. Rocky suggest meet up in an hour up Bethnal Green Road in that Fry Chicken place opposite the Blade Bone pub. One with the machine them. Zafar knowed that shop and figure him could probaly walk it just about in that time but now the time fe walk is over and him need to get on and do them things. Him better not be late fe Rocky. No way man. Him still have a tenner left and a bit of change out a that twenty so him nip back up Stepney Green Tube and get a day pass. Quickest way him figure a get up there is go Liverpool Street and walk from there. Is only like ten minute walk init so him hop on the first Hammersmith train and sit tight.

Now let me take you on a little walk.

Follow me up past Shadwell DLR and the Crispy Cod. There nuff rude boy hang out neath them archway there by the DLR. And nuff tag on them wall init. Man like Elament and Buzz and Cash and Bisto and Rex is all tag there seen. Plus some name we know init man like Red-Eye, Ifty, Shah, Ranky and Shabbaz is got there tag there and all. Man like Zafar. Some rude boy is walk through them arch now init and chat upon him mobile and say like, 'You a pussy boy. Shut the fuck up! Shut the fuck up! You a pussy boy, you a pussy! No I said to you . . .' then him pass down Shadwell Walk and take him chat with him init.

That post office there is close now so there no one else about except some few man what come down the stair from the DLR and look around fe some type a sign that can tell them how fe reach the Shadwell tube station. Only there aint no sign so them sucker wander round this way and that till them either get rob or see some other older person what look like they know the way around. Them never gonna aks none a them rude boy the way believe me.

Straight up the road and now we walking past them brick up flats. No film crew here today is it. No police neither. No stabbing tonight. Not yet seen. No one live in them flat is it. All them window a brick up and the council fit up all them steel door. Some day you see that a different door been broke down so them local junky and tramp or whatever find somewhere fe sleep. But then the council come back down and brick it up again till they find the next one. One day them flat a go be demolish init either that or get a lick a paint and done up but they is well wreck now and empty for about three four year. Up at the end a them flat is Watney Market what is dead now. None a them shop even the Victoria Wine dont stay open past about six. Is fucking dead man. Was different when that Sainsbury was there but even that now a Iceland since Sainsburys move up Whitechapel init. And it no open late believe me. Only old people go shop in Watney Market these days. All them shop with like fake fag packet in there display init because them shopkeeper sick a get rob.

But we aint going there man we is walk along Bigland Street.

Normally man say we could cut across the grass there seen. Only as its been raining thats all mud there so we go around the long way and turn left onto Bigland up by the Watney Market bridge. Aint much go on here. There be a few Muslim kids dress up and hang about outside the school there. But apart from that and all them building works what go on outside Norton House it quiet man. And them builder gone home now and all. But walk with me now along Bigland Street past them low redbrick building of the Mulberry School and the infants yeah and check that turning past them two-storey low rise down by the Surma Town Cash and Carry. Like a old cobble street what seem like maybe it use fe go somewhere one time only now it just a dead end except for another one of them old block of flat. Sometime you know there be like fifty rude boy hang around down there in that turning. Spar and joke and smoke some little weed or whatever and listen to them sound system them. For a while man use to be able to get down there and check fe some brown except that scene move along. That scene never stay no where long is it through that type a rude boy always keep move and find some quiet place where them can attend them business without get disturb. Only tonight it quiet down that turning init just a couple of beemer park up with there lights off so man cant see if there anyone sitting in them or not except you know there is init and if you hang around fe long enough then another car go come and park up and there be some swapping around and one car drive off then come back and someone get out and drive away in still another car you never notice before. Thats the kind of runnings that goes on down there only you never gonna hang around and watch it man because them heavy thing man and you never want fe know about them kind of things. But one a them car might be Rocky sitting in it you know. You dont want fe know what kind of runnings him a deal with believe me.

So maybe we just pop in the Surma Town Cash and Carry and check the vegetable from back home. Check them nice river fish and all fresh caught and freeze back home. Them big motherfucker too them river fish. Maybe get some cigarette then walk out quick man because them meat bin round the side of the shop is all the butcher waste and it only collect like twice a week so it stink man believe me. Same with that other Cash and Carry opposite. Shit no wonder fe rats is it. Sometime man hear them fighting in a them bin and rattling around in there fe fight over some scrap. But we no bother with rats now. Not like Shabbaz who pick up some dead rat by the tail man and chuck it at him sister! Shit man you could hear them girl scream in fuckin Watney Market way him scare them!

See like I say Bigland lead direct on to Cannon Street Road. That building opposite you can read the writing on the wall there init. Say 'Raines Boys School'. Only Raines is now up Bethnal Green init and now its the Sari Centre and use to be the old Quality Food Store before them buy the bigger place next door. Then down the left is the One Stop and the Eastern Fried Chicken. But we is going right. Past the Golden Lion social club where one time man could check fe a game a pool. Use to be a pub init. Golden Lion seen. Thats why it called that still. But I tell you man there barely any pub south a Commercial Road now cause the Muslim man no drink is it. There one little pub up Watney Market then another one close by Cable Street but even the Dolphin and Anchor there shut down and is flats now. Even the Britannia mate. Down opposite them rag and bone men shed back down Shadwell by the arch yeah. Even that close down and is now a fry chicken shop. Even many of them pub on Commercial Road shut down now. And believe me is a surprise if many of them pub there stay open as long as them did. Man if you ever went in one a them pub for like a game of pool would all be just old lady in them make up go down a lunchtime and sit there with one little drink all afternoon and eye up all the brothers and hope for one last fuck before them die. No wonder them landlord sell up is it. Then opposite the Golden Lion is a old close down Jewish shop use to be call Roggs. Left from time man. Since year ago man say this a Jewish area init only it aint no more fe real. Just that man kept open him deli fe sell all that Jewish food init but since none a them Jew live round here him no do no business and him close. Is all board up and them upstair windows open fe let in the weather and the pigeon so man know in a couple year time this all be demolish and turn into flat or whatever.

All a them shop a closing now init cause is late. Man sweeping up outside and stack up them empty mango box an chicken box and drum a cooking oil out by the bins and that. All them flip-flop and plastic goods and mops and shit outside the £1 shop is getting carry in side while the old Sikh man what run it him a wind up the awning fe the night. Only a few place still open now. Like two a them place what does catering. Man there always couple a van outside and loading up with big pan full a food or else bring back them pan empty. Seem like every day is a wedding somewhere. And the butcher still got him light on and all init and if you look in you see them a sweep up all a that sawdust on the floor and wiping down the counter them then out the back you can hear that circular saw going and smell them burning bones what they cutting. That butcher dragging one a them meat bins out the front of him shop and all. They rank them bins man believe me. Even the barber done close now and roll down the shutter fe the night. A couple a people waiting at the D3 bus stop and looking at there watch and they is roll there eye and tut to each another and take turn fe try an stare down to Cable Street fe figure out where that damn bus gone and one a them is a little boy what is kicking coke can and thing out into the road then watch them car run over them things. Opposite side a the road some rude boy is laugh there way down the pavement on the way fe check them spar or whatever but is quiet apart from that except the lights coming from the Cannon Video and the music what pump out the door from there speaker them. And except for the kids what is letting off fireworks down in the Bigland or where ever. So man just hear all them rocket and air bomb going off in the dark somewhere. And its quiet except for that and except outside the hostel where some rude boy is shout up at a open window, 'What you doin in bed, bitch? You should be out here working fe me init!' But man cant hear what she a say back is it.

But the E-Z Call still open. There be one or two people in there still. Look there Ruji-Babes sit in the window like usual and Foxy-T a mess with them computer them. Couple a people working at them computer and all and check fe them email or whatever. Or maybe some a them Russian type what live in the flats round here is checking fe some Russian porn site. Cause believe me normally when you log on them machine thats what you get init. Then there be just maybe one youth a sit upon that computer at the far end and he be writing something there. Tapping at him keyboard init and furrow him brow in concentrate upon what him writing. And occasionally him may turn around when him catch little bit a conversation between Ruji-Babes and Foxy-T or fe check Foxy-T fit arse in them tight jeans she is start wearing now. And believe me Foxy-T looking well fit these days init. She aint wear them trackie bottom and fleece type a thing now. She like a new woman with them tight tiger stripe T-shirt fe show off she tits and them jean cut off at the waist so man can practicly see her bush. She one fit bird I tell you man and if that Zafar could see this him may well think she make a effort fe try and impress him init. Only she aint expecting no visit from that boy tonight is it. She done change fe her own reasons. There something a go on inside her head what no man know and I aint about to guess what she thinking believe me.

But now them talking init. And Ruji-Babes come out from behind the counter and Foxy-T take her turn there while Ruji-Babes a walk cross the shop and disappear upstair for a bit. Only not for long cause she back down in a second or two with her coat on and say, 'Sees you later T. Best go up the airport now,' or whatever.

And Foxy-T say, 'Yeah laters. Take it easy Rooj.'

And a couple of them other people what was on the computer finish up there one hours for one fifty or whatever and log out and then stand up and stretch there legs and put there coats on before going, 'See you, thanks,' or whatever and stepping outside fe go back home or wherever. Till is only me there now still just a sit right here up the end of the row a PC and I'm like looking around and Foxy-T looking at me and smiling and pointing to her watch like she telling me its time fe stop. I check me counter though in the corner of the screen and its like five minutes left and I paid for it and I aint go nowhere till I use up me time is it so I put my hand up with all me finger outstretch and with me other hand I point at the screen as if to say, 'Five more minutes,' and she laugh and nod.

But me five minutes is up in no time seen. So I'm soon doing Save As business onto like my floppy disk and logging out. Then I check fe my bag and coat and put the disk away and sort my things and make fe leave.

As I walk like past the desk and give back my bar code thing so she can scan me out she goes, 'How's my best customer today then, eh? You is always work so hard init.'

And I'm like, 'Seen, seen. No safe man really. Cool.'

And Foxy-T goes, 'Good luck man,' only I aint really listening or whatever and I think she is saying 'Goodnight' like usual. It's only later I remember this.

So I'm just, 'Yeah, good night man. See you tomorrow I spect. Easy now.'

Then when I'm turning to like leave or whatever the door open and I get like a blast of fresh air and CK-1 and its Ruji-Babes cousin a stand there. And him must just have reach from back home init. Him must have come back a day early and him have a back home type of hair cut init. And I can see him beemer outside only that driver no with him tonight is it just him on him own and him dress more casual than normal init. Pure expensive clothes fe true but no suit now.

And I say, 'Night.'

And Foxy-T say, 'Yeah goodnight man.'

I aint exackly sure what happen next man but I'll tell you some things what I seen. As I'm like walking down the street I turn back and I can see Foxy-T pulling down the shutters like normal when they close up. Only thing is when I get down the road and turn back down onto Bigland Street fe reach me yard I just catch a glimpse of someone a climb over the gate of Mulberry School. I cant be sure is it but just in them few second before him disappear into the shadows it look to me like that Zafar. This worry me a little believe me. So I figure I better maybe go back round the front and tell them that I seen him or something init only by the time I get back up by the E-Z Call them shutters is well down and the place all lock up and the lights off. I knock but no reply. Ruji-Babes cousin beemer still park up outside though init. So I check in the Halal Kebab and Fish and Chips over the road and get a table in the window. Order some fry chicken and chip. The light is on upstairs in the flat above the E-Z Call and they aint draw the curtain yet so I just look up at there front room while I'm waiting for that food and I dont see nothing much except when Foxy-T come fe pull the curtain and I see Ruji-Babes cousin come stand behind her and slip him arm round her waist so him a hold her against him. I can see her laughing as him bend down fe kiss her neck. Then she pull them curtain close and I aint see nothing else is it. But I man just sit there for a bit init. Eating me dinner. Keeping an eye.

Listen like I say there was nuff fireworks a go off all around that night since it was November. So I aint sure if I heard nothing later or not. Nuff banging and flashing everywhere seen so what difference one more little bang gonna make is it?

I tell you already that Ruji-Babes uncle who is probaly just fly into Heathrow right this very minute while me sit there I told you him a business man seen. And him own many a them business and property down this way. Well just think for a second man. Think about that. And I know say not every business man a gangster fe true but every gangster sure enough a business man. Money is money init.

Some little time pass and my food arrive so I just sit and eating that chips and chicken and next thing I know is the shutter going up and I see Ruji-Babes cousin a stand there and chat upon him mobile for a second before coming out and crossing over to the butcher next door to where I'm sitting. And this butcher own by her uncle and all. And that cousin a chat quietly on the pavement outside a second then that butcher nip back inside him place before come out rolling one a them blue meat waste bin on its end and him take that over the way and into the E-Z Call. Few minutes later him brother bring the van up front and I seen them other two man struggle fe carry that meat bin out of the E-Z Call and when they done that them push it in the back of the van with all them other bin them. And while this all a going down I see another beemer pull up and this cousin driver what I reckonise and some other couple of guy what I dont just get out and touch fist with Ruji-Babes cousin then slip inside the E-Z Call. And like I say I dont know none of this fe true but you know what me think was in that bin.

Cause what I figure happen is this. I reckon that was Zafar what I saw a climb over the Mulberry School gates. Makes sense man. He done it before init. And since him stop that robber him also figure that without no Zafar a live in the E-Z Call there be no one fe stop him a broke in himself. And thats what him try fe do I reckon. Him try fe broke in and shoot Ruji-Babes with this piece what he buy off Rocky in it. With him sister child benefit. Only him no reckon upon Ruji-Babes being off at the airport fe pick up her uncle is it let alone figure that

Foxy-T may be have some serious shit with Ruji-Babes cousin all this time and her just use this stupid Zafar as a excuse fe split up with Ruji-Babes.

That Zafar man!

Believe me him no know women is it so him obviously no realise that them women might have other plan in mind than just play along with what simple-minded scheme him a hatch. Anyway I reckon him must and this is Zafar now I is a talk about I reckon him must still have got some like spare key fe the back door and gone a blunder in there. And perhaps him well cold now from spend all day a walk from Dagenham to Whitechapel so probaly the first thing him a do is check fe that Gucci jacket what him nick off the robber before and maybe if it was still hanging there next to the downstair toilet him maybe just slip it on and feel well cool. Him love the smell of that good quality leather even if it aint real Gucci and maybe Zafar even check himself in the mirror there fe see how cool him look and check fe him hair and all just fe see him look well crisp before him creep upstairs and slip into that front room there with him gun cock and ready. Only him no reckon upon what him gonna find in there. Stead a finding Ruji-Babes sitting and a watch the TV him must a find Foxy-T. And maybe him go like, 'Where Ruji-Babes?' but all him find is Foxy-T a stand there with that baseball bat or machete and maybe him no notice Ruji-Babes cousin at first cause maybe him stand behind the door or whatever. Cause fe sure them would a heard him downstairs and just think him another robber. And I reckon Ruji-Babes cousin step out from where him hid behind the door and shoot him first. That's what I think happen seen. Cause even if maybe man would never think yeah Ruji-Babes cousin would carry a gun is true that the type a business Ruji-Babes uncle a deal with and way them tax them shopkeeper and them type a runnings is pure gangster business seen. So if at least you can say that if Ruji-Babes uncle a gangster then her cousin a gangster and all. Like father like son init.

And listen. No one a see him arrive and no one not even him sister out Dagenham knowed about him scene here with Foxy-T. All Zafar sister know is her benefit book nick and him gone. He never even tell him spar is it through him embarrass. And not even Ruji-Babes would know nothing about him come fe call tonight since her cousin spar will maybe a clean up or whatever. No one except me that is. Cause I figure I seen it all happen or like I seen some of it and put them piece together through just be there. Cause like Foxy-T say I'm there best customer init. I seen everything since him first show up. But believe me man no one a go miss some little thief like that Zafar. Even him so call spar would just figure that him move on or back inside init. So where ever them butcher took that meat bin in there van I aint sure probaly just a burn him up with all that other shit from the other butcher them. But whatever they done they got rid of him good.

Few minutes or maybe half hour later I seen Foxy-T coming out the E-Z Call with a suitcase. Ruji-Babes cousin soon come too along with him spar who all shake hands business like and then get in there car and drive off. And after him watch them up to the lights him pull down the shutter and lock up or whatever then the two of them open the car doors and get in him beemer. And I tell you man once they was in the car and he turn the key and switch on him sound system there I swear that Foxy-T look over where me sit and catch me eye. And without even think she smile at me like normal as if to say 'Laters.' And that's when I realise like I say that she never say 'Goodnight' to me earlier on but she say 'Good luck' as if she plan it all the time. This was the night that she was gonna leave Ruji-Babes whatever and she was gonna do it when Ruji-Babes was off at the airport. Only she wasnt gonna leave her for that fool Zafar is it but for Ruji-Babes own cousin. And if him never come a blunder in the middle of all this that Zafar probaly still be alive and living out Dagenham with him sister.

I dont know man I mean maybe I just got a active imagination init. Maybe none a this mean what I think it does. Maybe is all just some story I make up fe tell myself. But I think I'm right man. So I smile back at Foxy-T and wave at her and I say 'Good luck' to her and all only she cant hear me cause a the glass but she know what I'm saying.

And believe me yeah as they pull away that night headed for where ever I knowed right there that this was gonna be the last time I ever see that beautiful Foxy-T. Only sometimes I still see her tag here and there init left from time where it aint yet wash off or paint over and I maybe stop and trace out them lines with my finger and think to myself, 'Yeah. Good luck man.'

Acknowledgements

I would like to thank Sarah Such for lots of things – helping to make this novel possible is one of them. I would also like to thank Antony Harwood, Lee Brackstone, Charles Boyle, Jon Riley, Steve Beard, Stewart Home, Gordana Stanisic, Michael Bracewell, Stella Duffy, John White, Bronac Ferran, Nicholas Blincoe, Matt Thorne, Borivoj Radaković, FAK, as well my family and other friends, for their support.